VERDICT REALITY THE COMPLETE SERIES
From the dark mind of Sea Caummisar

VERDICT REALTY #1
JUDGE. JURY. TORTURER.

By Sea Caummisar

Verdict Realty: The Complete Series (Books 1-3...

Copyright © 2019 by Sea Caummisar

All rights reserved. No portion of this book may be reproduced in any form without permission from the publisher, except as permitted by U.S. copyright law. For permissions contact sharoncheatham81@gmail.com

This is entirely a work of fiction, pulled out of my own imagination. All characters and events are not real (fictitious). If there are any similarities to real persons, living or dead, it is purely coincidental.

Remember this is a book based on a fictional realty company.

CONTENTS

VERDICT REALITY THE COMPLETE SERIES	1
RULE # 19 COVER YOUR TRACKS	16
RULE # 8 NO HAIR	24
RULE # 12 WIFE BEATERS MUST DIE	27
RULE # 4 DISPOSE OF DEAD BODIES PROPERLY	34
RULE # 1 MARRIED PEOPLE SHOULDN'T CHEAT	37
RULE # 32 LEAVE NICE PEOPLE ALONE	40
RULE # 27 GLOVES	46
RULE # 24 IGNORE YOUR DICK	52
RULE # 6 GET AS MUCH INFORMATION AS POSSIBLE	74
RULE # 13 HIDE IN PLAIN SIGHT	79
RULE # 2 DENY DENY DENY	84
RULE # 16 THE HOBBY IS FOR ANGER	88
RULE # 11 CLEAN UP IS IMPORTANT	95
RULE # 20 NO WITNESSES (EVER)	99
RULE # 7 THIEVES MUST DIE	103
RULE # 26 DISGUISES ARE GOOD	108
RULE # 33 THE PUNISHMENT SHOULD FIT THE OFFENDER	113
RULE # 9 KEEP YOUR FRIENDS CLOSE, YOUR ENEMIES CLOSER	121

RULE #22 SHOW THEM THE ERRORS OF THEIR WAYS	126
RULE # 3 ALWAYS BE ALERT	129
RULE # 15 LAY LOW IF THERE'S ANY DOUBT	137
RULE # 31 KEEP IN SHAPE, ESPECIALLY FOR TOUGH OPPONENTS	140
RULE # 28 KNOW YOUR OPPONENT	144
RULE # 10 USE YOUR BRAIN, NOT YOUR BODY	147
RULE # 29 MAINTAIN A GOOD REPUTATION	151
RULE # 18 TAKE CARE OF GUESTS TO MAKE IT LAST	155
RULE # 35 USE THE JOB TO YOUR ADVANTAGE	163
RULE # 5 DON'T LET THE HOBBY CONSUME YOU	166
RULE # 21 BULLY A BULLY	173
RULE # 14 BE HUMANE WHEN POSSIBLE	178
SLY's JOURNAL OF RULES (INCOMPLETE)	184
CHAPTER 1:	190
CHAPTER 2:	196
CHAPTER 3:	200
CHAPTER 4:	203
CHAPTER 5:	208
CHAPTER 6:	214
CHAPTER 7:	218
CHAPTER 8:	222
CHAPTER 9:	231
CHAPTER 10:	235

CHAPTER 11:	239
CHAPTER 12:	242
CHAPTER 13:	246
CHAPTER 14:	249
CHAPTER 15:	253
CHAPTER 16:	257
CHAPTER 17:	260
CHAPTER 18:	268
CHAPTER 19:	271
CHAPTER 20:	275
CHAPTER 21:	280
CHAPTER 22:	285
CHAPTER 23:	289
CHAPTER 24:	295
CHAPTER 25:	298
CHAPTER 26:	301
CHAPTER 27:	305
CHAPTER 28:	308
CHAPTER 29:	311
CHAPTER 30: ONE LAST KILL	313
Verdict Realty #3	321
SLY's JOURNAL OF RULES (INCOMPLETE)	323
Chapter 1	329
Chapter 2	333
Chapter 3	336
Chapter 4	341
Chapter 5	348
Chapter 6	353
Chapter 7	358
Chapter 8	363
Chapter 9	368

Chapter 10	374
Chapter 11	379
Chapter 12	384
Chapter 13	388
Chapter 14	393
Chapter 15	397
Chapter 16	404
Chapter 17	408
Chapter 18	413
Chapter 19	417
Chapter 20	422
Chapter 21	426
Chapter 22	433
Chapter 23	437
Chapter 24	440
Chapter 25	443
Chapter 26	447
Chapter 27	450

RULE # 34 WAIT AT LEAST ONE YEAR

Sly Verdict was busy in his basement, trying to get some of his cleaning done. It was time to clean the basement of his guest house, tucked away in the far corner of his large farm. He didn't really like having guests, so he appropriately had the guesthouse built near the pigsty. He never actually intended on having guests. At least not guests who would stay against their own will.

As he swept the corner of the dank room, he found himself distracted, not wanting to follow through with his chores. Sly rationalized that was normal. How many other men would rather look through their old nude girl magazines they stumbled across in a box in their garage, than to actually clean their garage?

Sly's vice wasn't nude girl magazines. Instead, his distraction was his current guest. A guest who was there against his own free will was finally waking up.

Chester Harris had been trying to get Sly's

attention, trying to speak despite the ball gag strapped around his head. Chester could make noise, but he couldn't produce words.

Sly set his broom aside, curious as to what his guest might want. He unlatched the leather strap from the man's head, and stepped away.

Chester spit a large wad of phlegm towards his captor, but the projectile missed and landed on the floor.

Sly sighed, knowing that now he would also need a mop.

Chester used the opportunity, while the gag was removed, to finally speak. "Untie me you sick-o!"

Sly quickly reattached the ball gag and forced the thick mixture of rubber and leather into the man's mouth. "I can tolerate you screaming. But the spitting? No. That's just gross."

Sly remained calm, despite the rude gesture his houseguest had just displayed. Sly wanted to go get the mop, and clean up the messy substance of saliva on his floor, but instead decided to show his guest some hospitality.

"I'm gonna take this out of your mouth. We're gonna talk, like men. I dare you to spit again. I'll cut your tongue off. And pull all of your teeth. Do you understand?"

Chester's eyes widened, contemplating his captor's words. He slowly shook his head yes.

Sly very gently unstrapped the gag from the

man's head, and stepped aside, just in case he decided to try and spit on him again. After Chester didn't spit, Sly pulled a chair from the corner of the room, and slid it next to his victim. The wooden legs dragged along the concrete floor, creating a sound that echoed off the room's concrete walls.

The sound made Chester cringe. As if Sly's words weren't enough to induce terror, the empty room was equally scary. Even though it was clean, it was dark and hollow. Since the temperature was cool, and Chester hadn't heard an air conditioner running, he assumed he was underground.

Chester kept his temper controlled, waiting for this man-to-man talk.

Sly sat in his seat backwards, and rested his face on the back of the chair. "First of all, welcome to my guesthouse. Do you know who I am?"

Chester shook his head yes. "You're that guy on all the commercials, and the sides of buses. I almost hired you to sell my house about a year ago. But you were too busy or something."

Sly remembered his own rules. He had strict guidelines he followed to ensure he wouldn't be caught doing what he did.

Rule #34: Wait at least one year.

Sly prided himself for being known as the guy with his picture on the side of public transportation buses. "Very good. It's actually one year exactly, since we last met. I remember that you, Chester, had a temper." Sly pointed a single finger in the man's face when he said his name.

Chester tried to shrug his shoulders, but his hands were chained tightly to his metal chair behind his back, restricting his movement. "I'll show you a temper! Untie me! Let's not talk man-to-man! Let's fight man-to-man!"

"Good. At least you're not spitting like an animal." Sly watched as the man squirmed. "This is about your wife."

Chester looked puzzled. "What's about my wife?" His face looked like it had just been struck with fear. "Did she hire you to do this to me?'

Sly laughed and shook his head no. This victim might be easier than he thought. Maybe this man had already realized the errors of his ways. It was a shame that it was too late for him, though.

Sly liked to drag things out. He enjoyed giving his victims time to think about everything they've done wrong. "Why would she hire me?"

Chester calmed himself. Maybe he could rationalize his way out of this. "Untie me. Then we'll talk about it."

Sly stood from his chair, and walked over to a small workbench. He looked at his selection of tools. He picked up a paring knife, and a whetstone. He glided the blade of the knife along the side of the whetstone, enjoying the scraping sounds. He made sure to turn around so Chester could see him.

Chester peed on himself a little bit. "There's no need for that. I'll be better to her! I promise!"

"Better?" Sly paused long enough to give the man time to think. "Have you done something bad to her?"

Chester's lips moved, but he didn't make a sound. His eyes were glued to the blade, watching as it got sharper with each stroke down the stone.

"Um. Well, maybe. We've been married so long. Who knows? I never cheated on her. But yeah, we've had some fights."

Sly didn't like this answer. He was looking for a very specific answer.

Without saying a word, Sly placed the stone down, and swiftly moved across the room, holding the blade out from him. He walked behind his victim.

Chester felt the blade break the skin of his ring finger, and screamed.

As Sly started to cut into the soft flesh of the man's finger, he shushed the screaming man so he could speak. "What have you done to her?"

Chester didn't respond. He just screamed. The blade hit resistance, and Sly knew he must have already sawed down to the bone. He applied more pressure to the blade, and put more elbow grease into the sawing motion. He could've used a better tool for this task, but what fun would that be? He wanted it to take some time so it would hurt longer.

The finger dropped to the floor, and Sly bent down to pick it up. He waved the finger in front of Chester's face.

"Do you see this ring? This wedding band? You don't deserve this!" Sly removed the ring from the detached finger and pressed it firmly into Chester's delicate eyeball. The edges of the jewelry dug into his eyeball, leaving a circular impression. The metal made a juicy sound as it penetrated deeper into his eyeball. Sly pushed hard so that the ring was embedded deeply into Chester's eyeball and it hung in place.

"I want you to see this!"

Chester tried to close his eyes, but he was helpless. He couldn't close his eye due to the metal ring.

Chester knew he had pain in his finger, but he couldn't see his hand since it was tied behind him. He bunched up his other fingers, rubbing his thumb across his palm. He felt a stump where his ring finger used to be.

Chester realized the seriousness of the situation he was trapped in. "You're crazy! Are you screwing her? You want my wife! You can have her! I won't tell anyone. Let me go!"

Sly lashed out. "No! I want you to admit it!"

Chester gulped. "Admit what? I don't deserve her! I admit it!"

Sly's backhand collided with Chester's face

and the solid noise echoed. Quickly, Sly re-attached the ball gag to the man's head, and climbed the ladder, leading him into the upstairs of his guesthouse. The small door opened into the floor, like a hidden opening. Sly closed the door behind him, and covered it up with his large area rug.

RULE # 19
COVER YOUR TRACKS

Sly stepped outside and felt the warm summer sun on his face. This was his favorite time of year, when it was warm like hell. He could smell the stench of the farm filling the air.

As he walked past the pigsty, he was greeted with snarls and grunts. Sly threw Chester's ring finger to the pigs, and watched as they fought over which pig would reap their owner's reward. Pigs were interesting creatures. Not only could they dispose of an entire human body, they were also smart animals.

Sly had actually trained his eldest pig, Betsy, how to fetch. He loved her just like he would love a dog. She seemed to change after the first time she consumed human flesh. He wasn't sure if it was his imagination or not, but Betsy seemed more viscous. Her growls seemed more baritone after he corrupted her diet.

The cluster of pigs made it impossible to tell which pig got to eat the finger, but he could tell it was happy by the sound it made. When Sly heard the squeals, he knew the finger was properly disposed of.

Sly walked over to his farm truck and and made the short mile drive to his house, the house he actually resided in. A small foreign car was parked next to his house, and Sly was on high alert. He wasn't expecting any visitors, and he didn't recognize the car. He reached behind the seat of his truck, and grabbed a small handgun, and slid it in his pocket.

After walking the full perimeter of his house, and finding no one, Sly knew this intruder must be in his house. He pulled the gun from his pocket, just in case he needed it.

Sly could feel his blood boiling. He was used to being the person doing the hunting. Now he feared that he was the hunted. He retraced last night's steps in his mind, and knew that he had been careful when he abducted Chester.

The night before, Sly went to a bar and had a couple bourbons while he waited for nightfall. It was Sunday night, the night of the week that Chester's wife, Sara had yoga class.

It was a beautiful night to walk the two miles to Chester's house. Sly looked at the house, and verified that her car was gone. Sara had faithfully went to yoga every Sunday for the last month.

Cleverly, Sly let himself into Chester's house with his key. At one point, Chester was selling his house, and wanted to hire Sly to be his realtor. Unfortunately for Chester, Sly didn't like him. Who would like a guy who hit his wife?

The first time he met with the couple, Sara had on sunglasses and refused to take them off. Sly suspected foul play, but wanted proof.

After they hired the realtor to sell their home, Sly claimed he would get an appraiser to look at the house, and used the key a year ago, when they were both at work, to allow himself time to snoop around the house.

After finding old hospital bills, Sly knew that Chester was a wife beater. Sly had a copy of the key made, so he could come back in a year and take care of business. Then told Chester he was too busy to sell his home. Luckily, the couple never pursued selling their home. The old key still worked.

Once inside the house, and finding a sleeping Chester, Sly used a needle to inject sleeping medicine into Chester's bloodstream. He did a few quick internet searches.

How to leave your wife
Titty bars
How to relocate

Rule #19: Cover your tracks

Content that a computer search would make

Sara think that Chester had left her, he loaded Chester into Chester's car, and drove him to the farm. He would later take a taxi back to the bar to get his own car.

He tied up Chester in his guesthouse basement, and dumped the car in the woods on his property. He made sure that no one had seen anything suspicious.

Opening the door, in a silent motion, Sly quietly crept into his living room. He saw the brown Sheriff's jacket thrown on the back of his couch, and raised his gun.

Swiftly, Sly turned the corner. "Freeze! Or I'll shoot!"

Edward dropped his coffee cup, and glass shattered on the kitchen tile. The Sheriff reached for his own gun. "You jerk! Look Sly. You made me break the cup. Now, you've gotta make another pot of coffee."

Sly just laughed at his best friend, Edward. "Well, Sheriff Haskins, I thought a man of the law would be prepared for anything. If I was a bad guy, you'd be dead right now."

Edward just laughed. They had been best friends ever since Sly had moved to the small town. Back then, Edward was just a Deputy. Now he was Sheriff, but Sly still just thought of him as a friend.

"What's with the little car?" Sly glanced out

the window at the tiny car. "It doesn't suit you. Don't tell me. You're gay now? I mean, I got no problem with that. I kinda suspected it for a while."

Edward threw a piece of his toast in Sly's face. "Nope. Not gay. My patrol car broke down again. That was all the rental place had."

Sly held up two fingers. "Here's two options. Option one. Drive an hour into the city and get a real rental. Or B. Let me buy you a new car. Business is good."

Edward stuck to his stubborn personality. "Uh-uh. Nope. You already financed my election when I ran for Sheriff. I'm not taking anymore money from ya. And you can stop reminding me how successful you are, any day now. I won't complain. Nor will I forget."

"You should've been a realtor. Tell ya what. I'll pay for you to go to school and get your realtor license. Then you could have a real income." Life seemed so simple for someone like Sly, who thought he had it all figured out.

Edward started to get a tad upset. "I'll tell you once again. I enjoy what I do. I didn't get in law enforcement for the money."

Sly looked at the rental car parked next to his high end German car. "Obviously. And you need crime to do any law enforcing. The worst crime around here is kids trying to tip cows. I think you're just lazy." Sly laughed so his friend would know he was just joking with him. "Anyways, speaking of incomes, I have a showing in a couple hours. I gotta get going."

"Fine. But I dropped by to tell you Cindy is visiting this weekend. She's staying with me. Three full days. At my place."

Sly felt his mouth begin to water as he thought about his best friend's sister. She had been the prettiest girl in the whole county, until she moved away. Then she became the prettiest girl in the whole country. At one point in time, they almost dated. But she thought it was weird because he was more like a bother to her.

That was probably the worst insult any man could hear. Ever.

"So, I was thinking, Friday night, the three of us hit the bar. Are you game?"

Game? Of course Sly would go. He just had to get through the week first.

Driving an hour to the office everyday didn't bother Sly. He enjoyed the time alone with his thoughts. Today, his thoughts drifted to Cindy.

What he felt for Cindy, was probably the closest thing to love that he had ever felt. She was so sweet. And pretty. Naturally, as any warm blooded man would, he thought of her tiny waist that was situated between the perfect amount of curves.

She was more than just a pretty face. Being

Edward's best friend, Cindy was often around. He grew attached to her, and found himself in a drunken stupor one night, telling her everything about his past.

Sure, his life had been rough. Daddy beat up Mommy. Mommy ended up in the cemetery, and Daddy in prison. Very few people knew that about Sly.

His childhood was spent moving from one foster family to the next. Until he became an adult, and decided to become successful. He changed his name, legally, to Sly Verdict. At first he was going to use the last name Kinder, because it sounded great with his realty business. He had already named his business Kinder Realty. At the last minute he decided to use the last name Verdict, and changing the business name was a pain in his side filling out all the necessary paperwork.

He felt like changing his name would change his future, even though he knew it couldn't change his past.

Realty school was a short course, less than a year. And your income was infinite. How much money you made only depended on how hard you worked.

Now, he was the owner of Verdict Realty, the most successful realty office in the whole big city. Having created such a successful business didn't only give him a sense of pride and large amounts of money, but also a way to meet new people.

The way he had grown up, he found out that most people weren't worth meeting. So he liked to have his own kind of fun with people that he deemed not worth knowing. Everyone needed a hobby. His just turned out to be torturing people and feeding them to the pigs.

Sometimes he felt like he was doing the world a service by eliminating the world of people that he deemed bad. Hence his legally changed last name, Verdict. In his own mind he was judge, jury, and torturer.

Of course, he wasn't some sloppy serial killer. He had his own set of strict rules for his hobby.

RULE # 8
NO HAIR

Sly parked his expensive car, right in front of his expensive office. The whole storefront was nothing but windows. From floor to ceiling, you could see everything that was happening inside.

For this reason, Sly hired Stacy as his secretary. Stacy was a blond haired, blue-eyed all American girl. She had all the curves in the right places. Her large chest was stunning, and she always wore something low-cut to work, so the clients could see her cleavage. Sly thought of it as a smart business tactic.

He hadn't become the best paid realtor in the state just because he sold houses. There was a whole business aspect to it. Sly made sure to cover everything from sexy secretaries to a great name to a firm handshake. The sign on the building read 'Verdict Realty... The Verdict is that you deserve a new home.'

He always hated that slogan. He had

thought about changing the sign. His ads on the sides of buses read 'Verdict Realty... The Verdict is that your loan is approved.'

Anymore, he was just the face of the business. It took almost a decade, but he had fifteen realtors that worked under him. He took clients from time to time when he was bored, and when he was looking for new prey.

Sly checked his reflection in the glass window, and noticed how his brown eyes sparkled. His parents never gave him much of a life, but at least they gave him good looks. Standing at 6 foot 2 inches, he was taller than the average man. Plus, he took care of himself. He had a large concrete pool poured at his farm so he could swim laps everyday. Swimming was great exercise.

Stacy stood as Sly entered the building, and he noticed how short her skirt was today.

"Mr. Verdict, you have a showing in half an hour. Plus you have your appointment with the hair salon after that." Stacy shook her head. Her boss was bald, yet he paid $100 at the most exclusive salon in town for them to shave his head. And the rumor was that he also got a full body wax.

Rule #8: No hair. Not on head. Not on body (except eyelashes and eyebrows) IT LEAVES BEHIND EVIDENCE

"Right. I'm heading out now. I just needed some papers. It's gonna be a sale today. I just know it." Sly was confident. "Oh yeah. And you're looking good, as usual."

Stacy blushed and went back to her desk.

Sly just wanted to get this day over with. He had to sell a house, get his head shaved, his body waxed, and then he had to tend to his houseguest.

RULE # 12
WIFE BEATERS
MUST DIE

Rule #12: Wife beaters must die

After a not so long day that Sly couldn't wait to end, he sped home. He wasn't being the best host right now to his guest.

After quickly changing his clothes, Sly drove to his closest barn for some supplies. Then he made the drive to his guest house. He rolled up the rug, opened the door in the floor, and climbed the ladder down into his guest basement. Of course, Chester was still there, tied to the chair.

The man reeked of urine where he used the restroom in his clothing. He had no choice, being tied up and all. Sly wrinkled his nose, and reached for the garden hose. He had installed the water spicket all by himself.

The hose was also handy to clean up the puddles of blood, and the water drained nicely into the ground under the home.

The only other people who knew about this basement were dead.

After sufficiently spraying the man down with the clean water, and spraying away the blood puddle of the man's cut off finger, Sly laid down some ground rules.

"If I remove your gag, you won't spit, right?"

Chester shook his head in agreement. The man already looked defeated. The pain of losing a digit showed in his face, along with the fear that death was imminent.

Chester did not spit after the gag was taken out.

"What do you want from me? I'll do it. Please. I'm beggin ya."

"I want you to admit it. Then we can get this over with." Sly didn't even want to hint at what the 'this' part was that he referred to.

The man's face turned red. "Okay. I give. I admit it. Can you untie me now?"

Sly did not get the specific answer that he was looking for. Sly got the supplies he retrieved from the barn, and held a cup with a lid in the air.

Chester tried begging once again. "Water? Please, I'm so thirsty."

Sly set the cup on the concrete floor, and grabbed a pair of scissors. He started cutting away Chester's pants. Chester was begging and pleading for him to stop, but he never admitted to what Sly needed to hear.

After Chester was nude from the waist down, Sly picked the cup up. He used a gloved hand to grab Chester's penis. Chester started crying. Sly flicked the lid off the cup, and inserted Chester's pecker into the cup.

"These are the largest fire ants I could find. There's hundreds, possibly thousands in here. They will attack and sting your dick. I will remove the cup, once you've admitted it."

Chester wailed in pain. "Admit what? I wasn't a perfect husband. But I love her!"

"You're getting closer. What did you do to her?"

The stings from the ants made Chester feel like he was on fire. The ants started crawling up the shaft of his cock, and closer to his anus. The ants were angry for being removed from their home. They were ready to attack. The radius of the stings grew larger and larger.

"I loved her! When I was drunk, I wasn't good to her! But I've been sober for almost a year now! Things have been great with Sara!" With all the pain, Chester found it almost impossible to carry on a conversation.

"Did you hit her?"

"Yes! I hit her! Is that what you wanna hear? I hit her!"

Those were the words that Sly needed to hear. Now, with good conscience, he could do the world a favor and dispose of this man. Very slowly, like sloth-slow, Sly grabbed the water hose, and watered the man down knocking off all the fire ants. Except the ones that had crawled inside his rectum.

Chester's penis and ball sac were red and swollen. Tiny red, puss-filled bumps, began to form on his delicate skin.

Sly enjoyed the role of passing judgement on another human being. "Now, you know what you've done. I'm gonna leave you alone to think about it."

Chester's tears had soaked his face, and the snot ran down to his mouth. As he spoke, the bodily fluids sprayed from his mouth. "Think about it? I've been sober for some time now! I haven't hit her in a while. I'll never hit her again. We've even been seeing a therapist."

"So you're saying you know what you've done wrong?"

Chester shook his head yes.

"I usually let my victims think about what they've done wrong before I kill them. But since you know, I guess I can get this over with."

"Kill me? Call Sara. She misses me. I guarantee it. I've been really good to her lately. I changed." Chester paused to cry. "I'm sorry. Please, don't kill me."

Sly spoke like a child mocking a friend. "I'm sorry. Please don't kill me." Sly laughed harder than he had all day. Even harder than when he accused Edward of being gay.

Sly's face turned into a very serious facial expression. "I'm not gonna just kill you. I'm gonna torture you!"

Over at the workbench, he glanced over the tool choices in front of him. Chester cried and screamed and begged, but it all fell on deaf ears. Sly didn't care that the man changed. He was a wife beater.

Now, it was time to play executioner, Sly's favorite part of his hobby. He wanted to make this man suffer. Make him feel what Sara had felt.

First, Sly chose a hammer. He held it close to Chester's face as he questioned him.

"Did you ever black her eye?"

Chester's eyes were fixed on the hammer, and very slowly shook his head yes.

Sly drew the hammer up into the air, and landed the claw side right into Chester's eye. Chester cried out in pain, and the sound echoed off the concrete walls.

"Did you ever knock out her teeth?"

Chester wasn't stupid, but he knew that if he answered yes, that the realtor would knock his teeth out. Chester shook his head no.

"I don't believe you! Open your mouth!"

Chester shut his mouth as tight as he could, but that didn't stop Sly from raising the tool and slamming the hammer against his jaw.

Chester opened his mouth to spit the blood, and Sly saw an opportunity. He faced the claw side towards the victim, and shoved it in his mouth. Sly began tapping on teeth with the hammer, from the inside of Chester's mouth.

Chester was a bloody mess of tears and snot. The spots on his dick (from the ants) only grew larger and pussier. After breaking off a few teeth, Sly got bored.

Sly went to the corner, and grabbed his chainsaw. Chester was screaming, but the motor of the powertool was louder than his cries for help. He began with Chester's feet, and swiped the blade across both of his legs. Both of Chester's feet fell to the concrete floor, and a steady stream of blood began to puddle up beneath them.

Sly knew that Chester would die soon from bleeding out, but wanted the man to feel as much pain as possible. He quickly glided the chainsaw through the man's knees, and his shins dropped and splatted as they hit the cold concrete.

Chester wasn't screaming anymore, so he was probably dead, but Sly still continued cutting the man's body into small sections. It was easier that way to feed him to the pigs. Plus, that ensured each pig got something to eat.

Sly looked down at his ruined clothes, and knew that he would have to burn them. He decided that next time, he would do this nude. It would be easier to hose blood splatter off his skin than to burn his clothes each time.

Sly hated the mess. It would take him a long time to hose all the blood down the drain.

RULE # 4
DISPOSE OF DEAD BODIES PROPERLY

Since the body was cut into smaller pieces, Sly carefully placed each body part into plastic bags, and carried each bag up the ladder. The pigs went crazy with their noises, like they could smell the blood radiating from him. They knew it was feed time.

Sly reached into his bag, and pulled out a thick thigh. "C'mere Betsy! I have a treat for you."

The fat black sow waddled her way to the owner, pushing smaller pigs out of her path to the food. Sly placed the thigh in her mouth, and patted her on her head, and she scurried away with her treasure.

There were a dozen other pigs staring at Sly through the fence, and Sly turned the bags upside down, and pieces of Chester's body fell onto the dirt.

Each pig tried to force their way through the other pigs, until they got their snout on a body part. Once they got their piece of Chester's dead body, they would start making a chomping sound with their teeth. Their teeth easily tore into the bloody flesh. They could eat bone too, if it was cut up small enough. Sly had learned that the hard way.

Originally, he tried feeding a whole human body to the animals, and parts of the skeleton remained. That was a messy clean up. He didn't know what to do with the bones. So he tried cutting them up smaller, and covering them in pig feed. He learned that cutting up the bone into smaller pieces did the trick. Then they would eat that, too. There wasn't much that his pigs wouldn't eat.

Sly loved watching his pigs feed. They were very fast eaters, so he didn't have to watch them very long. He just watched them long enough to ensure the body had been properly devoured.

Rule #4: Dispose of dead bodies properly

Normally, Sly would leave his victims in his basement of doom for at least another day or so. He wanted them to know what they had done wrong. He wanted to give them time to think about it.

Chester was different. Sure, most people that he kidnapped would plead their innocence. Chester admitted that he had been wrong, but said that he changed with the help of a therapist.

It did NOT make a difference to Sly whether or not Chester had changed. His hobby was fun. He looked for any excuse to kill people. In the past, he had even killed innocents. That was before he had set his rules.

Before he had rules, there was a chance that the law would catch on to him. He could have possibly been caught. Now, he was just too smart for that.

After a long day of work, running errands and ridding the world of Chester, it was time to put his freshly waxed swimmer's body to use and swim a few laps.

RULE # 1 MARRIED PEOPLE SHOULDN'T CHEAT

"Good morning, Mr. Verdict. I wasn't expecting you today. I have no schedule for you today." Stacy, the secretary, was worried that maybe she had messed up. She was paid well, and she couldn't afford to get the boss's schedule wrong.

Sly noticed the worried look on the woman's face. Her young forehead was full of wrinkles, yet she was still beautiful. "It's fine Stacy. I just had a free day today. Maybe a fresh call will come in."

Sly went to his office, and checked last

year's planner. If a name was circled in red, that meant Sly planned to make them his houseguest a year later. The next name circled on his calendar was Charlene Burris, and her year was up on Friday.

Friday he was supposed to have drinks with Edward and Cindy, and was torn between abducting Charlene before or after his trip to the bar. He wanted to do it sooner than later. He had already waited a year, he didn't want to have to wait another day.

Charlene Burris was a horrible mother. Her three children ran around looking dirty, while she always looked like a supermodel. She and her husband had bought a house from Chester, and he learned that she was very self-absorbed. She even made a few passes at him.

He hated it when married people cheated. Especially when there were children involved. When her husband wasn't around, she had invited Sly out for drinks. Women seemed to like Sly. What woman wouldn't want a good-looking, wealthy man?

Rule #1 Married people shouldn't cheat

She would be easy to take back to his place. He would just have to figure out a way to get her there with no one else knowing. He checked his charts for where she worked. A makeup counter at an upscale store. How appropriate for the diva.

Friday he could go do some shopping, and accidentally bump into her.

He made the appropriate plans in his head. This would be too easy. With Chester, he had to do some spying to figure out his schedule. He watched Chester for a full month, until he decided to take him while Sara was at yoga. With Charlene, it would be as simple as asking her out.

Sly's desk phone rang. "Mr. Verdict, we have a call. From a Mrs. Combs. She's looking for a realtor."

He felt his heartbeat just a little bit faster. The only thing he enjoyed better than killing was making money.

"Great. Put her through.

RULE # 32
LEAVE NICE
PEOPLE ALONE

Mrs. Combs was happy that the realty office had an available time slot today. She was told that they just received a cancellation, so Mr. Verdict would be meeting with her.

A very expensive car pulled into her driveway, and she watched as the tall man exited his car. She greeted him at the door, before he even had a chance to knock.

"You look so much taller in real life than you do in the commercials. I'm so happy that I got you. Your commercials say that services might be provided by other realtors in your office."

Sly raised his finger as to point as his client. "The Verdict is that you're selling your home."

Sly chuckled. "Your home is lovely. I can sell this fast."

Sly stepped inside, and saw how well taken care of the home had been. Other things caught his eye. The fireplace had a bible on a stand, propped up. The walls were adorned with crosses. This woman had a very religious house.

Sly hated religion.

"So, Mrs. Combs, please tell me, why are you selling such a beautiful home?"

"Do you want some sweet tea? I have a fresh batch of sun tea. I just brought it inside a few minutes ago."

Sly accepted the drink, and it was the best tea he had ever tasted. He looked at the feeble woman, and realized that she must be a wonderful grandmother to someone.

"My husband died about a year ago. This house is too big. I want a condo. Somewhere with a pool, and lawn service."

Sly sat on the elderly woman's couch, and realized how comfortable it was. He looked at all the woman's wrinkles, that came with age, and was envious of her grandchildren. He had never known his parent's parents. He never had a grandmother. He wondered if this was what it felt like having grandparents. Sitting on comfortable furniture, drinking the best tea.

Sly was at a loss for words, and only knew of one thing to say. He didn't know how to handle other people's pain. Usually, other people opening up to him made him uncomfortable. Not this time. "I'm so sorry to hear that."

The old woman just kinda lowered her head. She mumbled a quiet thank you, and got lost in her own thoughts for a moment.

Sly broke the silence. For some odd reason, he was more concerned about the woman than the sale of her house. "What about children? Grandchildren?"

Mrs. Combs just sighed, and got teary eyed. "My daughter died quite some years ago. My grandson... well, he's partly why I'm selling my house."

Sly sat on the edge of his seat, and leaned in towards the woman. He was interested in what she had to say. "Mrs. Combs, I've sold many houses. You shouldn't sell unless you want to."

A tear slowly ran down the woman's face. "I have to. My grandson, he got messed up in those drugs. When my Harry died, he left me enough life insurance to pay the house off. My grandson, he came to visit me. He took my checkbook. He took all the money. But I think I have enough equity in this house to get a condo if I downsize."

Sly controlled his temper. Here he was a few minutes ago envious of a child that had a grandmother, only to find out that grandchild was a waste of flesh. "Did you press charges?"

"Against my grandson? Oh no, I couldn't live with myself if I did. I pray for him morning, noon, and night. Hoping he gets the help he needs."

Rule #32: Leave nice people alone

But that didn't mean that he had to leave her grandson alone.

"Mrs. Combs, do you mind if I take a look at the house?"

The old woman sat and waited patiently as Sly explored the large home.

In an upstairs bedroom, Sly saw pictures of the woman's family. He found a picture of a young boy, dated ten years ago. He pulled the picture out of the frame. On the back was the date and a name, Elliot Combs.

Sly intended to find this Elliot, and teach him a lesson. The only part he struggled with was whether or not he should wait the one year before he dealt with this man.

He had no direct ties to this man. Nothing could be traced to him. It's not like he sold or bought a house from him. Plus if he's so into drugs, nobody would miss him.

Sly would have to think on the *Rule #39 Wait one year*. Maybe that rule didn't apply to this situation.

Sly nestled his butt back into his spot on the comfortable couch, and Mrs. Combs brought him another glass of the most refreshing tea he had ever drank.

"Let's talk numbers."

Mrs. Combs shook her head.

Business talk was something that Sly was actually good at. "I'm not an appraiser, but I'd say this house will sell in the quarter of a million range. How much do you owe?"

Mrs. Combs sighed once again. I just called the bank. "Somewhere around fifty thousand. They want me to refinance. They say it will help me. But I don't know. Harry used to take care of all that stuff." The woman began to cry. "Elliot left me with nothing. I can't afford much of nothing!"

Sly did something that was not in his nature. He stood up and walked over to the woman, and awkwardly placed his hand on her shoulder, in hopes to comfort her. Without even thinking, Sly spoke.

"I'll pay off your house. You can stay here. But, expect a visitor for some tea from time to time."

Sly shook his head. He didn't know why he just said that. Sure, fifty grand was nothing to him, he had many times that in the bank. But he wasn't usually the helping kind of person.

Mrs. Combs crying came to a halt. "What? Why would you do that for me?"

"Well, Mrs. Combs, I never had a grandmother. And it just feels like the right thing to do."

RULE # 27
GLOVES

Friday couldn't come soon enough. Not only was it the day that marked the year of his last meeting with Charlene Burris, but Sly also had plans to see Cindy that night.

It was the perfect day to go do some shopping.

Once inside the upscale department store, Sly wandered over to the glove section. His hobby required gloves, and he loved to be fashionable.

Rule #27: Gloves. When in someone's house/car, wear gloves

Being warm weather, winter gloves were out of season, but driving gloves were always in season. After not being able to decide between the black or brown pair, Sly chose to buy both. They were a slick leather in size large, that molded perfectly to his fingers. He tried them on, and felt the fuzzy lining grace his fingers with luxury.

Proud of the choice he made, he ventured into the cosmetics department. He was meeting with Cindy that night, and could pick up a nice cologne that made him smell manly.

Casually walking past the make up counter, and not looking in that direction, Sly heard a woman calling out his name.

When he turned around it was none other than Charlene Burris.

"Hey stud. Is there anything, anything at all, that I can interest you in?" Charlene used her pretty, long fingernails to fiddle with her necklace drawing attention to her low cut blouse.

Sly felt his skin crawl as this married woman practically threw herself at him. "I remember you. Mrs. Burris, how is Mr. Burris doing?" He tried to give her one more chance to redeem herself.

Charlene flipped her long blonde hair over her shoulder and just giggled. "I'm at work. Why don't you tell me what you're interested in, and we'll see if I can get it for you." The woman thrust her chest forward.

Sly was still just a man, and his eyes focused in on her large fake breasts. He cleared his throat. "I need cologne. I need to smell good."

"Big date? If not, I'm sure we can arrange something." Charlene stuck her fake red fingernail in her mouth and playfully sucked on it.

Sly felt the response from his dick, which was at full attention. "Is that so? Why don't you pick me out something that smells good?" Sly leaned in just a little bit closer, and spoke just a bit quieter. "I'm going to the park across the street after I leave here. I'm gonna feed the ducks."

"Yes sir, I have something in mind for you." Charlene grabbed a sample bottle of spray, and released its fragrance on Sly's shirt. She leaned in extra close, nuzzling her nose into his chest. Then she spoke in a whisper. "I get off work in an hour. I love feeding ducks."

Sly's plan was working perfectly.

Sly was throwing some old bread in the water, and felt a petite hand on his shoulder. When he turned around it was none other than Charlene.

She didn't waste any time. "What do you say? Me and you get outta here? Go somewhere private?"

"I have a large farm, about an hour from here. All the privacy we could ever want. We could even go skinny dipping in the pool, if you want."

Of course, Charlene wanted to.

"Just leave your car here. I have some business in the city later on tonight. I'll bring you back to it." Sly had checked and double checked, there were no cameras in the park. Nobody would ever know where Charlene disappeared.

The hour drive felt so short as he sped down the expressway, the whole time her hand on his knee, her tongue in his ear. He didn't have to worry about talking. Charlene wasn't interested in talking.

He drove into his long driveaway, and Charlene was amazed by how private his farm was.

"I own the land all around here. A couple miles in each direction. Here's your privacy." This was probably the easiest target, ever. She willingly came to his property. Now, there was no chance of survival for her.

Charlene didn't speak, as she walked past the house to the large pool around back. "Come here, lover." She really emphasized the word lover, and Sly couldn't say no.

Charlene grabbed the bottom of her shirt, and raised it over her head, revealing two large mounds of saline implanted under her skin.

Sly fumbled with his belt, lowering his pants, exposing his hardened dick to her.

Charlene giggled, and dropped her skirt. She either wasn't wearing any panties, or she took them off at the same time. But she stood nude, before him. She jumped in the pool with no hesitation. Sly followed.

She reached out her arms, pulling his lean body into hers. Sly felt her small hand wrap around his large dick, and his blood really started pumping.

He grabbed her by the hair of her head, and firmly turned her around.

Charlene was pleased. "You like it rough, huh? Give it to me."

Sly placed his large hands around her larger titties, backing her ass into his dick. He tried to wiggle his way into the small opening of her rump, but she tried to pull away.

Charlene didn't like where this was going. "I don't like anal."

Sly didn't care, her words meant nothing to him. He pushed her up against the edge of the pool, and wedged her body between the wall of the pool and his body.

"Stop! That hurts!"

Sly used her hands to spread the cheeks of her ass, and his penis found entry inside of her. She continued to scream, and Sly just pumped his body even further into her tightness.

After a few pumps, he couldn't control himself, and he blew his cum inside her tight ass.

As soon as he backed away from her, he decided to give her a chance. "You can scream for help. Right now, you could even run. The choice is yours."

"You bastard! Take me to my car now!" Charlene climbed out of the pool, feeling pain in her backside with each movement.

Sly just laughed. "If you're smart, you'd run! I like a chase."

Charlene stopped at the edge of the water to gather her clothes. "Chase? What does that mean? I'm gonna ruin you. I'll tell everyone how you raped me! Think about what that would do to your business." Then her whole demeanor changed "Unless you pay me. Then, I'll be quiet. I won't say a word."

"Money. You want money. Sure, I can do that." Sly took his time, climbing up from the water. He loved it that his prey didn't realize the danger she was in.

Pure adrenaline started pumping into his bloodstream, and he got high, thinking of what he could do to her. He hadn't even gotten to sample her vagina yet, and that was definitely on the to do list.

Still naked, he looked into her eyes. "I'm sorry. How much do you want?"

As Charlene started calculating numbers in her head, Sly charged at her, and she fell backwards on the wet concrete. Charlene's world went black.

RULE # 24
IGNORE YOUR DICK

Sly was lightly slapping a naked Charlene in the face when she came to. She tried to focus her eyes to see better, but everything still looked blurry. She blinked a few times, and all she could see was a naked Sly, and concrete walls. Her head hurt, and she tried to reach with her hand to feel if there was a knot on her head. But her hand wouldn't move.

She felt something digging into her wrists, and realized that her hands were tied to the arms of a chair.

"You are so easy, in more ways than one. You're an easy lay. And you're so thin, you were even easier to bring to my guesthouse."

Charlene couldn't make sense of anything. "Guesthouse? I have to go home. Take me to my car."

Sly just laughed.

"I won't tell anyone. You didn't really rape me. I came on to you. I mean, I don't like anal, but maybe I deserved it." Charlene was trying to think of the right words to say, any words that might save her in this moment.

Sly laughed even harder. Amused at her lack of recognition of what was happening to her, he truly enjoyed these moments. His heart was pounding, his mind was racing. His head was flooded with thoughts of the worst pain he could inflict upon her. He wanted her to be his houseguest for a few days.

He enjoyed Charlene, and wanted her visit to last.

Charlene looked at the heavy chains that bound her wrists. As her eyes scanned the concrete room, she saw how dreary her predicament was.

"Look. I'm sorry. I won't tell anyone. You don't even have to pay me off. I just wanna go home." Small tears fell from her eyes.

Sly looked at her face, and knew that she was lying. She didn't want to go home. She just didn't want to be here, in this moment, right now.

"I saw how you don't take care of your kids! So why would you wanna go home?"

"I love my kids. It's hard being a mother! Please. I'm begging you. Just let me go." Charlene trembled with fear as she tried to struggle against the chains.

"Your kids run around in old clothes, full of holes. But you! You get your pretty nails did, you got your tits done, and by the way they're nice." Sly ran his large hand around her even larger breast implants. "But maybe you're too selfish to be a mother. You don't deserve your children."

"Who are you to judge me? You're being a crazy person! Please. Just let me go."

Sly turned his back on the woman, and grabbed a small box from the workbench. "I'm Sly Verdict. I'm the person that deems you unfit for motherhood."

Sly used a slight motion of his wrist to shake the small box in his hand, and a sound of wood crashing together startled Charlene.

He slid the box open, pulling out a large match. "I want you to see this. I want to show you how easy beauty fades." The wooden tip of the match looked like a large square piece of wood. "There were more important things in life. It's just a shame that you didn't see that." He purposely spoke in the past tense. He wanted her to know that she was gonna die.

The sooner she realized that she would die, the sooner he would see true fear in the woman's face.

Sly took the match, and ran it along her fingertips. He firmly placed the wooden tip of the match under the fake fingernail. Very quickly, he shoved it between the skin and fingernail, until the skin cracked and she bled.

He ignored Charlene's screams of pain, and enjoyed every second her pain was audible.

Very slowly, he pulled out nine more matches. "Here's one for each finger." Sly wanted the bad woman to know exactly what was going to happen to her.

Each time he separated the skin from the backside of her fingernail, she wailed. Each finger, he shoved the match even further, embedding it deeper into her frail flesh. The skin of her fingers seemed to give away so easily to Sly's strength.

Blood was dripping from her fingertips as she begged for him to stop. The matches were wedged into each finger, and Sly waved a lighter in the air.

"Let's see if those fake fingernails melt with heat."

Sly lit the tip of the first match, and watched as the small flame traveled closer to Charlene's fingertip. Eventually, the flame engulfed the fake acrylic fingernail. As it started to melt like wax, the warm soft substance dripped its heat onto her skin.

Charlene was trying to blow on the flame, she needed to extinguish this pain. But her breath didn't get close enough to the match.

Sly lit all the other matches, and Charlene turned her head back and forth, trying to blow onto each hand. The wind of her breath seemed to make the fire angry, and it just spread and traveled faster to the tips of her fingers.

Charlene was crying and screaming and breathing so hard she started to hyperventilate. Sly watched as the beautiful mess of a woman slowly succumbed to the pain and fear.

As each flame extinguished itself on her soft flesh, the melted acrylic dripped onto the floor. The tips of her fingers instantly blistered, forming water filled sacs of flesh.

He noted that burning fingernails smelled very similar to burning hair.

Sly shook the box again, letting her hear the sound, letting her know that he was equipped with more matches. He counted as he pulled each match from the box. "One, two, three, four, five, six, seven, eight, nine, and ten."

She looked at him, horrified as to what else he might have planned for her. His naked body slinked down, onto the cold concrete floor.

He firmly grabbed a freshly painted toe. "This one looks pretty."

It felt like he was diving nails into her skin as he methodically shoved each match behind her toenails. No matter how much Charlene wiggled her small digits, it didn't do her any good. Sly was strong, and determined to invade the sensitive flesh.

Sly glanced up, and he was eye level with her smooth, shaved pubic region. His cock responded by engorging itself with blood. He was torn between burning her toes, or pleasing his own needs. But if he gave into what his body wanted, then he wouldn't be any better than her.

Rule #24 Ignore your dick

He buried his nose in her snatch, taking in the aroma of estrogen and tuna. Sly picked up the lighter, once again. He lit a match, and stuck the flame into her exposed womanhood. The sweet smell dissolved and was replaced by a sulphuric, burnt flesh smell.

The flame fought to stay alive inside of her moist region, and Sly heard the faint sizzle of her cavity burning. The woman moaned, but it was not a moan of pleasure.

Realizing that he had lost track of time, he knew he had to meet with Cindy and Edward soon. He left the woman, with the matches still sticking out of her toes.

RULE # 17 TELL NOBODY. EVER

After Sly showered, he did his full impress

to dress routine. He always dressed well and looked nice for work, but tonight was different. He wanted to impress Cindy.

The local bar wasn't but a few minutes drive from his farm. The place was always lurking with locals, mostly farmers, drinking beer. Sly hardly ever ventured here, unless he was with Edward. The Sheriff found it beneficial to hang out at the bar. It was the easiest way to know about anything that was happening in the countryside.

As soon as he opened the door, Cindy caught his eye. She stood apart from the rest of the crowd. Her hair was perfect, and her face was accented by the correct amount of makeup. She had natural beauty, and didn't have to apply too much war paint to look nice.

Sly stood for a moment, just taking in Cindy's presence, feeling the warmth in his bones. This was the only woman who ever had that effect on him. She was his comfort zone.

Edward looked up from the bar, and noticed that his best friend had arrived. "Yeah. That guy! The one in his fancy clothes. He said he's covering my tab, tonight." Edward laughed and the bartender just kinda rolled her eyes.

Sly wanted to say hello to Cindy first, but didn't know which form of hello would be proper for this situation. Naturally, he wanted to kiss her hello on her cheek. But maybe she wouldn't like that. He always felt out of place in social situations.

Work was different. He was like a machine and had his buying/selling routine down pat. But when it came to social outings, he functioned like an awkward teenage boy unsure of himself in the world. Other than Edward, Sly didn't have too many friends.

He had plenty of employees. He had plenty of clients. And his role was bluntly designed with them. He knew how to be a boss. He knew how to be a salesman. He even knew how to be an abductor. With Cindy, he wasn't quite sure what his role was.

"This man's right." Sly gestured towards his friend. "I can afford to buy him a beer or two."

The bartender looked puzzled. "A beer or two? Some nights he drinks a dozen!"

Cindy took it upon herself to greet Sly. She gave him the slightest peck on his cheek. "You're looking good, Sly. What've you been up to?"

Sly looked into her glowing eyes, and lost himself for a moment. He forgot where he was, and had to think carefully to choose his words.

Rule #17: Tell nobody. Ever.

"Ya know. The same stuff. Working." Sly felt a small ping of anger inside of himself. Maybe he should tell her that he missed her. He felt an even smaller bit of guilt. That was a lie. He had been killing more often that he had been working. But he couldn't tell her that.

Edward noticed his sister kiss Sly on the cheek, and decided to leave them alone for now. He wanted his sister to move back to the country where she belonged. He hated it that she lived so far away. Maybe Sly could use his salesman skills to convince her to move back home.

There was a pregnant pause of silence, neither party speaking. Just them looking at each other. Sly wondered what kind of thoughts could possibly be stirring about in that precious mind of hers.

The bartender broke the silence. "So, was that a yes or no on who's paying the Sheriff's bill?"

Sly shook his head and looked around. He saw the bar full of people, and knew that the bartender was trying to get his attention. "Buckets. Let's start with a bucket of beer. Eddy's choice."

Edward let out a small grunt. He hated it when people shortened his name. His name wasn't Eddy. His name was Edward, and Sly knew he hated it when people used the sloppy version of his name.

Edward put his hand around Sly's shoulder. "I guess if you're buyin', you can call me whatever you want. Just don't call me late for dinner."

Cindy's giggle aroused Sly. Everything about her was so dainty, and amusing. She was the perfect woman.

After grabbing their bucket of beer, Edward ushered the trio to a table in the corner. A quiet place where they could all talk.

Sly mustered up a few words, and asked Cindy how her flight in had been. He wanted to know everything about her. Ever since she moved many hours away, he had lost touch with her. Sly was so glad that she was back in town, even if it was only for a brief stay.

Edward grew impatient. Small talk wasn't in his nature. He wanted to get this conversation headed in the direction that he had intended for all along.

"Cindy's in between jobs right now. That's why she came to town. She had some free time." Edward used his fingers and made air quotes when he said the word free.

Cindy didn't like how her brother had brought up her unemployed status. "Yes, in between jobs. But I've got something wonderful lined up. It's practically a sure thing." She didn't like it when her brother talked down to her.

Edward shrugged his shoulders. "You belong here, in the country, with me. You could do like Sly here. You could commute to the city. It's just a bit over an hour." Edward checked his tone, and realized that he sounded harsh. After calming his voice, he spoke again. "I really wish you'd come home."

"I'm here now. Let's enjoy it while we can."

That was what Sly intended to do. He would enjoy every moment of Cindy that he could.

RULE # 23 DON"T BREAK THE RULES

After drinking just a couple too many, and having to catch a ride home from the Sheriff, Sly decided to break his own rule. He was just drunk enough to throw caution to the wind.

The perfect end to a perfect night was a visit with his houseguest. He would have rathered his houseguest had been Cindy, but for now, he would have to settle for Charlene.

Charlene heard the door-in-the-floor creak, and she opened her eyes wide. She had been left alone for hours, and she was in dire need of a potty and a glass of water. She was surprised when she saw that the realtor had brought her the latter.

He held the glass of fluid to her mouth as she drank it too fast. While she was drinking, he was checking out her melted fingernails and bloody toes that still had the matches stuck in them.

Charlene's voice was raspy as she tried to speak. Her throat had been so dry from screaming for help the past couple of hours. Unfortunately, help never came. All she got was the echoes of her own hollow voice bouncing off the concrete walls. "I've gotta pee."

She was blunt with her statement. She

knew it would do no good to reason with Sly. But maybe if he let her loose to take care of business, maybe she could get free.

Sly held up both of his hands. He held up a single finger on one hand, and two fingers on his other hand. "Number one? Or number two?"

"One."

"I'm gonna untie you. Then you can squat over that drain. Then, I'll hose you down."

Charlene agreed, but she knew she was gonna fight the man. That was her only chance of survival.

He untied her bindings, and pointed to the drain. Sly turned his back and was gathering his hose as he watched the woman squat out of the corner of his eye. His dick responded to the naked woman squatting, and stiffened in his pants.

He waited until the faint sound of her urine splashing off the grate ended before turning around. As he turned around, Charlene leapt into the air, pushing the full weight of her small body into him. With the beer in his bloodstream, he couldn't balance himself, and fell to the cold floor.

Charlene scrambled up the ladder, and tried to raise the hatch. She knew she was close to freedom. But the door didn't budge. In the darkness, her hand felt along the edges for a latch, and she felt a lock dangling from the wood. The crazy man had locked himself in with her. Now, she would have to fight him for the key.

Sly's laughter sounded like many men laughing as the echoes kept reciprocating. He knew that she couldn't escape. Now he was just having fun with her.

He rubbed his crotch with his hand.

Rule #23: Don't break the rules.

Being drunk, Sly didn't care about Rule #24: Ignore your dick.

He was listening to his dick, and he was going to give it what he wanted. He wanted to feel her tight, wet snatch wrapped around him. He knew that the rules were in place for a reason. It was for his own safety.

He made the rule about his dick when he figured out his dick would let temptation get the better of him, maybe leading to him getting caught.

But tonight, he outsmarted his own rules. He had locked the door, and the girl couldn't get out.

Charlene slowly made her way down the ladder, feeling the pain in her toes with each rung she climbed. Even though she had removed the matches, her digits were already damaged and she felt the pain.

Sly pointed the water hose in her direction and released a cold spray on her, making her nice and clean for him. Charlene fought against the force of the stream of water and stood within an arm's reach of Sly. He stanced his body like a fighter, and she kicked towards his crotch but missed. Sly quickly dropped the hose and wrapped his large hands around her arms, pulling her close to him.

Her fake breasts slapped his chest, and he could feel his hard dick next to her naked pussy. His dick fought against his clothing, wanting to snake out of the cloth and into her warmth.

Sly pushed her to the ground, and as she fell backwards her head made contact with the cold, concrete ground. Charlene fought the urge to pass out, and tried to get back up. Instead, she felt Sly's body weight on top of her, pinning her to the ground.

Sly firmly grabbed her implants and squeezed so hard that Charlene thought they might burst. As she cried out in pain, she tried to look down at her breasts. She wanted confirmation that they hadn't exploded. She saw that they were still intact.

She swung her arms and each time her fingers landed on Sly's skin, the pain from her ruined finger tips resonated down into her hands. Each time she hit him, he seemed more determined. Sly grabbed her head, and repeatedly slammed it into the concrete until she was unconscious.

Her body went limp, and Sly unzipped his pants and gave his member the freedom it desired. He separated her thin legs, and soon his penis found entry into her still warm body.

Sly thrust himself into her, and her unalert body flailed around like a ragdoll, giving way to each pump.

After he was satisfied, Sly easily threw her body over his shoulder. He sat her up in the metal chair, and balanced her weight evenly so that it would sit on its own.

After he tied her wrists to the arms of the chair, he was confident that she couldn't get loose. Her large fake breasts distracted him, and he didn't like it that her body was a strong enough force for him to break his own rules.

Determined to not break his own rule again, Sly grabbed a small knife from his workbench. As soon as he plunged the tip of the blade into her exposed nipple, Charlene woke up, unable to stand the pain. Sly laughed as he slid all three inches into the implant, and watched as its contents oozed out. Her titty slowly deflated and shriveled up like a prune.

Charlene was screaming in terror, watching the fluid mixed with blood drain down her body.

As he squeezed her breast, the saline mixture flowed even flaster, leaving a slime-like trail down her body.

After he was sure that breast was no longer something that would persuade his dick to betray him, he laughed as he looked at her other breast.

Wanting to have some fun with her, and

punish her for having such a stupid cosmetic surgery, he put the knife aside. Instead, he grabbed a larger blade, a machete. He made sure to display it in front of her, the dim light bouncing off it's sharp edge.

The look on her face was priceless. Her mind was scanning each corner, wondering if this was the end for her.

Sly didn't intend to kill her, yet. Instead, he raised the weapon in the air, and dropped it as he flicked his wrist down. The sharp edge sliced through the skin of her other fake breast.

When he pulled the machete out of her ruined body, it was covered in a red gooey substance. He watched as she leaked out of her body. Before leaving her alone for the night, he politely offered her another glass of water. She needed to stay hydrated if he was gonna visit her the next day.

RULE # 30 DON"T GET SLOPPY

Sly was woken by the buzzing of his phone. He knew it was early, just not exactly what time it was. His head was pounding from consuming the beer at the bar, and he tried to remember what he had done the night before.

He remembered the bar, and especially the time he got to spend with Cindy. After that, he could only recall bits and pieces. He knew he had visited Charlene also, but he didn't know how he had left her.

His mind scrambled. Did he kill her? If he did, did he dispose of her bodily properly? He couldn't afford to be sloppy. If he had done anything stupid when he was drunk, it could cost him his freedom.

Rule #30: Don't get sloppy

Sly answered his phone, even though he didn't want to. He didn't even speak. He just waited.

"Sly? Are you there? Sly? Hello?"

He tried to make sense of the woman's voice. Even though it sounded familiar, he couldn't place who it was. Maybe it was his secretary. Did she by chance have a cold and sounded different?

"Yeah. I'm here."

"It's Edward. He's so mad at me. He took off this morning. Can I stay with you? Just for a couple of days? I hate to ask. But I refuse to stay here."

It was Cindy. She wanted to stay with him? Of course, he had to oblige.

Knowing that it would take Cindy a few minutes to get to his house, he quickly threw on a pair of running shorts, and darted out to check on his houseguest. He had to know what Charlene's status was.

He jumped on his small four-wheeler and sped back to his guesthouse. He raced inside, and unlocked the hatch and braced himself for what he might see.

Charlene was a mess, with the blood stains where her breasts had drained down her abdomen. Her eyes barely opened, and he was relieved. She was still alive. He hadn't gotten too sloppy, yet.

After locking up the hidden door, he stepped outside, letting the sun soak into his face. The warmth made him smile, and the nearby squealing pigs got his attention.

He got a bag of feed, and threw the actual pig food into their pen. Their snarls weren't happy, he knew that the pigs would rather be eating human flesh, but he didn't have the time to give in to what they wanted.

He hopped back on the small vehicle. Maybe he would have just enough time for a quick shower. He didn't want Cindy to see him in the panicked state he woke up in.

Sly was wrapping the towel around him and he heard Cindy knocking on his door.

"Come in! I'll be out in a minute."

He took just a few seconds to check his appearance in the mirror. When he deemed himself appropriate, he jumped back into his running shorts, anxious to greet Cindy.

Sly felt his heart fall just a bit when he saw that her eyes were red and puffy. Tears had streaked her mascara, and portions of the black residue invaded her cheeks.

"What's goin' on? You okay?"

Cindy sniffled and looked at Sly's bare chest, but tried not to let her eyes linger too long. She loved how smooth his body was. And even after a few years of not seeing him, she was delighted that he still took care of his body.

"It's my brother. He's just giving me a hard time about moving home. When I lost my job, I was actually thinking about it. But now, I don't know. I just don't know. I'd probably end up killing him." Cindy tried to laugh, even though she was obviously sad.

Sly took a second to think about it. When other people used the word kill, they usually didn't mean it literally. So he figured that she must be joking. With Edward being his best friend, he knew he had to defend him. Plus, Sly would love it too if she moved back to the country.

"He just misses you. Sure, sometimes he can be a prick. But he loves you. You're his little sis. He just wants you close."

Cindy used her hand to wipe some of the moisture from her face. "Maybe. But then why's he so mean about it?"

Sly didn't have the right answer to that, so he decided to change the subject. "How about some eggs? Let me make you some breakfast. The chickens have been laying some pretty big ones this time of year."

Cindy was pleasantly surprised to learn that the man could really cook. They didn't talk about how pushy Edward was. Instead they talked about some of the times they had in the past.

There had been one drunken night, that the two of them hooked up, in the biblical sense. They made sure to not mention that night, even though Sly still remembered it as the best night of his life.

When Cindy was around, Sly didn't even think about Charlene. He didn't give her another thought. He knew that she was secured properly and had zero chance of escape.

After enjoying most of the morning with

Cindy, Sly realized he had other obligations. "I have to run into the city today. I have to do some paperwork. But make yourself at home here. You're welcome here, for however long you need a place to stay."

"Look at you, Mr. Successful. Let me guess, some big sale? And I appreciate the offer. Is the guesthouse unlocked?"

Sly couldn't let her stay in the guesthouse, it was already occupied, and he couldn't chance her hearing any of Charlene's screams. She probably wouldn't understand.

"Guesthouse? No. It's locked up tight. Stay here. In the main house, with me." Sly hoped that would make her happy.

Cindy shook her head no. "I couldn't. I don't wanna impose."

"It's not an imposition. We're both adults. And I miss you, too." Sly closed his mouth as soon as he recognized the words coming out of his mouth. He felt like an idiot. Now, she'd probably never wanna stay with him.

She put her hand on Sly's arm. "That was a long time ago. Can't we be just friends?"

Just her touch stirred something inside of him.

Sly tried to recover from his slip of words. "I meant as just friends. I know. I tell you what. I don't like it that you're upset. Why don't you ride to town with me today? It's not a sale. It's more like a buy, but not for profit. I can let the top down on the convertible. Maybe some fresh air would do you some good."

Cindy agreed, and Sly very much looked forward to spending more time with Cindy. At least this way, he didn't have to worry about her stumbling across anything that she shouldn't find in the guesthouse.

RULE # 6 GET AS MUCH INFORMATION AS POSSIBLE

Sly watched as the wind in the car whipped Cindy's hair back. She looked happy, for the first time all day. He felt the sun penetrating his bald head. It was a nice day for a ride into the city.

Sly made a quick pitstop to his office, picking up the required paperwork. He thought he noticed Cindy eyeballing Stacy through the glass storefront. He wondered if she was jealous of his well-built secretary.

Sly drove straight to Mrs. Comb's house, and Cindy offered to wait in the car. He wanted her to come inside with him. In a way, he wanted her to witness his noble deed.

Plus, maybe she could help to get Mrs.

Combs talking a little bit. He needed more information on her grandson, Elliot Combs.

Mrs. Combs seemed a bit confused for their visit. She was up in her years, but surely she had remembered the visit from man who told her he would buy her house for her.

She invited them in, and offered them some of the sun tea Sly loved. After a moment, Mrs. Combs started talking.

"Is this your secretary or something?"

Almost offended by the remark, Cindy quickly said no. Sly now knew for a fact that she had checked out Stacy, and maybe she was just a tad jealous.

Sly rectified the statement. "No, Mrs. Combs. She's just a friend. I think of this more as a social call than a business one."

The only person that didn't understand now was Cindy.

"Well, I almost didn't believe you when you offered to buy my house. What's the catch?"

Sly placed a hand in front of him, and gestured towards Mrs. Combs. "There's no catch. I'm just being a nice guy."

Cindy finally wanted to know what was happening. "Okay, I'm lost. Who wants to fill me in?"

Sly just looked at the older woman.

Mrs. Combs slowly opened her mouth. "I was gonna sell my house and move. My husband died, and I can't afford this house no more. I could have, but my grandson robbed me blind. Mr. Verdict here told me he would buy my house for me. Now, you have to understand, I didn't believe him at first. But it looks like he's come back with the paperwork." The elderly woman smiled.

Cindy almost choked on her tea. She couldn't believe it either. Sly must be doing well for himself if he can buy houses for strangers.

"It's just that Mrs. Combs here is so kind. It's kinda peaceful here. As you know, I never knew my grandparents. But this is what I would imagine visits with them would feel like."

Cindy looked at Sly in a different way. That was the kindest thing she had ever heard in her entire life. She always knew that Sly was a good guy, she just never imagined that he was this good of a guy.

As Sly pulled out his laptop and started getting to work, Cindy took it upon herself to keep the conversation going with Mrs. Combs.

"Your grandson? That's horrible. What happened?"

Sly did not look up from the screen of his laptop, but he made sure to pay attention to what Mrs. Combs had to say.

Rule #6: Get as much information as possible

"My husband left me a healthy life insurance policy. My grandson knew this, and he stole my checkbook. He forged my signature, and took every last penny of it. It left me in this situation. I hated the thought of selling my home, but sometimes you have to do things that you don't want to in life. All I can do is pray for him."

Cindy's heart broke for this old, feeble woman. "What would possess him to do such a thing?"

"Drugs. They're bad. The last I heard, he was homeless. So I offered for him to stay here. He had been bouncing around the homeless shelters downtown. I wanted the company. I thought I could help him if he lived here. Instead, he did what he did. The thought of him staying at that men's shelter down on Eighth Street broke my heart. I saw that place on the news. That's no place for a good kid like him."

Sly's skin crawled when Mrs. Comb's referred to her grandson as a good kid. He absorbed the information. Now, he knew which shelter the boy had stayed in. Now, he could possibly find him.

Sly interrupted the women's conversation. "Once I push this button, the money will be wired to your mortgage company. You will own this house free and clear."

Mrs. Combs stared off in space, almost in disbelief. "That's the nicest thing anyone has ever done for me. And I can't believe you can do all of that from that little machine. We didn't have technology like that when I was growing up."

Once the screen confirmed the transfer of the money, Cindy and Sly congratulated the old woman on being a proud homeowner. They drank tea, just like Sly imagined he would have with his family.

RULE # 13 HIDE IN PLAIN SIGHT

During the drive back to the farm, Cindy looked at Sly in a different way. Sure, she had heard about how successful he was, and learned of the many awards his real estate office had won. But she didn't know that he was using his money for such great acts of kindness.

Cindy's heart softened just a little, and her mind wandered as to how good he would treat a woman. Being his best friend's sister, she knew that hooking up with Sly would strain that relationship. Plus, she lived so far away.

There were so many reasons that it was a bad idea, and Cindy tried to push the thoughts of hooking up with Sly away from her mind.

She was enjoying the sun on her face, and the wind in her hair. Before she had lost her job she was working sixteen hour days editing for a newspaper. She appreciated this little bit of down time that she could actually enjoy life.

When Sly's house came into sight, the Sheriff's truck was parked right in front. Cindy and Sly looked at each other and raised their eyebrows. They both knew that Edward must be looking for his sister.

Edward was pacing back and forth, until he saw Sly's car come into view. Then, he casually leaned against Cindy's car and folded his arms across his chest.

Sly just shook his head as he got out of the car. "I'm innocent, Mr. Officer." He laughed at his little jest with his friend. "She came to me. I haven't touched her."

Edward loved to joke around with the best of them. But he didn't smile. Instead, he had a very solemn facial expression. "Cindy, go in the house. I have to talk to Sly."

Cindy didn't like her big brother bossing her around. "Anything you have to say to Sly, you can say in front of me." She waved an angry finger in her brother's face. "And I'll have you know, I'm staying with Sly. I'm not coming back to your house. I don't care what you say."

Her brother started to get a little angry. "It's not about that. I'm working right now. Go in the house. I have to talk to Sly."

Sly told her that the front door was unlocked, and to go into the house. Cindy stomped her feet every step she took. As she opened the front door, she stuck her tongue out at her brother, like a child would do teasing their sibling.

Sly tried to speak. He wanted to joke around with his friend, and make light of the whole situation. But Edward started to speak, and got right down to business.

"Do you know the Miller's little boy? They share your property line to the west of you."

Confused, Sly just gave a slight nod. His mind couldn't make sense as to why the Sheriff would be asking him about his neighbor's kid. He realized that his friend was there on a business call, not a social call. He only hoped that it didn't have anything to do with his hobby.

"Well, he was playing on your property. The very far corner of your property. He stumbled across a car. Now, I have to ask, do you know anything about it? I'm just doing my job, okay?"

Sly did know about a car hidden on his property. He knew that it belonged to Chester Harris. He hid it there. Apparently, he hadn't hid it well enough. He couldn't confess that to his friend. He had to lie and deny it.

Rule # 13 Hide in plain sight

Sly kept his cool, and focused on relaxing so the good Sherriff wouldn't see the spike in his blood pressure. It was years ago that Edward had done his cadet training, but he knew that he had been trained in the basic elements on how to tell when a person was lying.

"A car? No. I have a lot of land here, and

I have to be honest. There's much of it that I haven't even explored yet."

The Sheriff continued. "It's a stolen vehicle. I guess it's the largest crime this county had seen in some time. The state wants to take it over. They're sending some troops here to question you. They also want to inspect the land for themselves.

Sly couldn't make sense of anything. He abducted Chester in Chester's car. He knew that since he had fed Chester to the pigs that Chester couldn't have reported his own car stolen. "I don't understand. What's a stolen car have to do with me?"

Edward stepped in closer to his friend, as if he was about to tell a secret. "I'm not supposed to tell you this, but you're my friend. If you breathe a word of this to the state boys, I'll deny telling you anything. But at first, it looked like a classic story of husband leaving his wife. But he was stupid enough to take the car that was solely in his wife's name. So she reported it stolen. And now, since the car popped up here, they're suspecting foul play."

If Sly wasn't standing there talking to the Sheriff, he would've kicked himself for being so stupid. He didn't check to see whose name was on the vehicle. Now he was in danger of state troopers inspecting his property. What if they checked out the pigsty? Would there be traces of blood? What if they looked in the guesthouse?

Would they find his secret basement?

Sly just wiped his brow. "It sure is hot out here. Why don't we go inside and talk about this? I'm sure there's an explanation for all of this."

Edward looked down at his feet, and kicked the ground. "That's what I'm gettin' to Sly. The state boys, they want me to take you in for formal questioning. I hate doing it. But it's my job." Edward chewed on his lip for a split second. "There is a stolen car on your farm. I know you're innocent, but they don't."

Sly hid his panic very well, and tried to keep up with his playful banter. He held his wrists out in front of him. "Okay, I'll go willingly. You can cuff me and all. I'm okay with that."

Edward slapped at his best friend's wrists. "I'm not gonna cuff you. But c'mon. I gotta take you in. I'm sorry."

Sly just sighed.

RULE # 2 DENY DENY DENY

Edward didn't even make Sly ride in the back of his official police vehicle. He rode in the passenger seat, and Sly could feel the tension. He knew his friend would be mad at him for spending the day with his sister.

Sly just looked at his friend as he was driving. "So, when are we gonna talk about Cindy?"

Edward cringed. "What's there to say? She don't wanna move home. Plus she ran to you to get away from me. I'm her brother. I know what's best for her."

Sly shook his head in agreement. "I want her home, too. She belongs here.

They rode in silence to the police station. Edward was relieved that his best friend was on his side.

When the state troopers arrived at the small police station, Sly had been waiting in the very small interrogation room. He had never been questioned by the police. All he could do was sit and hope that the police wouldn't find any evidence against him.

He knew that he wore gloves when he was in Chester Harris' car. But he also knew that Charlene Burris was currently being held hostage in the dungeon of his guesthouse.

Sly showed no signs of concern, as two officers questioned his relationship with the missing man. When they asked if he knew Chester Harris, Sly simply stated that he did business with many people in the city. He didn't remember all of his clients by name.

Rule # 2 Deny Deny Deny

Unfortunately for Sly, Chester's wife remembered briefly doing business with him, even though the deal had fallen through.

Sly had to sit and wait while the police were at his farm, looking for any form of evidence that they hoped to find. Sly just very calmly asked if he could call his lawyer. He knew that he had rights. And he thought it was unfair that they were detaining him for no reason.

Even though the officers eventually let him

go home, they made it very clear that they found it odd that his past client just happened to go missing, and his car was found on Sly's property.

Paranoia set in as Sly remembered the tortured Charlene awaiting her fate in the basement of his guesthouse.

Edward could tell while he was driving Sly home that his best friend wasn't happy. He had been questioned by the police officers for a few hours, and his mood was really sour. Even though Edward knew that Sly was innocent, it was an inconvenience.

They had been friends long enough that the Sheriff knew his best friend had nothing to do with the disappearance of that man. But the law still had to do their job. Edward didn't want to discuss the current legal situation, he wanted to talk about his sister.

"I know this isn't the best time, but can we talk about Cindy?"

Sly steadied his breath, and remained calm. Naturally, the only thing he was thinking about was getting back to his farm. Sly literally had his fingers crossed that the state troopers hadn't discovered any incriminating evidence.

Sly just looked at his friend. "She already told me. I want her to move home, too. But it's not like we can make her."

Edward smiled, happy with his friend's response. "But she's only in town for a couple days. Think you can convince her to come stay with me? I miss her, ya know."

Sly wanted her to stay with him, but he also had another houseguest to tend to. Sly obliged. "I'll see what I can do."

RULE # 16
THE HOBBY IS
FOR ANGER

Cindy had a hundred questions for Sly as soon as he stepped in the door. After the day he just had, he didn't want to answer anymore questions. All he wanted to do was spend time in his guesthouse basement.

Sly remained cool and collected after hearing Cindy's account of how there were plenty of police officers searching his home. Apparently, it wasn't a pleasant ordeal for her either.

One important piece of information that one of the policemen told her unofficially was that the missing man's wife didn't believe that Chester had left her willingly. She had a brother in the city that was on the police force.

Sly was so mad at himself. He should've known that Chester's brother-in-law was an officer of the law. There was no reason for Sly to overlook such an important detail.

Knowing that he couldn't change that situation now, all he could do was try to be more careful in the future. He only hoped that whichever cop was Chester's brother-in-law wouldn't keep pursuing him since they didn't find anything on his farm.

After a quick chat with Cindy, she agreed to go stay with her brother. Sly noticed a hesitation as she left. He could almost feel a longing inside of him, he wanted to beg her to stay. But he had other things to tend to.

The second that he saw her taillights exit the driveway, he jumped in his car and drove to his guesthouse.

He walked along the pigsty, and the animals turned their snouts in the air, growling from their want of food.

Sly patted Betsy on her head. "Soon. I'll have some dinner for you soon."

He entered his guesthouse, and saw that a few objects had been moved. Now it made sense to him as to why they got a search warrant so easily. When you're related to a cop and go missing, they take it seriously.

Sly laughed as he ran his foot along the unmoved carpet. They weren't smart enough to find his secret room.

Like a child waking up on Christmas day full of excitement, Sly was eager to unleash his anger.

Rule # 16: The hobby is for anger

A bloodied Charlene was sitting in the chair, her eyes only half open. He knew that she was on the brink of death, but he wasn't done with her yet.

He inspected her damaged breasts. She let out a small groan as he ran his fingers along her wounds.

He held a cup of water to her face, and the woman drank.

"You've lost a lot of blood. You need this."

Sly couldn't help but laugh about the whole situation. "You're still alive, right? Did you hear all that movement upstairs earlier? It's almost funny. There were cops up there. They could've saved you. If only you had screamed."

Charlene's eyes rolled back into her head. She could barely make out the words he was saying. There was no way that she had enough energy to scream.

Sly enjoyed every minute of seeing this shell of a woman in pain. She had spent her whole life trying to look good, and ignoring the important parts of life. He hated it when people were self-centered.

"Wake up! Can you hear me?"

Charlene groaned. Sly grabbed her long

flowing hair, and pulled her head straight up in the air. Her ruined body adjusted so that her back was straight. He pulled on her hair so tight that the skin on her forehead smoothed out all of her wrinkles.

"Look at your pretty hair." Sly mocked her as he gave her silky strands another tug. When he released his grip, her neck fell limp and Charlene's head wobbled onto her shoulder.

Sly went to his workbench and grabbed a large hunting blade.

Charlene tried to keep her eyes open to see what her captor was doing, but she barely had any energy left.

Sly grabbed her by the head of her hair once again, and slid the blade into the hairline of her forehead. Her skin cracked easily, and a line of blood ran down her face.

He pulled harder on her hair, raising the skin away from the bones in her head. He glided the blade down the center of her skull, just deep enough to remove her scalp.

Charlene tried to scream from the pain, but instead it sounded like a high pitched heavy breathing sound.

Blood flowed from her head, pooling up, and her hair absorbing the red sticky substance. Her breathing became labored, and Sly could hear her sounds whistling in the air.

Sly grabbed a mirror and forced her to look at herself. "Look at your pretty hair now! Do you see how easy that was! Now, you have not only a bald patch but it looks like I went a little deep right there."

Sly was waving the mirror around, and Charlene refused to look. She had just enough energy to keep her eyes held shut tight.

"Open your eyes!"

Charlene refused. Sly grabbed a small pair of scissors from the workbench. As Charlene squinted, she saw the small object, thinking that maybe he was going to cut the rest of her hair.

Instead, Sly plucked at her eyelashes, separating her eyelids from her eyeball. He held the scissors at an angle, and forced her eyelid between the two blades. When he squeezed the blades together, the metal made a snipping sound. The blades were so sharp that they easily cut through her eyelid.

Once again, he held up the mirror.

"Look now. Now! You have to look!" Sly laughed as he looked at the mess of a woman in front of him.

Charlene tried to cry, but due to dehydration she had no more fluids in her. She whistled her last labored breath before giving in to death.

Sly smacked her around. He wasn't done with her yet. But it was too late now. She was dead.

Sly made sure to remove all of his clothes. He didn't want to get her blood in his laundry.

He picked up his circular saw, and felt the

tiny motor revving in his hand. He started with her head, and he cut her across the neck. When he cut through her spinal cord, a clear fluid leaked out of her neck.

Then, he cut off each limb. As the blade of the saw was spinning, it was throwing blood all over the cement walls and floor. Sly loved the mess. He enjoyed the splatter of fluids.

She was an unworthy human being. She didn't deserve to be. She especially didn't deserve to have children. He knew that now her children would be better off without her.

As Sly got to her breasts, the saw ate its way through her implants. For a second, he wondered if it was safe to feed her implants to the pigs. But then he remembered that his pigs will eat anything.

He carefully cut off each finger and each toe. By the time that he was finished, Sly's naked body was covered in blood from head to toe. The pigs seemed to enjoy their dinner in smaller chunks.

After the long hard day that he had, this was the kind of relaxing evening that he needed. After Charlene's entire body was cut up small enough, Sly carried the pieces of her body to the pigsty.

As the pigs fed on the tiny pieces of the dead woman's body, their snarls were glorious. Sly smiled as he enjoyed the sounds of his pets feeding, destroying any evidence that Charlene was ever a guest. He laughed at the thought of the police being too stupid to check the pig dung.

RULE # 11 CLEAN UP IS IMPORTANT

Sly was awake all night. First, he used the hose in the basement to hose down his naked body. As Charlene's blood drained off his naked body he felt alive. As much as he hated to see the stains of her sins washed away, he knew he had to do it.

Rule # 11: Cleanup is important

He splashed his feet in the red puddles and felt the gooey substance in between his toes. After his body was clean, he pointed the hose at the concrete walls.

Blood was difficult to wash away, and he used high pressure to remove the substance. The red flowed down the walls until eventually the floor was a mess of crimson red.

He hosed the floor thoroughly, leading the

water into the drain.

Afterwards, he used bleach and a mop on the stubborn spots, and repeated the rinsing process. Before he knew it, it was morning.

Sly got in his car after talking to his pigs, and drove to the main house. As he was getting out of his car, he saw none other than the Sheriff driving up the driveway.

He realized he was still naked and quickly scampered into his house. As he was getting dressed, he heard Edward walk right into his home.

Edward chuckled to himself. "Sly! Were you just naked? I think I saw your butt!"

Sly slightly blushed as he put on a pair of running shorts. "All I was doing was feeding the pigs. Plus, I need a tan."

Edward's laughter filled the room. "You're gonna get a sunburn on your balls! Don't tell me that you're tanning for Cindy? Is there something you aren't telling me?"

Sly blushed even redder as he thought of Cindy. He felt his blood pressure rise, and his heart beat just a little bit faster. "There's nothing to tell. She was mad at you, so she came here." Sly paused for a very brief moment. "Why? Did she say anything about me?"

Edward stopped laughing, and he looked at his best friend and gave him a nudge on the shoulder. "Do you want her to have said something about you?"

Sly felt like a child in school, back when he had his first crush on a girl. But this time it felt more real and more serious. Edward never knew of his best friend's drunken night with his sister years ago, and Sly intended to keep it a secret.

He just shook his head no.

Edward reached into his pocket, and pulled out a sealed envelope. "I already took her to the airport. She said to give this to you."

Sly held the letter in his hand, fighting the urge to tear it open and read it that very moment.

"Well, open it. I wanna know what it says."

Sly refused. "If she wanted you to read it, she would've wrote it to you."

The two grown men bickered like children until Sly slipped the note in his pocket.

"She said you were shook up yesterday. I don't understand why those state boys put you through the wringer. I vouched for ya'. I told'em that you're a good guy."

"I appreciate that." Sly just sighed. Due to his lack of sleep, he really didn't have the energy to have this conversation. "I don't understand. My lawyer said they had no grounds. But I heard a rumor that the missing man has a family member in law enforcement. Plus, he was almost a client of mine at one time. They say that I've met the man. But I've met a lot of people. That don't mean nothin'."

Edward slapped his friend on the back. "It'll

be okay. They just wanted the car. They towed it in. They're checkin' into it. Your name will be clear in no time."

Sly only hoped that was true.

As soon as Edward left, Sly ripped the envelope open. He swore he could smell Cindy's sweet perfume in the paper.

Sly,

I'm sorry that I left without saying bye. Maybe I'll be back sooner than later.

Cindy

Sly felt warmth from his heart as he held the letter close to his chest. He only hoped that her words were true.

He gave in to his exhaustion, and went to bed. He wanted to be rested up for the next day. Sly had plans to go to the city and check out the men's shelter where Elliot Combs might be residing.

RULE # 20 NO WITNESSES (EVER)

Sly slept until three in the morning. It was still dark outside, and he was surprised when he looked at the clock. Not only had he slept an entire day, he also slept most of the night. The coffee maker had an aroma that filled his house, and after a few cups he was alert.

He knew that if he drove fast enough he would make it to the men's shelter on Eighth Street when they made their residents get out. They let out everyday at five thirty in the morning when it was still dark. Perhaps it was to encourage the homeless to find jobs.

Sly sped for the hour drive, and checked his expensive watch. He still had a few minutes to spare. He hoped that he would recognize Elliot from the picture Mrs. Combs had on display.

He parked his car a few blocks away, and knew there was zero chance that Elliot would be coming home with him today. At best, he might just learn the kid's routine. He walked across the street from the shelter and waited in a dark alley.

It wasn't long until a swarm of men came from the building. There were dozens of them, and Sly knew that this would be much harder than he anticipated.

As he leaned against the building, he squinted to try and get a good look at the men, but it was so dark that it was difficult. None of the men got into a vehicle. Instead, they all walked, each in different directions.

Sly was too busy trying to find his target, that he hadn't realized there was a man behind him. He felt a tap on his shoulder.

"Man. You're in the wrong place right now."

Sly turned around and saw a man holding a knife in the air.

"Empty your pockets. I'll take that watch, too."

Sly looked at the young punk. Was it possible that he was looking at Elliot? It could be the man from the picture, if the picture was a couple years old. Also, this man had a long scruffy beard that made his appearance even harder to decipher.

Sly held his wrist away from him, pretending to fumble with the clasp of his watch. "I don't want no trouble."

As the robber was watching Sly try to remove his expensive jewelry, Sly quickly shoved his elbow into the man's face. His elbow connected with the delicate cartilage of the man's nose, and he heard a slight crunching sound. The robber dropped the knife, and held his hands to his bleeding, broken nose.

Sly stepped on the blade, just in case the man tried to pick it up. Instead the man just held his nose, screaming obscenities.

Sly looked around, and apparently, everyone from the shelter was already out of hearing distance, because nobody came to see what the man was cursing about.

Rule # 20 No witnesses (Ever)

Making sure there was no one around, Sly picked up the knife.

"What's your name?"

The man refused to answer. Instead he turned around to run, even deeper into the darker part of the alley.

Sly chased the man, and tackled him, barely catching the man by his shins as he dove to the ground. The man fell face down into the pavement. The robber tried to kick Sly, so Sly raised the blade, and cut a large gash behind the man's foot. As the man's leg started bleeding he screamed out in pain.

Once again, there was nobody coming to

rescue this man. Sly grabbed the man by his head and slammed it into the asphalt until the man went unconscious.

Sly looked around, not once, but twice, to reassure that there were no witnesses. He still had just a few minutes of darkness. He quickly ran to get his car, and then loaded the passed out man into his vehicle, and sped to his farm.

RULE # 7
THIEVES
MUST DIE

Sly drove, keeping his fingers crossed that this man wouldn't wake up. He still had the blade, just in case. He could quickly stab him and kill him, but what fun would that be? He drove fast, hoping that he wouldn't get pulled over.

Another thought crossed Sly's mind. Was he being stupid by taking another houseguest so soon after learning the police were watching him?

It's not like he planned to take a houseguest today. He had only planned to find out something about Elliot. He wasn't exactly prepared to be speeding down the expressway with an unconscious man in his passenger seat.

The sun was rising in the distance and it was a beautiful sight. Sly tried to keep his focus on his passenger, hoping that he wouldn't wake up. Blood was clotting on his forehead of the thief, where his face had been smashed into the concrete several times. A large red bump was already forming.

Sly made it to his driveway when the man started opening his eyes. It took the man a second to realize what was happening, and he looked at his blood soaked hands before rubbing his broken nose and knotted head.

"What's going on?"

Sly played stupid and hoped that the man wouldn't remember what was happening. "I found you in an alley. I'm taking you to the hospital."

The man looked around. "There's no hospital here. You're the man with the watch."

Sly put the knife to the man's throat. "That's right. And with the head wound and your cut leg you're in no position to fight me. I just wanna talk."

Sly drove past his main house until he reached his guesthouse.

"Get out! Now!" Sly knew the man couldn't run due to the large gash in his leg.

As the man lifted himself from the passenger seat, Sly noticed the blood that the man had left behind and made a mental note to thoroughly scrub his car with bleach.

With the blade dug into the man's side, Sly led the man into his guesthouse.

"Raise the rug! Right there!"

The man scampered to a corner of the rug and lifted it until he saw the hidden hatch to the basement.

"Open it!"

As soon as the man opened the door in the floor, Sly pushed the man down the ladder, and he heard rumbling crashing sounds as the man's fragile bones hit each rung of the ladder.

Sly lowered himself down the ladder and saw the man's broken body lying on the concrete floor. He propped the man's body into the chair, and handcuffed him to the metal arms.

Sly said nothing as he left the man alone. He had to go scrub his car clean.

After cleaning his car, Sly went back to his basement of doom. He looked at the man in disgust. Only hoping that he was Elliot Combs.

"What's your name?"

The man spit towards Sly.

"I admire your gumption. Even after being stabbed in the leg, even after I broke your nose, even after I banged your head on the street, and even after falling down a ladder, you have gumption. Unfortunately, you tried to steal from me."

Rule # 7 Thieves must die

"I'm just trying to figure out who else you have stolen from."

Sly grabbed at the man's pockets, but the man tried to kick him. Sly picked up a large chain, and forced the man's legs against the chair so he could chain him up.

Sly searched the man's pockets. He pulled out a lighter, a single key, and a napkin.

"Where's your wallet? Who are you?"

The man refused to answer. The man tried not to cry. "Why are you doing this?"

Sly laughed as he answered the man. "I have to feed my pigs."

Sheer terror formed on the man's face.

Sly grabbed a pair of scissors from his work bench, and stuck them in the man's mouth. "If you ever want to speak again, you'll tell me your name."

The man peed on himself, and the stench was undeniable. Very meekly, he looked at his captor. "David."

Sly shook his head. He had a thief, but it wasn't Elliot. "Your name isn't Elliot?"

A flash of recognition showed in the man's eyes. "You mean that druggie? I'm not a doper like him."

Relieved that he was finally getting somewhere, Sly set the scissors down, and crossed his arms across his chest. "Where can I find Elliot?"

The man started shaking from fear. "I don't know. I mean he's at the shelter sometimes. But then he came across a lot of money. He's usually at the crackhouse."

"Do I look like I know where a crack house is? Where's this crackhouse?"

The man rattled off an address. Sly was on a mission.

Once again, Sly left the man alone. He had to go to the crackhouse.

RULE # 26 DISGUISES ARE GOOD

Before making the long drive back to the city, Sly went to his main house for a change of clothes. He dressed in an all black running suit, and a black baseball cap. He firmly folded the bill of the cap around his face. He looked in the mirror, and he looked just like any other man on the streets.

He carefully took off his expensive watch and stored it with his dozen other watches. Then the finishing touch was a dark pair of sunglasses.

Sly went out to the barn, and retrieved his old car that he referred to as 'The Beater'. He had this car for many years, and mostly it sat in the barn collecting dust. It was an older model vehicle, and had plenty of rust spots and dings. His car still smelled of bleach, so this was his best option. Plus, he would be traveling to what they called a crackhouse.

Sly had never been to a crackhouse, and it was a term he had only ever heard of on the news or in movies. He remembered one specific movie that had a crackhouse in it. It was just basically an abandoned house that homeless drug addicts went to and did their drugs.

He questioned whether he was doing the right thing. He already had one guest staying in his basement, did he really need another? Sly tried to push the paranoia from his mind. Surely, the police were content with their search that yielded no results.

Paranoia kept Sly in check. That's why he had the rules. For his own protection. His paranoia also gave him an adrenaline rush. He loved it that the police could have caught him, but they didn't. He felt alive knowing that he had outsmarted the law.

He started 'The Beater', and made the drive back to the city, not sure what to expect.

He pulled up in front of the old house that looked abandoned. The windows had boards covering them. The roof was caved in at one section. The paint was peeled off nearly every piece of siding.

It was starting to get dark, and Sly took in his surroundings. The road and yard was littered with beer cans and cigarette butts. The neighboring houses were run down, with knee high grass. Perhaps they were abandoned, also.

There were no people in sight, and the evening was very silent. Sly made sure his ball cap was pulled tightly around his face, and thought about taking off his sunglasses. It was getting almost too dark to see through the dark shades, but he had a very recognizable face and couldn't chance it.

His face was in almost every advertisement for Verdict Realty. He only hoped that crackheads never noticed realty adverts.

He stepped on the first step of the small porch, and the creak was the loudest noise of the evening. He reached for the doorknob, but it was absent. The door had a hole where the knob should be.

He took his shoe and lightly tapped the door, and it swung open freely. Sly stuck his head in the doorway, and saw that it was too dark with his sunglasses. Clouds of smoke lingered in the air, and they smelled of a scent that he didn't recognize. He could hear people shuffling around inside, and wondered if he should make his presence known.

Instead, he decided to call out a name. "Elliot!"

He stood in the doorway, waiting to see if someone actually responded.

He heard a faint voice cry out. "In the dining

room."

Sly took that as his invite into the house. He stepped into the rubbish lying around the entryway, and was glad that he had chosen to wear his running shoes.

There were people on the floor, half of them looked to be sleeping. The few who weren't passed out didn't even raise their head to look at Sly. It was like they were in their own little world, obviously high from whichever drug they were doing.

The kitchen stank of rotten food, or perhaps dead mice. Sly didn't know, but he held his breath as he trudged through the room. The interior of the house got darker in each room, but his eyes had started to adjust to the darkness.

When he was in a room that he assumed could be a dining room, (it was too difficult to tell without furniture) he called for Elliot once again.

A small framed man, who looked like he hadn't eaten in weeks, pointed to an unconscious man sprawled out on the floor.

"What do you want with him? Does he owe you money? He owes me, too. His pockets are empty."

Sly pondered how Elliot had blown through fifty grand and still owed people money. It didn't matter. He picked up his frail body and threw it over his shoulder. He was so glad that he stayed in shape from all his swimming, otherwise he wouldn't have been able to move this man.

The toothless man that had pointed Elliot out took another smoke from his pipe. "Just bring'em back when you're done. K?"

Sly carried Elliot out of the crackhouse, and kept his head down. But it didn't really matter. Nobody was paying any attention to him, plus it was dark.

When he got Elliot to his old car, he checked his face under the streetlight. He compared the face of this man to the picture he saw at Mrs. Comb's house. It was a perfect match.

Sly had brought along some duct tape this time, and taped the man's arms and legs together in the backseat. He looked around and saw that there were no witnesses. He drove the man back to his guesthouse.

RULE # 33 THE PUNISHMENT SHOULD FIT THE OFFENDER

When Sly carried Elliot into his guesthouse, his muscles relaxed as he got to the ladder. He threw the taped up man down the ladder, and heard a heavy thud hit the concrete.

Sly climbed down, hoping that he hadn't busted the man's head open. There was no blood. The man opened his eyes and looked up at Sly.

"What the hell man?"

David was still chained to his chair. "Elliot? Is that you?"

"Yeah. What's going on, dude? Why am I tied up?"

David finally smiled. "I don't know, and I don't care. This guy wanted you. Now he has you. You owe too many people money." David looked at Sly. "Can I go now?"

Sly laughed. "I'm not done with you yet, David. It's not that easy."

Elliot was so scared that his voice was trembling. "How much do I owe ya? I can get it. I'm good for it."

Sly answered with one word. "Fifty."

Elliot sighed out of relief. "Whew. I can do that."

"Thousand."

Elliot began to panic. "What the? Fifty thousand? Where am I supposed to get that kind of money?"

Sly hoped the boy would realize his sin. But instead of acknowledging his crime, he just panicked.

Sly slammed a pallet of wood on the ground next to Elliot. The board fell to the concrete. SMACK. Elliot tried to jump, and fought against the tape on his hands. Elliot tried to get to his feet, but kept tripping over himself since his ankles were taped together.

Sly climbed on Elliot's back, like he was riding a horse. He slid the frail man's body on top of the pallet, facedown. He grabbed Elliot by the wrist, and led his hand until it was centered with a slab of the wooden pallet.

Elliot tried to fight, but he was so weak and his strength was no match for Sly. Sly held the man's hand in place with his knee, and reached for his hammer and an extra long nail.

David was watching in terror. "Dude! What are you doing?"

Sly centered the nail to the back of Elliot's hand, and raised his hammer. He swung the hammer down and it connected with the head of the nail. Elliot screamed out in pain, the sound echoing in the room.

David flinched, even though he was only watching. "Dude! Stop! That's some Jesus Christ shit there!"

Sly continued hammering the nail until it found its way deep into Elliot's hand. Eventually, just the head of the nail was visible.

Sly could hear David and Elliot screaming, but he didn't care.

After one of Elliot's hands was sufficiently nailed to the pallet, he untied the tape. Elliot was writhing in pain. It didn't deter Sly. Sly took Elliot's other hand, and spread it shoulder width and forced his palm flat to the wood. Sly grabbed another nail, and started pounding it into the backside of Elliot's hand. Each time the hammer slammed into the metal, it made a slight ping noise that was barely audible due to the screaming.

Sly heard a gagging noise, and looked up to see David spewing vomit down the front of his body.

Elliot's body laid face down on the pallet, with both of his hands above his head, nailed to the wood. Sly stood and kicked him in the ribs to see if he could move. Elliot's body slightly raised as he groaned in pain, but his hands were stuck in place, blood running down to his wrists.

David, no longer watching, turned his head and closed his eyes. "I ain't in this man." He started to cry. "Why can't I leave?"

Sly shook his head and spoke in a very calm manner. "Simple. You're a thief."

David started apologizing, but his words of sorry fell on deaf ears. Sly didn't care if he was sorry, he had to rid the world of this evil creature.

Elliot wasn't speaking, just making sounds of agonizing pain. Sly enjoyed the sounds of the men. It was the simple things in life that pleased him.

Sly reached under Elliot's waist and unbuttoned his blue jeans. He slowly unzipped the man's pants. He stood at Elliot's feet, and tugged on the pants pulling them down his legs. He then removed his underwear, exposing his bare bottom.

David couldn't take no more. "What is this? Some gay shit? Man, I don't wanna watch this." Tears mixed with the dried up blood and snot running from his broken nose, creating a mixture of a gel-like mess.

Sly bent down and grabbed Elliot by the face, and turned it to the side to face him. "Put your butt in the air!"

"Huh!" Elliot had a look of confusion on his

face.

"You're either gonna do it, or I'm gonna do it!" Sly was stern with his command. He wasn't gonna take no for an answer.

As Elliot tried to pull his body weight up on his knees, the strain on his hands hurt too much and he couldn't stand it. The metal nails tugged at his skin. "I can't!"

Sly kicked Elliot in the ribs, and the boy started coughing. He slowly got up on his knees until his butt was in the air.

Sly bent down and screamed directly into the half-naked man's face. "Since you like to take from people, David is gonna take from you!"

Rule # 33 The punishment should fit the offender

Elliot was defiant. "Take! I ain't got nothing to give!"

Sly just chuckled. "You got your body, and David is gonna take it."

Through his sobs and sniffled, David tried to produce words, but he could only create a fragmented sentence. "I can't." Sob "Take." "Not gay."

Sly approached David. "I'll untie your feet, but not your hands. Don't try anything funny. And you're gonna either get it up and give it to Elliot, or you're gettin' a nail in your dick. Are we clear?"

David cringed at the thought of a nail in the

soft, sensitive tissue of his cock. "Clear. I got it!"

Sly slowly undone the shackles at David's ankles, and held the hammer to his head. Sly leaned in to whisper in David's ear. "Don't try anything. I'm warning you."

David limped over to Elliot's rump in the air, feeling the gash in his calf with each step he took. He fumbled with his pants, which was difficult with his hands handcuffed together, but got the zipper loose and they fell to his ankles.

David tried to stroke his dick. He tried to get erect. He just couldn't. But the thought of this crazy man hurting his manhood was too much pressure. He rubbed on his penis, but it stayed flaccid. He tried to guide his pecker into Elliot's anus, but it just kept mashing against it and not into it.

Sly got tired of watching him try to get erect, and drew the hammer back, swiftly bringing it down on his kneecap. The crunching sound of the bone was audible, and even Sly cringed. David fell to the concrete floor, grabbing onto his knee.

Sly wasn't a man to make hollow threats, he was a man of his word. He grabbed another nail, and dragged David closer to the wooden pallet. He pressed the man's dick against the wood, and pressed the sharp tip of the nail into the head of the penis.

The nail started to penetrate into the tissue, and David squirmed, causing the nail to scratch the shaft, leaving a trail of blood behind. Sly had already raised the hammer, and was in mid-swing. Even though the hammer missed the nail, it collided with the head of the penis, mashing it against the hard wooden pallet.

David made the highest pitch sound Sly had ever heard in his life and it made his ears hurt. David's penis had burst open, and blood and goo oozed all over the pallet.

Elliot turned his head, even though everything was happening so fast only inches from him, he refused to look.

The sight of David's penis even made Sly's crotch hurt. He pulled David by his long beard and slid him across the floor to the metal chair. He lifted the sobbing man and chained him to the chair once again.

Sly wanted to call it a night, but he remembered that he still had hungry pigs to feed, even if it was only a snack.

Sly took a saw to each of Elliot's fingers, cutting off snack-size pieces for his pigs. Elliot eventually passed out from the pain. He wanted Elliot to realize the error of his ways. He wanted the boy to know that he shouldn't have stolen from his grandmother.

He decided to teach him a lesson the next day.

As he went up the ladder, Sly looked at Elliot's damaged hands, the metal nails barely visible from the caked-up blood. He held all ten of his fingers in his hands, and hoped the boy wouldn't bleed out before the morning.

Sly fed the pigs, and they were more than happy to eat the fingers. They snarfed the digits in seconds, and grunted wanting more. He promised his pets a large meal for the next day. He needed to get some sleep.

RULE # 9 KEEP YOUR FRIENDS CLOSE, YOUR ENEMIES CLOSER

The morning sun was sneaking in through the windows, and Sly could feel the warmth on his face. He knew it was time to get out of bed, but his body wanted to lay in the comfort of the blankets just a few more minutes.

As he was enjoying his moments of solitude, there was a loud banging on his front door. He looked at the clock, and figured with it being early in the morning it was probably Edward, wanting some coffee while he was making his morning rounds around the small town.

"Hold your horses, Sheriff. I'm coming."

He stumbled out of bed, and wiped the sleep from his eyes. He went to the front door, and opened it, without even looking to see who it was. "I'm starting the coffee now. I was sleepin' in today."

An unfamiliar voice startled Sly.

"Mr. Verdict, I'm not here for coffee."

Sly turned around and found that he had just invited a complete stranger, a police officer, into his home for coffee. He froze in his tracks. "I'm sorry, sir. Can I help you?"

The cop held his uniform hat in one hand, and pointed a finger from his other hand in Sly's face. "Buddy, I'll have you know that I'm watching you."

Sly held his hands in the air. "Whoa, I'm innocent, and I just woke up. You wanna tell me what you're talking about?"

"I know it's not a coincidence. Chester's car didn't end up here by accident. I don't buy the businessman vibe from you. There's something off about you."

Sly sighed. "Officer, am I under arrest for something?" Sly looked at the name tag on his police uniform. "Officer Williams?"

The cop shook his head no. "No. But I'm watching you. Apparently there was a scuffle in the street yesterday, and the description of the car fits your car to a tee. That's fishy if you ask me."

Sly looked as innocent as he could. "I

don't know what you're talking about." Sly realized that the cop had no evidence, otherwise he would already be in handcuffs. He turned his back on the officer. "I'm gonna make some coffee."

Officer Williams followed him inside. "You're not getting away with this."

"With what? Tell me what I've done." Sly continued into the kitchen and pressed the button on the machine that made the caffeinated liquid his body desired. "If I've done something, arrest me."

The officer lost all confidence. He wasn't exactly sure why he came here. He wanted to get a feel for his suspect, but he was getting nothing. "Well, the witness didn't get the license plate. But it's fishy, after my missing brother-in-law's car was found on your property."

Sly held a mug in the air. "Do you want a cup?"

Rule # 9 Keep your friends close, and your enemies closer

Officer Williams was caught off guard. He had expected Sly to be an ill-tempered hooligan. Instead his suspect was calm and collected. Even though he had a bad feeling about him, the man wasn't showing any bit of worry.

"No. I'm leaving. I just want you to know that I'm on to you." The cop turned around to leave. "Mark my words. I will get you."

The man's threat resonated throughout Sly's body. But he knew that was all it was, a threat. If the cop had any evidence, he wouldn't be standing in his kitchen drinking a cup of coffee.

Sly followed the man onto his porch, relieved when he saw Edward's truck pulling up to his house.

Edward got out of his truck, and gave Sly a puzzled look.

"I'm the Sheriff here. I think your authority ends at the county line. Can I ask why you're here Officer Williams?"

Officer Williams turned to Sly. "I'm watching you." He ignored Edward as he got in his truck and drove away.

Edward was concerned about his friend. "He's out of his jurisdiction. Friend of yours?"

Sly shook his head no. "Brother-in-law of a missing man whose car was found here."

"Yeah. I know. I've talked to him. When I told him that I've known ya for years, he didn't take kindly to me. He has a hard on for you." Edward tugged at the star on his shirt. "I'm the Sheriff in these parts. You've got nothing to worry about. I'll take care of him."

Sly invited his friend in for a cup of coffee. In the back of his mind, he was thinking of his own ways to deal with Officer Williams.

Sly tried not to act upset with himself, even though he was fuming inside. How had he been so stupid to let somebody see his car. He knew he should have never picked up David.

Edward reassured his friend that everything would be okay. He knew in the pit of his heart that Sly was completely innocent. To keep Sly's mind off of Officer Williams, he changed the subject to one of Sly's favorite subjects.

"So how's work going? You been to the office lately?"

Sly took a sip of his too hot coffee, and winced as it burned his tongue. "Just a few days a week. That's the privilege of being the boss. The last time I went in was a few days ago. I even took Cindy with me."

"She told me. She didn't say much. But she did ask me about Stacy."

Sly mentally patted himself on the back. Cindy was jealous of his secretary. Perhaps there was still a chance that she would still come around.

RULE #22 SHOW THEM THE ERRORS OF THEIR WAYS

After Edward left, Sly needed a distraction to keep his mind off of Officer Williams. What better distraction than his hobby? He had two perfect specimens of a waste of human beings locked in his guesthouse, waiting for him.

He wasn't shocked to see Elliot passed out facedown on the pallet. David was possibly dead. His crotch covered in blood, matching the blood on his face from his broken nose. David had lost a lot of blood.

He didn't want Elliot dead yet. He needed him to know what he had done wrong.

Rule # 22 Show them the error of their ways

Sly kicked Elliot in the ribs, and the man let out a groan of pain and exhaustion.

"Wake up." Sly stood in his nakedness and knew what would wake the scum up. He held his pecker in his hand, and emptied his bladder on the back of Elliot's head, and on the back sides of his hands.

From the noises that Elliot made, the urine burned the wounds on his fingerless hands.

"Do you know why you're here?" Sly demanded a response from him by stepping on the man's damaged hands, and grinding the heel of his shoes into the metal nail.

Elliot cried and tears streaked his face. "I don't know. You said you want fifty thousand dollars."

Sly hoped that this was getting through to the thief. "Why would I want that much money? Does that number mean anything to you?"

Elliot sobbed louder and tried to turn his head to look at Sly. "Grandma?"

"Ding ding ding. We have a winner." Sly was so mad and he saw red. This piece of filth had admitted to stealing from an innocent, sweet old lady.

Sly picked up the hammer. "You don't deserve a grandma! You took from her, now I take from you!" He used the claw side of a hammer to beat on the bottom of the man's feet. "I'll take your ability to walk."

"No! Please. I beg you!"

Sly didn't care what he said. He kept raising the hammer over his head and slamming it down, breaking every bone in Elliot's feet. Then he grabbed Elliot's wrist and pulled so hard that his injured hand lifted from the nail. The head of the nail was larger than the hole and gave so much resistance. But Sly kept pulling until the hole in his hand was large enough to allow the head of the nail an exit.

When Elliot's hand was free, Sly tugged on his other hand, lifting it from the nail.

Sly flipped the man over. "You're free to go now."

Sly laughed as the man looked at his fingerless hands with holes in them. He tried to stand, but couldn't stand the pain from the broken bones in his feet. Elliot just cried like a baby.

Between sobs, Elliot tried to speak. "I'm sorry. I'm so sorry!"

It was comical watching the grown man cry. Sly laughed maniacally as Elliot squirmed. Hopefully now, he had made his point.

He beat Elliot in the head with the hammer, spilling grey matter all over the concrete floor. Sly looked at the two dead men, and was proud of the feast he would be giving his pigs.

Like a madman, Sly grabbed his chainsaw and began to cut Elliot and David into sections.

RULE # 3
ALWAYS BE
ALERT

Sly was so tired from his long night of cleaning up the mess in his guesthouse basement. He woke way too early, but at least he had a smile on his face. He remembered the feast he had given his faithful pigs. He had given them more meat than usual, but they had quickly eaten every bit of it, disposing of the evidence.

He slowly got out of bed and made a direct path to the coffee maker. The sweet aroma of liquid caffeine filled the house, waking his senses. After a quick trip to the toilet, he made plans for his day in his head. He felt like he had earned a relaxing day, lounging by the pool after swimming his laps.

As he poured his first cup of java, his phone rang.

"Sly here. Speak."

"We have an open house today at noon." Stacy, his secretary, sounded rushed and panicked. "Jan called in. There's nobody else available."

Sly picked up on the hint. This was one of the joys of being the boss. "I'll cover it. I'll be there."

Just like that, his day of relaxing was done. He had to go to work.

Sly looked his best in his high dollar suit. He showed up to the vacant house a few minutes early to set up a table of donuts for the potential buyers. If he wasn't busy making the world a better place by killing one useless person at a time, he loved to be at work.

He was good at selling houses. He could charm a man with no feet to buy a pair of shoes. He learned the gift of charm during his rough childhood. When he was a child being moved from one foster home to the next, he learned that it was best to be nice to his new foster parents. He honed his charm to an art. As a child, his new parents were more apt to keep him around if he played nice.

After picking up the keys for the open house at his office, Sly drove to the large house. He pulled into the driveaway, admiring all of the windows on the frontside of the home. It was a three floored Victorian Style home, and it was absolutely stunning. Sly dreamed of the large commission he would get from selling this home.

Sly slid the key into the front door of the home, and noticed a car pulling in behind him. Pleased that there were potential home buyers eager to show up and see the home extra early, he turned to greet them with a smile.

His smile quickly turned sour when he noticed that it wasn't a potential home buyer afterall. It was Officer Williams in a civilian vehicle. Mental note to self, Officer Williams drives a small, black compact car.

Rule #3: Always be alert

The real estate agent didn't let the stalking police officer bother him. After setting up the donuts in the entryway of the home, Sly picked up a napkin, and grabbed a donut.

He carried the junk food to the police officer's car, thinking to himself how appropriate it was to give a cop a donut.

"Good morning, Officer Williams. Thought you might like a snack." Sly extended the food to Williams. He thought how it was a shame that he didn't have any poison with him.

Officer Williams snarled up his face. "I don't want that. I'm just here to keep an eye on you. I figure it's my responsibility to protect these innocent people from you." Williams glanced Sly straight in the eyes. "You aren't fooling me. I'm gonna get evidence against you. I promise you that."

Undeterred from playing Mr. Nice Guy, Sly just smiled at his nemesis. "I appreciate your dedication to your job. But trust me, I'm innocent. Your time would be better spent somewhere else."

"This isn't my job. It's personal. For my sister." The cop shifted his weight in his car seat, leaning his hand out the car window. "I know it's not a coincidence. My sister and her husband were your clients. Then he goes missing, his car found on your farm. Do you think I was born last night?"

"Not at all officer." Another vehicle pulling up to the house caught Sly's attention. "Now, if you'll excuse me. I have a job to do.

Sly broke away from the cop car to greet the potential buyers. He made a mental note to himself. Keep an eye open for Officer Williams. Apparently he wasn't gonna let Sly go so easily.

Several interested buyers showed up to look at the beautifully restored mansion. Sly watched out the window at the off-duty police officer hoping he would leave. It took a couple of hours, but eventually he left.

Even though he was trying to be attentive to his clients, his mind kept wandering to how he should handle Williams. He contemplated getting a restraining order, but he hated doing anything through the legal system. Most criminals avoided legalities if they could. Then he thought about maybe making Williams the next guest in his guesthouse basement.

That was what Sly wanted to do. He wanted nothing more than to make this man disappear forever. But that went against every rule in his book. It would be sloppy. He would possibly be the first suspect.

There was another option that he hadn't thought of yet. Until he remembered the day that Officer Williams woke him up, and Sly invited him inside for coffee. Of course! Edward took care of Williams then, maybe he could take care of him now.

Sly's mind eased just a bit, and he couldn't help but to watch the potential homebuyers extra close. He needed new prey to add to his calendar a year from now. He also needed to check last year's calendar for any red circles.

Unfortunately, he didn't see any signs of abused wives or children. There weren't any creepy men trying to steal the homeowner's silver flatware.

Sly knew that he was going to have to work more to start filling next year's calendar with red circles. He hated waiting a year to kill his prey, but he knew that he had to play it safe. Especially with Officer Williams breathing down his neck.

RULE # 38 PROFESSIONAL. PERSONAL. HOBBY. KEEP LIFE ORGANIZED IN SECTIONS

Sly enjoyed his day at work, and watched for any sign of the police officer that might be following him home. Instead of heading straight home from the open house, he stopped by the office to check last year's calendar. Also, he was going to tell all of his workers that he was scheduling himself for more shifts.

He had to start filling his schedule with red circles for a year from now. New prey. But he couldn't tell his employees that.

Rule # 38: Professional. Personal. Hobby. Keep life organized in sections.

Everyone who had ever worked under Sly loved him as a boss. He was lenient with their hours, and he paid well. He always had the feeling that Stacy his secretary carried a secret crush for him, but he knew that he couldn't give in to her. The less that people from the office knew about him, the better.

Stacy greeted him in her super short dress, with her large breasts overflowing from the low neckline. He had to admit that she did look good, but he was her boss. He had to keep this strictly professional.

Some days, he felt as if he wore different masks for each section of his life. Professionally, he was a likeable, charming salesman. In his personal life, he was a cut-up. A funny guy that everyone wanted to spend time with. But in his hobby, he was a totally different creature.

He was happiest during his killing sprees, and wished that he could dedicate his whole life to ridding the world of bad people. If only there was a surefire way to not get caught, that would be how he spent his life.

"Stacy. Do me a favor? Put me on the schedule for every day next week?"

Stacy's eyes got large, like she was happy that Sly would be spending more time in the office.

She shook her head yes. "Of course, boss. Anything you want."

Sly got the feeling that her offer of anything that he wanted wasn't just pertaining to the job. He quickly walked into his private office and checked last year's calendar. There weren't any red circles for two more days. Just enough time to try and do some stalking of his own.

But first, he had to lose his own stalker.

RULE # 15 LAY LOW IF THERE'S ANY DOUBT

His next target was one that he had been waiting for a while. He remembered Chuck Bingham vividly. Chuck was a large, muscular man, who visited the gym regularly. Even looking at him, you had to wonder if he was on steroids. Especially after seeing Chuck's temper, Sly was almost sure that he was on steroids.

Chuck had bought a house from Sly last year. He had a pretty wife, and three cute kids. The children were well behaved at each and every house that Sly showed the family. Usually, the kids would run around the empty houses and act crazy and loud. Not Chuck's children.

They were the quietest kids that Sly had ever met. They actually reminded Sly of himself as a child. He knew what it was like to have an abusive father, and how important it was to abused children to keep quiet.

When Sly was getting Chuck's signature on some of the final paperwork for the sale of the home, Sly excused himself to the restroom. He snooped through the medicine cabinet, and found what he had suspected. Steroids. Sly knew all about what they refer to as roid rage. When you've been on steroids for too long, and it causes the drug addict to have a temper and be violent.

Sometimes, in cases like this, he wished that he didn't have to wait the whole year, but a rule is a rule. Maybe if someone had intervened when he was a child, then his Father wouldn't have murdered his Mother.

Sly knew the gym that Chuck frequented.

Before leaving his office, Sly checked to see if Officer Williams was following him. He didn't notice anything suspicious, so he drove to the gym.

Sly sat in his car outside of the gym. It was one of those twenty four hour work out places, that had a storefront made of all windows. He saw the buff Chuck pumping iron on a weight bench, and checked his watch to see what time it was He wanted to know approximately what time Chuck usually left the gym.

He watched the man do various types of lifts with the weight bar full of large, heavy weights on the ends. Then a car behind him caught his eye. It was a small black vehicle, but he couldn't tell exactly what kind of car it was due to it getting dark outside.

He started to panic, wondering if Officer Williams had followed him to the gym. He couldn't tell if it was Williams for certain, but he felt the need to leave anyways.

Rule # 15: Lay low if there's any doubt.

Sly started his car, and slowly drove down the street, watching to see if the suspicious vehicle followed behind him. It didn't.

Sly recognized his paranoia. Was it just in his head? Was this cop actually getting to him?

He wanted nothing more to get close to Chuck.

First, he had to get Williams out of his way.

RULE # 31
KEEP IN SHAPE, ESPECIALLY FOR TOUGH OPPONENTS

Sly had no guest in his guesthouse. He wasn't scheduled for work until the new week. He was downright bored.

He was feeding his pigs some boring pig food. Their snarls weren't as thankful as when he fed them human flesh. It might have been in his head, but he would've swore that they actually growled at him.

He had placed a quick phone call in to his best friend. Not only was he lonely, but maybe the Sheriff could help him with his problem with William. Plus, maybe he could motivate him and help him work out.

Rule # 31: Keep in shape, especially for tough opponents.

Edward used to be in shape. When he first started on the police force, he had to stay in shape. But now, he was the Sheriff. The boss. He enjoyed beer a tad too much, and it showed in his pudgy belly.

Sly picked at his friend. "C'mon lazy! Race me in some laps around the pool! It'll be fun!"

Edward ignored Sly as he sat in the lounger chair and removed his shirt. Sly heard the pop of the aluminum can as Edward opened another beer.

Sly swam to the edge of the pool, and splashed Edward, hoping to get a response from him.

Edward just took a long gulp of his cold beer. "Thanks buddy. It's hot out here. That water feels good right now."

Sly swam around the edges of the pool as fast as he could. He didn't need anyone to motivate him to keep in shape. Chuck was all the motivation that he needed. In his mind, he kept picturing Chuck tied to the chair in his basement. He knew that the steroid monster wasn't gonna go down without a fight.

When Sly got out of the pool, Edward was

laying in the long chair, baking his bare chest in the sun.

Sly threw his towel at his friend. "Aren't you on duty?" He liked to tease his friend. Ever since they had known each other, they always found ways to pick at each other.

"I'm always on duty. I'm the Sheriff. Always on call. But we don't get much crime here anyways. 'Cept you. Your farm had a stolen car on it." He threw the wet towel back to Sly.

Sly frowned as he towel dried his hair. "Not fair. I had nothing to do with that."

Edward set his beer down, and cocked his head sideways. "You don't think I know that. Relax, grab a beer." He motioned towards the cooler.

Even though he wasn't thrilled with the idea of the excess calorie intake, he grabbed a beer and held the cold can to his forehead. "That guy. He still won't leave me alone. Ya know he came up to work the other day, and followed me to an open house." *Pop.* Sly opened the beer and enjoyed the first drink so much that he drank nearly half the can in one big gulp.

Edward sat up real fast. "I checked that guy out. I found out he's been in trouble with Internal Affairs before. It turns out that he don't always follow the law. The rumor is that he's gone rogue before."

Thinking that maybe he could work that to his advantage, Sly stored that on an imaginary memo note in his head.

Edward crunched the aluminum in his fist. The can was no match for his strength. "I'm gonna call his superior. Let me take care of this."

Sly smiled. That's exactly what he wanted. It was great to have a best friend that was the Sheriff.

Immediately, Edward pulled out his phone, and held a single finger in the air. Sly knew that meant to leave him alone to speak on the phone. After killing his beer, Sly jumped back into the refreshing pool, and swam more laps. He wanted to swim until his body was completely exhausted.

Sly swam until Edward threw an empty beer can at him while he was swimming. His head was submerged underwater, and he was so dedicated to his workout that he didn't hear Edward calling his name.

After getting his best friend's attention, Edward patted both of his hands together, as if he was shaking dirt off of them. "Problem solved, buddy. You won't hear from Officer Williams ever again."

RULE # 28
KNOW YOUR OPPONENT

Sly had a full year to study up on steroids. Chuck was an easy man to characterize. He could easily be found at the gym. Taking him though would be a different story. Sly would have to get clever with Chuck because it would be almost impossible to strongarm him.

But Officer Williams. He was different. Sly knew hardly anything about him. If he ever had a nemesis, it would be Officer Williams. If it weren't for Cindy, then Sly would have never known that he was Chester's brother-in-law. If it weren't for Edward, Sly would not have ever known that he had been in trouble with Internal Affairs for not always following the law.

That was it. That was the full extent. Sly basically knew nothing about Officer Williams. He figured it was time to level the playing field.

Rule #28: Know your opponent.

Another advantage of owning a real estate company was the opportunity to get to know someone. And not just in the general terms of meeting them.

It was getting to know someone the good old fashioned electronic way. Sly had a spectacular company program. Once you entered their social security number, you could find out anything about a person. Mostly about their debts, but debts revealed a lot about a person.

For example, you knew if they gambled. You knew if maybe they used the ATM too often and was somehow blowing too much cash. You could see how much they charged, and when. As to where a person shopped truly said something about their personality.

Sly had used this method many times to get to know someone for his own benefit. Checking Chester's wife's credit was how he found out that she went to yoga once a week. When he ran Chuck's credit, that's how he found out which gym collected a payment each month.

But Officer Williams was different. He had no debt. No credit card charges, no house mortgage, no car payment. It was almost impossible to live on a cop's salary, nevertheless to live debt free on a cop's salary.

For the first time, The electronic method of getting to know someone let Sly down. If he wanted to know anything else about Officer Williams, he would have to get his hands dirty.

RULE # 10 USE YOUR BRAIN, NOT YOUR BODY

Sly had always heard the expression, 'The bigger they are, the harder they fall'.

He understood it was some motivation bull to tell the underdog. Encouragement for what would usually be the loser. However, it never really had meaning until he chose to take Chuck as his next houseguest. Chuck outweighed him by at least a hundred pounds of muscle. Chuck's neck was larger than his head.

In reality, Sly knew that he had no chance against this beast.

Until he got smart.

Rule # 10: Use your brain, not your body

Physically, Sly couldn't take down his opponent. But he was sure that he could outsmart him.

Sly signed up at the gym, on a trial basis. Under a false name, of course. They offered one free week of gym membership for possible new members. He wore a hat at all times, and if anyone were to recognize his face from his realty ads, he would deny being himself.

Knowing that Chuck worked out later in the evening, his quest was even easier. There weren't too many other members at the gym at that time of night.

Sly went to the locker room to change his clothes, and easily picked the lock to Chuck's locker. He changed out his vial of steroids with a fast acting sleep aid. Now all Sly had to do was hope that Chuck injected the tampered with steroids before leaving the gym.

Sly rented a car and sat in a dim alley across the street from the gym, watching for Chuck to exit. The sun was gone, and only the night moon illuminated the sky.

After waiting almost an hour, he watched as Chuck stumbled to his own car, rubbing his head with each and every step. Sly emerged from the shadows, offering to help the man to his vehicle. It was almost too easy leading the man to his own rental car.

He placed the sleepy man in his passenger seat, and watched as Chuck went to sleep. A loud snore confirmed that the man was unaware of what was happening.

Sly checked and then double checked to ensure that he wasn't being followed. He hated this paranoia that Officer Williams had gifted him with, but he also saw it as a blessing. His paranoia helped keep him on his toes, making sure that he wouldn't get caught with his newest houseguest.

Sly enjoyed the night drive back to his home. Chuck's snores reminded him of some of the sounds his pigs made when they ate. He eyeballed the muscle man, wondering if maybe the pig's feast would be larger than both of the skinny thieves combined.

Just in case Chuck woke up, he had slumped the man down in the passenger seat, and handcuffed each wrist to the corresponding ankle. Sly knew he would have a serious problem if the man woke. But he also knew that he gave the man enough tranquilizers to knock out a horse for a full night.

Getting his newest houseguest out of his vehicle was a feat that Sly dreaded. He used a wheelbarrow to transport the large man from the car into his guesthouse. Once he reached the threshold of the front door, he dumped the man on the floor. Luckily, he didn't wake up.

Sly slid the carpet, revealing the hidden

hatch to the basement. He drug the man across the floor by his feet, and flung him down the ladder. The man fell eight feet, making a thud noise when he landed on the firm concrete. It was so loud that Sly checked to see if the concrete had cracked. It didn't.

When Sly climbed down the ladder, he saw that the man's face had busted open, his nose bleeding down his face. Chuck opened his eyes momentarily, only to go back to sleep.

Sly kept the man's hands handcuffed to his ankles, and then chained the handcuffs to the metal chair. Unfortunately, he knew his guest wouldn't wake up until morning, and for tonight, his pigs would have to settle for normal feed.

RULE # 29 MAINTAIN A GOOD REPUTATION

Sly was excited to be back at work. When he arrived at the office, Stacy informed him that he had gotten an offer on that Victorian style home where he had just hosted the open house. His mind drifted to all the money signs and commissions he would receive for the sale of the home.

Each time he made a sale, his adrenaline spiked. He felt alive whenever he made money. But it wasn't just about the profit. It was the fact that he was the one that talked the buyer into making the purchase. It was a rush having a small bit of control over a person.

He checked the roster for which homes were soon to be listed on the market, and the ones that were already for sale. After familiarizing himself with his merchandise, he noticed there was a home in Mrs. Comb's neighborhood that the owners wanted to list.

Homes in that area tended to sell fast, and he assigned himself as the realtor for that home. Plus he looked at his almost blank calendar for next year. He didn't have many red circles for next year's victims. He told himself to keep an eye open for anything shady about the sellers. If he wanted any houseguests this time next year, he would have to be super critical, and punish for even the smallest of sins.

Sly knocked on the door, admiring the exterior of the home that he was hoping to list for sale. He was sure of himself. He could convince these owners to choose him as their realtor.

An attractive woman answered the door, and greeted him with a warm smile. She looked innocent, but if Sly knew anything about people, he knew that looks could be deceiving.

He scanned the walls for any signs of pictures in the home that would lead him to believe that the people living here would be capable of being evil. He saw nothing but pictures of wildlife. There were pictures of lions in the wild, and bucks standing amongst large mountains.

"Hi. I'm Sly Verdict. Nice to meet you ma'am."

She motioned for him to come inside. "I'm

so glad it's you. I wasn't too sure when I called that you'd be assigned to our house. Mrs. Combs referred your office to us." She walked into the living room, and offered him a seat on a black leather couch.

Sly couldn't help but notice a large deer head on the wall, with numerous antlers protruding from its head.

A slim man joined them in the room. "Hi. Harvey Watson here. It's a pleasure to meet you. I recognize you from the ads. Mrs. Combs told us what you did for her."

It took a few seconds for Sly to realize what they were referring to. The fondest favor he remembered doing for Mrs. Combs was killing her grandson, but she wasn't privy to that bit of information. "Oh yeah. I didn't want her losing her home." Then Sly forced himself to stop speaking. He didn't want to blurt out anything about Elliot.

Rule #29: Maintain a good reputation

After some small talk about how sweet Mrs. Combs was, Sly quickly switched into work mode, going over the normal contracts that come with selling a home. He couldn't help but to keep looking at the dead deer head on the wall.

Harvey saw him looking at the deer. "That's a ten point buck there. Took me an hour to drag it to my car." The homeowner was obviously proud of himself.

Sly loved animals more than anything. He never understood how people could hunt and kill innocent animals. "Oh, you're a hunter?"

Harvey stood next to his prize hanging on the wall. "I try. He's a beauty, isn't he."

Sly just smiled. Mr. Watson would officially be the next red circle on the calendar for next year. He would have the privilege of being his houseguest. Perhaps he could hang Harvey's head on his wall somewhere.

The best part of it was that after they signed the contract, he would have keys to their home. Then, if he sold them a new home, he would also have a key to that home. Most people didn't bother changing their locks when they moved. Some people just made it too easy for Sly to keep busy with his hobby.

RULE # 18 TAKE CARE OF GUESTS TO MAKE IT LAST

After a long, successful day at work, there was nothing that made Sly happier than going home to a houseguest.

By now, Chuck was bound to be awake, and probably starving. Sly had checked last year's calendar and knew that he wouldn't be having another houseguest for at least a week. He liked the game more than he liked the kill. He knew that he would have to make Chuck last, so he stopped for some fast food during his drive home.

Rule # 18: Take care of guests to make it last

The human body can go weeks without food, but he learned the hard way that victims tended to die sooner if malnourished. Water was easy to supply. The human body could only go days without water, but he didn't mind giving Chuck water. It was easy to turn on the hose and let him drink the tap water.

Sly climbed down the ladder to his basement, and noticed that the metal chair that Chuck was chained to was out of sight. He had never had a houseguest ever rearrange the furniture, but Chuck was a muscle bound beast, not like any other victim.

Sly lowered himself, and saw that the chair was scooted over to his workbench, but Chuck appeared to be passed out. Possibly from starvation and dehydration.

Sly got closer to his houseguest to check on him, and he saw the silver object shimmering in Chuck's hand. But it was too late. Chuck lunged at him with the knife he took from the workbench and lunged at him.

The blade of the knife pierced Sly's arm, and he immediately jumped back. Chuck tried to lunge further, but the sound of the heavy chair scooting along the concrete let him know that he didn't lunge as far as he intended to.

Sly rapidly climbed the ladder and closed the hatch, putting the lock in place. He checked out his arm, and luckily it was only a superficial wound. But it hurt so bad that Sly fought back the tears.

Sly had a mad strong man in his basement,

armed with his own weapons.

Sly rushed to the barn looking for a way to take care of this situation. Even though his farm wasn't a full fledged farm, he still had farmer's tools on hand.

He glanced around, and saw a pitchfork, thinking the length on that would come in handy. The tips weren't as sharp as they should be, but could easily pierce human flesh.

The farmer before him had cattle, and even though Sly hadn't kept the cows, he still had the farmer's cow prod. The only livestock Sly kept was the pigs, but in this moment he was glad that he kept the inhumane stick that electrified cows.

Sly held the tips of the pitchfork right above the hatch as he unlocked it and flipped it open. Luckily, he didn't see Chuck anywhere near the ladder, and wondered if he was feigning unconsciousness. He held the pitchfork and the cattle prod close and he jumped down the ladder, and saw that Chuck was still chained to the chair near the workbench.

"What do you want? Why me?" It was comical watching the grown man cry.

Sly kept his distance from the sobbing man, not willing to get cut again. He said nothing as his eyes adjusted to the dimness. He saw that Chuck had a hammer in one hand and a knife in the other.

Weighing out the odds as to which weapon he should use, he decided that it was best to use both. He extended the pitchfork and the cattle prod in front of him, one in each hand. He charged towards the muscle man.

Sly had the advantage. Being chained to the chair kept the man close to the ground, and he couldn't move too far away too fast. The tips of the pitchfork penetrated Chuck's forearm, and the cattle prod struck him square in the chest, making a zapping bolt of electricity.

The man's large body gyrated, dropping both the hammer and the knife. Sly stood perfectly still hoping that now Chuck truly was unconscious.

The man didn't move.

Quickly, while the man was out, Sly slid the lifeless body away from the workbench. He unchained the handcuffs from the metal chair, and grabbed a large chain. He threaded the chain around the man's arms, as tight as he could, multiple times, before placing a lock into both ends on the links. Blood ran along the chain from where he had been stabbed with the pitchfork. Now, Chuck's arms were tightly pinned to his sides, unable to move at all.

He wove another chain around Chuck's knees, locking it in place so that he would be unable to move his legs. Chuck's body laid flat on the ground, chained into something that looked like a mummy.

Sly was disappointed. All he wanted to do was have an uneventful night of no drama. He only wanted to torture Chuck, and make him be his houseguest for at least the next week.

He had to refrain himself from killing Chuck on the spot. He was so angry about Chuck cutting him. But he knew that if he made it a quick kill he would soon regret not having a houseguest.

He turned on the water hose, and felt the chilled water flowing from the hose fitting. He sprayed Chuck in his face until he woke up. Sly wanted to drown the man, yet he refrained himself.

Sly spit on the man, and he tried to roll around on the ground, but his chains were so tight that he couldn't get the momentum to roll himself over.

"Drink! Drink now!" Sly commanded the man to hydrate himself.

Chuck's eyes looked at Sly in horror still trying to figure out what was happening.

The bag of takeout food that Sly got on his way home was lying on the floor. He picked it up, and attempted to feed his victim.

"Please. You don't have to do this." Chuck begged for mercy, not knowing that his captor was merciless.

Chuck didn't want to eat, but Sly crammed the burger in the man's mouth, forcing him to swallow at least a little bit of it.

"You're my guest! I have rules here! Don't ever try to hurt me again." Sly glanced at the small wound on his own arm.

Sly ignored whatever words the man on the floor was saying. Perhaps he was having a bad comedown from his lack of steroids. The shape the man was in now, Sly didn't worry about him breaking his chains of bondage.

Since Chuck would be a houseguest for at least a week, he wanted to take things slow with him.

He stepped onto Chuck's crotch, sure that he was squeezing his genitals under his shoe. The chained mummy looked awkward, trying to maneuver his body from side to side.

"So, you're a muscle man?" Sly asked. "Do the drugs make you mean?"

"You sorry sonova bitch. Unchain me. You'll find out!"

Not getting the answer that he wanted, Sly placed a gag around the man's mouth.

"Mmmhmmm!"

Sly moved his foot higher to the part of Chuck's abdomen that wasn't covered by the thick, heavy chains.

"Nice. Firm abs. Let's see what these muscles do for you now."

Sly bent down and slowly raised Chuck's shirt a few inches, revealing his navel.

"Humm Umpp." The harder Chuck tried to

resist, the more energy he wasted.

Sly went to his workbench, examining all the tools before him. He tried to choose the tool best to hurt the muscle man's abs of steel. He chose the simplest of tools.

He hovered over Chuck, with a screwdriver in one hand, and a few screws in the other. He held the screw steady, pressing it into Chuck's abdomen, and used the screwdriver to slowly turn the screw even deeper into the man's hardened flesh.

Chuck twisted and tried to roll, but he just couldn't change position.

Sly turned the screw extra slow, until the full half inch of metal embedded and anchored into his muscle.

"Were the drugs worth it?" Sly laughed at his houseguest.

He placed another screw above the other, turning it even slower, letting Chuck feel every second of pain. Eventually, the head of the screw was engulfed in flesh.

"Now last, but not least. Let's save your muscles. This one is for trying to hurt me."

Sly centered the last screw on the man's belly button, and pressed it firmly into the gap. He fitted the star shaped tip into the head of the screw, and pressed even harder, before twisting it.

He twisted fast, feeling Chuck's muscles hardened as he squirmed in pain. After all the screws were in place, Sly stepped onto each and every one of them.

Chuck looked defeated, and it was getting late. Sly left his houseguest to rest for the night.

RULE # 35
USE THE JOB TO YOUR ADVANTAGE

Being good at his job, and actually listening to his clients, Sly knew exactly what the Watsons were looking for in a new home. Even though their requests barely fit in their price range, Sly was determined to find them the home of their dreams.

Mrs. Watson wanted a large kitchen with plenty of cabinet space. Mr. Watson wanted a large garage for all of his hunting supplies. The thought of hunting made the realtor sick to his stomach, but he was happy to oblige.

The budget would be the hard part to work around. Apparently Mr. Watson spent too much money on hunting supplies because he wanted to pay next to nothing for a home. He was very specific that he needed a garage large enough for two cars, and enough room for him to skin deer.

Most homes were equipped with two car garages. Not two garages with an additional room to torture poor, defenseless animals.

Sly wanted to make this sale. He wanted to have a spare key made for whichever house they chose to buy, so he would have easy access a year later when he would welcome Mr. Watson as his houseguest.

Rule # 35: Use the job to your advantage

Being a good salesman, Sly knew the easiest way to get Mr. Harvey Watson to reach deeper into his pockets and buy a more expensive home was to get Mrs. Watson to fall in love with a home. It seemed like the women were always the path of least resistance. They were easier to sell to.

The very first house he showed them was a tad out of their price range, but after checking Harvey Watson's credit, he knew that they could afford it. The house had a grand entrance with an arched door. And the kitchen was absolutely beautiful.

Mrs. Watson spun circles in the kitchen, admiring the marble countertops and the solid oak cabinets.

"Look at all the cabinets, Harvey. There's at least two dozen cabinets! I could prepare food on the island. And there's even a double oven. Thanksgiving would be so easy!" Mrs. Harvey was in love with the home.

Mr. Watson was obviously not as impressed. "Yeah, yeah, honey. Let's see the rest of it first. Plus, he hasn't even told us the price."

They toured the rest of the home. Each room larger than the one before it. There was plenty of closet space, and a wonderful bathroom off the master suite with a large garden tub.

When they got to the garage Mr Watson marveled at how spacious it was.

"A four car garage. There's even a separate room that I believe the previous tenants used as a mancave. Equipped with electricity and heating and cooling." Sly was proud of himself as he studied the buyer's face. "What do you think?"

Knowing that it was too good to be true, Harvey knew that it would be expensive. After asking the price, he protested since it was thirty thousand above his budget.

Then Sly stood back and watched as Mrs. Watson begged and pleaded for the home of her dreams. It didn't take long, and the Watsons put an offer in on the house.

Sly made a mental note to be sure to have extra keys made.

RULE # 5 DON'T LET THE HOBBY CONSUME YOU

As soon as Sly got home from work, he prepared food to take to his houseguest. Just a little bit of nourishment. Just enough to sustain him. Barely enough to keep him alive, but it would keep him clinging to life for at least a few more days.

He was getting on his four wheeler to make the short drive to his guest home, when he saw the Sheriff's truck speeding towards his house. Edward's car was blowing dirt off the back wheels, creating a cloud behind him.

Sly set the food down, and waited to see what Edward was in a hurry about. As the car got closer, he saw there was somebody sitting in the passenger seat. As he focused his eyes, he saw that it was Cindy. His heart skipped a beat. He wondered why she was here.

As soon as the vehicle parked, Edward jumped out of the car. "I got a surprise for you."

Cindy exited the vehicle slower.

Not sure as to whether he should show his excitement or play hard-to-get, Sly froze in position and didn't run up to her to welcome her. Even though he wanted to.

Cindy smiled her most innocent smile, and her eyes twinkled in Sly's direction. He felt his heart skip a few more beats.

"It was kind of last minute. That whole job thing fell through. I've decided to move back home. I didn't like the city much anyways." Cindy truly looked happy.

Sly opened his arms, hoping she would move in closer for a hug. "Welcome home."

Cindy stepped in and felt Sly's warm embrace surround her entire body.

Edward was all grins. His sister was home, and he knew in the back of his mind that maybe his best friend would be enough to get her to stick around. He knew that Sly was capable of making her happy.

Even though Cindy felt good in his arms, and even though he was so happy he wanted to scream from the rooftops that she came back to him, his mind wandered to Chuck in his guesthouse.

Rule # 5: Don't let the hobby consume you

Edward broke the silence of their embrace.

"Hey! Who's up for beers! Let's go to the bar."

Sly reminded himself that his guest could wait. Right now, he wanted to devote all his attention to Cindy.

As usual, Edward got sloppy drunk. Once again, Sly picked up the tab. While Edward was busy getting hammered and downing beers talking to the bartender, Sly and Cindy had a chance to talk.

"Have you had anymore problems with the cops? Anymore searches on your property? Inquiring minds want to know." Cindy flirted as she brushed her hand against Sly's arm.

Sly laughed. "Not exactly. No problems with cops. Just with one in particular. Nothing I can't handle."

Cindy took a sip of beer, and lightly placed the bottle back down on the table, with her usual gracefulness. "I hate to ask. But for now, I'm staying with him." She raised her finger and pointed to her drunken brother. "You don't by chance want to rent out your guest house, do ya? I mean, just til I find a place of my own."

A bead of sweat began to show on Sly's forehead. He couldn't chance Cindy in the guesthouse. That was used strictly for his hobby. Especially with Chuck being a current houseguest.

She held both hands out in front of her. "That's okay. You can just say no. I'm not made of glass, I won't break. It was just a question."

Sly cleared his throat. No it's not that. It's just that. It's just." Sly took a sip of his own drink as he tried to think of something good to say. "I'd love to have ya around. Just not in my guest home. I have a spare bedroom in my house. Why don't you stay with me? Of course, no strings attached. Rent free. Plus, I know a good realtor. Maybe I can put a good word in for ya."

Cindy delicately slapped Sly on his shoulder. "You kidder. It's okay. I'll stay with him, I guess." She pointed in Edward's direction.

Sly wanted nothing more than for Cindy to stay with him. But he wasn't willing to give up his hobby for her.

Even while he was out and having a good time at the bar, he got anxious to get home to Chuck. If anything, he wanted to at least give his houseguest some water before the night was over.

Since Edward and Cindy were too drunk to drive, Sly drove them home to his house. It took everything in him to not obsess about Chuck. He knew better than to let the hobby invade his every thought, but he felt like he was going mad.

It would be a shame if Chuck died of dehydration. There wasn't anything fun about that. He just kept telling himself that everything would be okay. Chuck could go a day without water.

Sly sat outside by his pool, gazing at the

night sky. Contemplating if he could sneak to his guesthouse for just a few minutes while his friends slept.

Then, he thought he heard something in the distance. The sound of a rustling bush. He turned on the flashlight on his cellphone, and looked around in the darkness but didn't see anyone. Perhaps it was his imagination. Maybe the madness of worrying about his houseguest was getting to him.

A creak from the patio sliding door heightened his paranoia. Sly quickly turned around. Luckily, it was Cindy.

Sly felt like he missed his chance to go water Chuck. "It's gotta be three in the morning. What're you doin' up?"

Cindy wiped her eyes. "I dunno. Thinkin' bout life, I guess. I'm a mess. No job. No home. I mean, I'm glad to be back. But it's just gonna be a rough transition."

Sly wanted to pull her beautiful body close to him. He wanted to comfort her. When it came to selling houses, he had a natural charm. When it came to women that he liked, or possibly even loved, he was socially awkward.

While Sly was thinking of the correct way to handle this situation, he heard another rustle in the bushes.

Sly jumped up on his feet and turned his head, on guard. "Did you hear that?"

Cindy confirmed that she also heard it, and

he was relieved that it wasn't just paranoia.

Sly clicked on his flashlight, and ran into the bushes. He searched for the source of the noise. Animals usually stayed away from the house, but he was thinking maybe it could be a stray. As he was traipsing through the greenery, he heard a cry from Cindy.

He quickly scrambled back to his patio and saw none other than Officer Williams.

"Get away from this man. Sly is dangerous." Williams waved his finger in Cindy's face. "I'm warning you."

Cindy's face was frozen in fear.

Sly grabbed Williams around his neck, and pinned him to the side of the house.

"Cindy! Get the Sheriff now!" Sly demanded she get her brother before he strangled Williams to death.

"I'm on probation thanks to you!" Williams started to cry. "I can't even work right now. You said I was stalking you. I'm gonna show you stalking you. And I'm gonna watch you. And I'm gonna warn everyone to stay away from you!"

Sly wanted so badly to strangle the life out of the crying man.

Edward rushed out of the house, wearing only his tight, white underwear, waving a gun. He aimed the gun at Officer Williams.

"Sly, step away. I got him now. Hands in the air! Now!" Edward moved in closer to the trespasser. "You're under arrest. You have the right to remain silent."

Williams lashed out at the Sheriff. "I know my rights! Shut up! This man is the one you should be arresting!" He pointed towards Sly.

"I said hands in the air! Cindy get my cuffs from my pants." Edward looked down at his half-naked body, almost embarrassed.

Williams of course kept blurting out his accusations against Sly. Edward was sober enough to arrest the trespassing police officer. He told Sly that he could now file for a restraining order against Williams. But Sly knew that he hadn't seen the last of the man.

RULE # 21 BULLY A BULLY

Edward arrested Williams, but knew since it was a minor infraction that he wouldn't be in jail any longer than twenty-four hours. After taking the man to the small town police station, he came back to Sly's house and picked up Cindy to take her home.

Finally, Sly was alone. Even though he was exhausted from the long, eventful night, he knew that he had to check on Chuck.

Sly also wanted to put an end to Chuck and clean his guesthouse thoroughly, in case Cindy asked to stay with him again. He had the hardest time telling her no. She had some sort of power over him that he didn't understand.

When Cindy was around, he felt like a totally different person. He felt like a better man just by being in her presence. He wanted to be better for her. He wanted her in his life.

Chuck was still laying in his mummified

chains when Sly got down to the basement. The man's eyes were only half opened, but at least he was still alive. Sly removed the gag from his mouth, and turned on the water hose, and Chuck tried to gulp down the water streaming in his face.

He also sprayed Chuck's pants that were urine soaked to try and get rid of the stench.

Chuck tried to speak, but the pain from the screws in his belly, and laying in the same uncomfortable position for a day had tired him out.

"Please. I'll beg. I have money! I have a family. I'll do anything!"

The mention of Chuck having a family caught Sly's attention. "A family, huh? Were you good to your family?" Sly hoped that Chuck noticed the past tense in the question. Hopefully, giving him zero hope of survival.

"I love my family so much."

Sly kicked the squalling man in his balls, and the man yelped out in pain.

"I didn't ask if you loved them! I asked if you were good to them."

Chuck sniffled, and thought for a moment. "I will be. If you let me go, I'll be the best husband and father there has ever been."

Sly stared at the defeated man, accepting that as his confession. That the man knew what he had done wrong. Now, the tables had turned for Chuck.

Rule #21: Bully a bully

Sly put the gag back in Chuck's mouth, and his victim tried to bite at him while doing so. He was just bored with hearing the man begging for his life.

He hated this victim. He hated a bully. This man had a family, and instead of cherishing it, he let his drug induced rage control him and push them around. Since his muscles were the desired result of his drugs, he wanted to take his muscles away.

Sly grabbed a large hunting blade, and started with the man's calf muscle. It was large, and protruded from his leg in a bulging fashion.

He inserted the tip of the blade into the man's Achilles tendon, slowly twisting it upward. The man's muffled screams echoed off the concrete walls.

He carved around the large bulge, inches deep into the man's skin. He very slowly guided the knife, higher up his leg. He stopped once he hit the large links of chains wrapped around the man's knees.

Blood poured from the wound, and the mass of muscle flopped onto the ground. Pieces of what could possibly be a tendon still hung from the backside of Chuck's leg.

Unpleased with there not being enough blood, Sly examined the man for muscles that were not wrapped up in the chains.

Chuck had the largest shoulders that Sly had ever seen in his life. They surrounded his head on both sides like curved domes around his neck. Not wanting his victim to die too soon, he started by just shaving off the top layers of skin.

He could now see the muscle, exposed and unburdened from the epidermis. Beneath the blood, the trapezius muscle looked like a pale red, almost pink, engorged pork roast.

The muscle was abnormally huge, and almost made Sly sick to his stomach as it pulsed and spurted blood out from where he nicked it too deep. It looked almost like a balloon, and Sly wondered if he punctured it, would it pop?

Tears were flowing down Chuck's face, and fell off the side of his face. They mixed into the puddle of blood, yet the blood was so much thicker.

Sly took the tip of the sharp blade, and made several puncture holes, releasing so much blood that he could now smell the copper in the air.

"Were these muscles worth being a bully?"

Sly knew that his victim couldn't answer due to the ball gag. Chuck's eyes were rolling back into his head. He was losing too much blood, and Sly feared that he would die before he had his fun with him.

He wanted to have enough time to cut the screws that were planted into the man's abdomen muscles. He quickly used his blade to cut squares around the screws. Then he had a better idea. He decided not to cut the screws out.

He ran over to the workbench in a hurry, and grabbed a hammer. He decided to use the claw end to pull the screws from the man's body, in the same fashion that you would pull a nail from a board.

The first screw gave resistance, and Sly had to pull extra hard. It was more difficult than he imagined. Chuck's muffled cries had stopped, and Sly feared that he had bled to death.

The ridges of the screw were full of human tissue and blood.

He smacked Chuck in the face with the hammer, trying to wake the man. He got no response. Bored with this muscle man, and disappointed by how weak he proved himself to be, Sly placed the blade by Chuck's ear. He sliced from his ear, to below his chin, and watched what little blood was left stream with no pressure to the concrete floor.

He looked around at the mess. He smelled the blood in the air. He began to cut Chuck into tiny little chunks of snack sizes for his pigs. His work had just begun. Muscle tissue was harder to cut than soft tissue. He grabbed his chainsaw and made an even bloodier mess.

He looked at all the blood, and knew it would take him a very long time to get it clean enough, just in case he decided to let Cindy stay there.

RULE # 14 BE HUMANE WHEN POSSIBLE

Carrying the body parts of the man up the ladder was a feat in itself. He had to make several trips, carrying him in portions. When he was a whole man, he must have weighed at least three hundred pounds.

He waited to give his pigs the feast until he had carried every bit of Chuck up the ladder. He carried the pieces of one arm and one leg on his first trip, and mentally noted how they weighed almost as much as the thieves he had just killed. Then he made a second trip with the remaining arm and leg. He saved the pieces of the head and the torse for the last trip.

The pigs could smell the rotting flesh and blood and greeted Sly at the fence, eager for their special meal. He wanted to give his favorite pig, Betsy, the thighs. They always seemed to be her favorite, but he didn't see her in the mass of pigs.

He called for Betsy, yet she didn't answer. He threw the human remains in the sty, holding a large thigh, specially reserved for Betsy. He opened the gate, and entered. He found Betsy under a small wooden covering, with her back turned to him. He waved the thigh in her face, but she didn't take it.

Instead, she turned her head to acknowledge Sly, but then just laid her head back onto the dirt ground. He noticed blood coming from her eyes and her nose. His first instinct was to take her to the vet, but he couldn't chance the veterinarian finding out that her diet had been dead bodies. He wondered if maybe she got some disease from the drug-addicted thieves.

All of the other pigs appeared to be fine, chowing down on Chuck.

Betsy looked miserable, and he knew what he had to do. He left the thigh for her, in case she decided to eat it. He retreated to his house for his shotgun.

Rule #14: Be humane when possible

When he returned the thigh was still uneaten. He patted Betsy on her head, and she moved just a bit, and Sly swore that he saw her smile. He said his goodbyes to his one true best friend in the world. Of course, Edward was his friend, but Edward didn't know of his hobby.

Betsy knew of his hobby and accepted him,

despite it. He remembered how much she used to love reaping the rewards of his hobby.

"I love you, Betsy."

He raised the shotgun and shot her between the eyes.

"Rest in peace."

After skinning Betsy, and storing the rest of the pork in his spare freezer, he decided he would eat a piece of her.

He cooked a piece of her up in the form of a tenderloin.

Sly was surprised by how moist and tender her meat was. This was by far the best piece of pork he had ever eaten. He wondered if her meat was so good due to her special diet of human.

Sly sat and contemplated if maybe he should start eating the results of his hobby. If eating people made Betsy taste so good, then people must taste good.

He decided that he would try eating his next victim.

See ya next read

Thanks so much for reading this book. I'm really excited about developing more of Sly as a character in the next book. He will be pushing his own boundaries. Find me on Facebook (Sea Caummisar) or on Twitter (@seacaummisar). I love hearing from my readers. Turn the page for Verdict Realty 2… Unhinged. Extreme Horror.

I like reviews, too. No pressure, but they really help out authors and give them encouragement to write more.

VERDICT REALTY #2 UNHINGED. EXTREME HORROR

By Sea Caummisar

Verdict Realty: The Complete Series (Books 1-3...

Copyright © 2019 by Sea Caummisar

All rights reserved. No portion of this book may be reproduced in any form without permission from the publisher, except as permitted by U.S. copyright law. For permissions contact sharoncheatham81@gmail.com

This is entirely a work of fiction, pulled out of my own imagination. All characters and events are not real (fictitious). If there are any similarities to real persons, living or dead, it is purely coincidental.

Remember this is a book based on a fictional realty company.

SLY'S JOURNAL OF RULES (INCOMPLETE)

(in no particular order)

Rule #34: Wait at least one year.
After doing business with a person, wait at least one year before abducting them. That makes it harder for police to trace their suspicions to Sly, or his real estate company.

Rule # 19: Cover your tracks.
Try to make it look like the person is missing, not dead. Try to throw the police off Sly's trail.

Rule #8: No hair. Not on head. Not on body. (Except eyebrows and eyelashes).
Many serial killers have been caught by their DNA linked at a crime scene. Hair leaves be-

hind too much DNA.

Rule #12: Wife beaters must die.

Coming from a broken home, and Sly's own Father killing his Mother, this rule is very important.

Rule #4: Dispose of bodies properly.

Without a dead body, there is no crime committed. The person is just assumed to be missing, not dead.

Rule #1: Married people shouldn't cheat.

Marriage is very sacred to Sly. Anyone who breaks their vows are not worthy of being married.

Rule #32: Leave nice people alone.

Nice people make the world a better place. Don't kill them.

Rule #27: Wear gloves when in someone's home or car.

Fingerprints can be traced to a person's identity. Leave nothing behind that can be traced to Sly.

Rule #24: Ignore your dick.

At all times, think with your brain. Not your manhood. Semen also leaves behind DNA in the event that a body is found.

Rule #17: Tell nobody. Ever.

The hobby is a secret. Many serial killers

have been caught by telling someone their secrets. Even if you feel close to a person and think you can trust them, you can't.

Rule #23: Don't break the rules.

Just a reminder to never break the rules. The rules are in place for a reason. They are not meant to be broken.

Rule #30: Don't get sloppy.

When you get sloppy, and don't think things through, you can get caught. Follow the rules, and keep your guard up at all times.

Rule #6: Get as much information as possible.

Know your enemy. Find out as much about them as possible. This makes it easier to abduct them.

Rule #13: Hide in plain sight.

Even though Edward is Sly's best friend, he is an enforcer of the law. Nobody would ever suspect that a serial killer would have such a close relationship with a police officer.

Rule #2: Deny. Deny. Deny.

Even if you have been caught, deny any allegations against you. They need evidence and proof before you can be found guilty. Following the rules ensures they will find no proof.

Rule #16: The hobby is for anger.

When angry, kill/torture someone. It is

very therapeutic. There is no better stress reliever.

Rule #11: Clean up is important.

Leave behind no traces of blood, or anything that can be linked to a missing person. Let the pigs dispose of bodies. Burn their personal items, such as clothes. Clean up blood with bleach.

Rule #20: No witnesses. Ever.

Witnesses are bad news. They could identify the criminal. When committing *any* crime, be sure to get rid of witnesses, even if it means breaking the rules.

Rule #7: Thieves must die.

Thieves should not be or exist. They should not breathe. The punishment for theft is death.

Rule #26: Disguises are good.

Sly is well known for his real estate company (Verdict Realty) commercials. When necessary, use hats and sunglasses or anything else to mask face.

Rule #33: Punishment should fit the offender.

Thieves do not need hands. Rapists do not deserve sexual organs. Abusers should be beaten. Etc…

Rule #9: Keep friends close, enemies closer.

Know your enemy. Get to know them. Kill

them (not literally) with kindness.

Rule #22: Show them the errors of their ways.
Make sure the victim knows why they were chosen.

Rule #3: Always be alert.
Even in personal life, be alert for enemies. Also, always keep an eye open for possible victims.

Rule #38: Professional. Personal. Hobby. Keep life organized in sections.
Do not let the different compartments of life blur and intersect. Know your role at the appropriate times.

Rule #15: Lay low if there's any doubt.
Even if it is just a small chance that you are being watched or followed, retreat.

Rule #31: Keep in shape. Especially for tough opponents.
Physical fitness is not only important for a healthy lifestyle, but also to abduct victims.

Rule #28: Know your opponent.
Know everything about your victim. That makes it easier to abduct them.

Rule #10: Use your brain, not your body.
Outsmarting the victim will help greatly.

Rule #29: Maintain a good reputation.

Being a public figure (real estate agent), it's important for the business to be represented by someone with an impeccable reputation. Do not do anything stupid. Don't get caught breaking any law, no matter how minor it may be. Do good things for the community.

Rule #18: Take care of guest to make it last.

It is impossible to get a new victim everyday. Make sure guest stays hydrated so there's always a guest to torture.

Rule #35: Use job to have the advantage.

Hang on to the spare keys of a future victim's house. Use the credit check to know their habits. Use spare key to snoop through their personal items.

Rule #5: Don't let the hobby consume you.

Make time for work. Money is important. Make time for personal life. Do not think about the hobby constantly. The mind needs a break from time to time.

Rule #21: Bully a bully.

Bullies are bad. Be their bully. Show them how it feels.

Rule #14: Be humane when possible.

It's important, especially in business and personal life, to be humane. Not every situation is an outlet for anger.

CHAPTER 1:

"Last year, when you told me that you couldn't buy a house near a school, I wanted to strangle you then!" Sly Verdict stared at the man chained to the chair. "I knew then you were a pervert!" Sly hated perverts. He especially hated anyone who committed a crime against children.

Victor Gonzo struggled against the chains holding him down, and the heavy links were hurting his wrists. He wasn't sure how he got here, but his head hurt as if he had been drugged. He wasn't sure if he was hearing echoes in his head, or if the screaming man's words were actually bouncing off the concrete walls.

The last thing he remembered was sitting home alone watching television and drinking beer. Then he woke up here, in some dungeon, with a crazy real estate agent screaming at him. He recognized the realtor, but he hadn't seen him in a year.

Sly heard many odd requests as a real estate agent, but when someone requests a home far from any school, he knows what that means. It usually meant that the buyer is probably on a Sex Offender Registry. That they had been convicted of a sex crime, probably against a child.

The only other reason to not live near a school could be noise. But when Sly plugged Victor's name in the Sex Offender Database, he found out he had been convicted of statutory rape. Rape against an underaged minor. Sly hated Victor for his supposed crime.

Sly grew up in foster homes, and he had lived with some female foster children. He remembered hearing them cry themselves to sleep at night, reliving memories of their foster parents sexually abusing them. Victor's crime really hit close to Sly's heart, and he wanted to really torture this man.

In Sly's eyes, Victor was scum. You had to be a low-down rotten person to rape a minor. There was no excuse for what Victor had done. That's why he kept the gag in his victim's mouth. He didn't want to hear any excuses from him.

"That's why I opted to not sell you a home. I won't do any favors for a pedophile!" Sly kicked the man in his knee so hard that it hurt his own foot.

Victor's knee buckled and he cried out in pain. His cries sounded like muffled screams of agony. His own screams echoed off the concrete walls.

The man groaned in pain, and tried to speak

through his gag. Yes, he had been convicted of statutory rape, but it was only because his girlfriend was a couple of years younger than him. Her parents didn't approve of their relationship, and they filed charges against him.

If only this gag wasn't in his mouth. Then he could tell the crazed real estate agent the truth of this situation. He loved her. He didn't rape her. She loved him, too.

He ended up marrying the minor that he supposedly raped. When she became of legal age, they ran away and eloped. They had built a beautiful life together. He hadn't raped anyone. He served his time in prison, and she was waiting for him when he was released.

Sly picked up a drill from his workbench. "So, I already know you're on the Sex Offender Registry. I didn't even give you a chance to tell me as to why you didn't want to buy a home near a school. Maybe you would've lied. Maybe you would've said it was because the noise."

He squeezed the trigger on the drill and the drill bit started to spin. Sly watched as the spirals started to blend in with each other as it rotated faster. He contemplated the many places that he could insert the drill and inflict pain.

"So, let's just pretend that you don't like noise." Sly laughed maniacally. "Hold your head still. This is gonna hurt, and I'm sure you don't want me to go too deep. If I go too deep, it would puncture your brain. But, see, I don't want to kill you. At least not yet."

Victor opened his eyes extra wide. His captor placed a hand on the top of his head, to hold it in place. Sly quit squeezing the trigger, and slowly ran the unmoving drill bit around the outside of Victor's earlobe.

"Hmmm. Hmmm." Victor was trying to explain. He wasn't a pedophile. If only the man would remove his gag. All Victor could do was cry.

Sly carefully fed the drill bit into the man's ear canal, but not too deep. He didn't want to puncture the victim's brain and kill him. He only wanted to reach the man's eardrum. He only desired to hurt the man.

With just the tip of the bit inserted into the ear canal, Sly squeezed the trigger and heard the tool spin to life. It slightly vibrated in his hand.

Victor tried to move his head away from the drill, but Sly was holding his head in place. The pain was so immense and Victor was sure he was going to die.

Blood was spinning off the drill, speckling Sly's face with drops of blood. Small specks of blood splattered on the concrete walls.

The noise in Victor's ear was so loud. Then it wasn't. His ear went deaf as his ear drum ruptured. Victor felt a small explosion in his head. He couldn't hear anything except a high pitched ringing tone.

"I'll leave you alone to think about what

you've done."

Then, Victor was alone, with nothing but pain and a ringing in his ears to keep him company.

Sly wanted to give Victor time to think about his offense. He wanted his victim to know what he had done wrong. The only problem in this situation was that Victor hadn't done anything wrong. His only sin was falling in love with someone younger than him.

If only he didn't have the gag in his mouth. Then he could have told him the truth of the situation. But he did have a gag in his mouth. Now he had to pay for his supposed sin.

Sly climbed the ladder out of the secret basement of his guesthouse. He closed the hatch behind him, and covered it with a rug. He looked at the blood on his naked body.

A quick rinse in the shower cleansed him of the blood. Washing Victor's sin off of him. Sly threw on yesterday's clothes and stepped outside. He stood on the porch, and watched the pigs in his pigsty.

It wasn't long ago that his favorite pig, Betsy, had gotten sick. He had to put her out of her misery. He missed her. He was thinking that maybe he should get a dog to replace her. He knew he would never find another pig as smart as she was.

The pigs saw him on the porch, and grunted, like they were asking for food. Sly kept them on a special diet of human bodies. After he killed Betsy, he ate some of her pork, and found out how good and tender her meat was.

He had never directly eaten human flesh before, but since Betsy's pork was so good he had already decided to eat some of Victor when he was done with him. He wanted to taste human flesh.

Sly approached the pigsty, remembering how Betsy would usually push the smaller pigs out of the way to greet him.

"I'm sorry little buddies. You're gonna have to wait another day or so."

They wanted red meat. They wanted bloody human body parts. For now, they would have to settle for normal pig feed.

Sly fed the pigs normal pig feed, and they turned their backs to him, not eating what he gave them.

"Soon. I'll have what y'all want, soon."

CHAPTER 2:

Sly's best friend, (Sheriff) Edward Haskins, was coming over for breakfast. Lately, Sly had the best sausage and bacon that Edward had ever tasted. Edward knew that he was eating Betsy, but he didn't know that Betsy tasted so good due to her special diet.

"So Sheriff, are you going to court with me?" Sly asked his best friend. Edward was the Sheriff in the small town they lived in. It was a little over an hour's drive to the next city. They called that the big city. That was also where Sly's real estate company was.

"Then who would fight all the crime here?" Edward laughed. The small town barely ever had any crime. At least not any crime that the Sheriff was aware of. He had no clue that his best friend was a crazed serial killer.

Sly committed many crimes butchering people in the basement of his guesthouse, but nobody was aware of that. It was his own little secret.

Edward popped a piece of bacon in his

mouth. "I swear. This is the best bacon ever. Sure, I'll go with you. I hope that Officer Williams loses his job over this. Scaring my sister like that. Men like that don't deserve to wear a badge."

Sly was going to court because he was getting a restraining order against a police officer. Sly had abducted and murdered Officer William's brother-in-law. The brother-in-law's car had been found on Sly's property. But the body was never found (because the pigs ate him).

Officer Williams was stalking Sly, trying to catch him doing something incriminating. He even snuck onto Sly's property late one night while Edward's sister, Cindy, was visiting. Officer Williams scared Cindy by warning her to stay away from Sly.

"Speaking of Cindy. What do you think about her staying with me?" Sly finally decided to let Cindy come stay at his guesthouse until she found a place to stay. She was moving back to the country after years of living in the city. He hated the fact that he wouldn't have access to his guesthouse basement. That was his dungeon and where he killed his victims.

He wouldn't be able to kill people in the basement with her living there. But he knew it was only temporary. She would find her own place in no time. He tried to convince her to stay in his main house with him, but she refused. She didn't want to impose on him.

If only she knew that staying in his guesthouse would be an inconvenience to his hobby. But it's not like he could tell her what he really used his guesthouse for.

Edward took a bite of sausage and smiled. "That is so delicious. Betsy sure was some fine pork." Edward chewed up his food and swallowed. "I'm just glad she's moving back to the country. There's too much crime in the city. She said it's only gonna take a couple days to get all her stuff packed up."

Sly made a mental note that he only had a couple of days before Cindy would be coming to stay in his guesthouse. That meant he had to kill Victor, and get the place cleaned up for her arrival. Cleaning was his least favorite part of his hobby. Blood was so hard to clean up.

Sly watched as the Sheriff ate Betsy. Every bite he took, he commented how good the pork was. It just made Sly miss Betsy even more. She was more like a companion than a pig. She was the most perfect pet ever.

Plus, Sly found it humorous that Edward was eating Betsy, and Betsy had eaten human bodies. So indirectly, the Sheriff was eating people. Sly patted his best friend on the back, and filled his plate with more pork. If only Edward knew what he was eating, maybe he would laugh, too. Maybe not.

Even if Sly had told Edward the truth of what he was eating, he probably wouldn't believe him. Sly and Edward had been best friends for years. Even when Chester had gone missing and they found his car on Sly's property, Edward vouched for Sly.

He knew that his best friend wasn't capable of hurting anyone. Edward was the Sheriff of the small town, so when he vouched for someone, his word carried a lot of weight.

Edward didn't know his best friend the way he thought he did. He knew the good guy side of Sly. He knew the Sly that had a good head on his shoulders and was great at business.

He told the state troopers that Sly couldn't have possibly had anything to do with Chester's disappearance. But Edward was wrong. Sly had abducted Chester, and killed him. He even fed his dead body to his pigs.

CHAPTER 3:

Sly and Edward went to the courthouse in the big city. It was Edward's idea that his best friend get a restraining order against Officer Williams. He suggested it when Edward arrested Officer Williams for trespassing on Sly's farm.

Normally, Sly wouldn't involve the law. He would just make the cop disappear. But Officer Williams had startled Cindy, and he knew that he had to do something soon. A restraining order was quicker than abducting the cop covertly and killing him.

Cindy was Sly's soft spot. She wasn't like other women. She didn't throw herself at him just because he was wealthy and attractive, like most women. She was beautiful, yet she wasn't conceited.

She was also very sweet. Sly loved that she was an all around great person. Naturally, he considered himself to be a good person. In his head he did the world a favor by ridding it of bad people.

When Officer Williams had warned Cindy to stay away from Sly, he wanted to kill him. Unfortunately, the Sheriff had been visiting, and arrested him for trespassing instead. So instead of killing the cop, Sly was now taking him to court to get a restraining order.

As the Judge granted a restraining order stating that Officer Williams must stay 500 feet away from Sly, Williams protested.

"But your honor! He's up to something. That man did something with my brother-in-law."

Yes, Sly had killed Chester, but he said nothing.

Sly's expensive lawyer stood in his expensive suit. "Your Honor. Hopefully now you can see the seriousness of Officer William's obsession. We would like to also have this sent to the Officer's superiors. My client does not feel comfortable with this man having a badge and a gun."

The Judge granted the order.

The chances of Officer Williams losing his job was great. Sly knew that he hadn't gotten rid of this man yet. He could tell by looking in Officer Williams' eyes that he still held a grudge.

Edward was happy leaving the courthouse. "I'm glad we got that taken care of before Cindy gets back. He really freaked her out that night."

Edward put on his sunglasses as he sat in the passenger seat of Sly's convertible.

Sly started the car, and looked up at the warm sun beating down on them. "I have a feeling this isn't enough. He's stubborn. A restraining order isn't gonna stop him. He already got arrested for trespassing and he still protested to the Judge."

Edward pulled his official police issued handgun from the glove compartment, and held it in the air. "I'd like to see him come back on your property."

Sly wondered if Edward was insinuating that he would kill Williams. Sly knew that most people weren't like him. They weren't true murderers. He knew that there was probably zero chance of Edward actually killing Williams.

But there was a million percent chance that Sly would love to get Williams in his guesthouse.

Nobody, other than Sly, had lived after seeing the basement in his guesthouse. The basement was where he spent a lot of his time, killing people that he deemed unworthy of life. This is what he referred to as his hobby.

Sly couldn't wait until he got home. Victor would be in the guesthouse basement waiting for him. He had plans for the sex offender. He was going to make him hurt worse than he had ever made anyone else hurt.

CHAPTER 4:

After Edward left, Sly drove the mile from his main house to the guesthouse. He walked over to the pigsty, and patted a few of the pigs on their hairy heads. He loved his pigs. None of them were as smart as Betsy was, but they were still his pets.

"Soon. You'll have some special dinner soon." He was referring to the fact that he would be feeding them some of Victor's dead body soon. The pigs loved to eat human flesh.

The pigs responded by snorting at him.

As soon as he stepped into the house, he undressed. Killing people was a dirty business. Blood stained clothes, yet it washed away from the skin so easily.

Sly unrolled the rug, and unlocked the hatch to his basement. He climbed down the ladder rungs and stared at Victor.

Victor looked defeated, chained to the chair. There was a trail of dried up blood running from his ear. When his captor offered him water, he took it and drank as if he hadn't had water in days.

"Can you hear me?"

Victor just looked at the man. One of his ears wasn't damaged, and he heard something, but it just sounded like echoes from his voice bouncing off the concrete walls.

Sly leaned in closer to Victor's undamaged ear. "You're a very lucky man. I have to evict you tonight, someone else is actually going to be staying in the guesthouse, and I need time to get it cleaned up. So your stay will be a short one. Also, I'm not going to feed all of your body to the pigs. I'm gonna keep a part of you for myself. You will be the first person I try to eat. I'm curious, did you have a good diet?"

Victor couldn't speak through his gag, but he heard some of the words the crazed realtor had said to him. If he heard him correctly, he was going to eat him. He knew it was pointless to struggle against the chains, he had tried that all day and couldn't get loose.

The pain in his ear was too much. Almost unbearable. All he could do was cry. Large tears fell down his face, and he tried to think of a happy place in his mind. But nothing he did took away the pain in his head.

Sly laughed at himself for speaking to the gagged man. It was just as bad as talking to the pigs. He knew they wouldn't respond, but he still got joy from talking to them.

Sly looked at the tools scattered across his

workbench. He picked up his trusty hammer and a nail. He held them in the air for the chained up man to see. He needed no words for Victor to know that this was going to hurt.

He stuck the nail in Victor's good ear, and barely pierced the thin membrane of the eardrum.

Victor flinched and Sly laughed. Sly didn't want to kill him yet, so he barely tapped the head of the hammer onto the nail, and the nail lodged itself further into the ear canal.

Victor felt the burst in the side of his head and the pain radiated throughout his entire body. He saw Sly's lips moving, but all he could hear was pain. He felt like a grenade had exploded in his head.

"Do you like medieval torture? Do you know what they did to rapists?" Sly had brought a glass thermometer with him. This would be something new that he had never done to a houseguest before.

Victor just looked at the madman waving a thermometer in the air, and wondered why he would want to take his temperature. Nothing was making sense to Victor.

Sly grabbed a pair of scissors, and cut Victor's pants off of him. He wasn't wearing any underpants, and his manhood laid limp on his lap. Sly grabbed Victor's pecker with one hand.

Sly squeezed the penis until Victor's urethra began to spread. It was a small hole, but it was just large enough to slide the thermometer into the opening. Sly forced the thermometer into the opening that Victor used to pee.

Victor screamed as loud as he could through the gag, but in his head he only heard the vibrations of his vocal cords.

Sly slid the thermometer as deep as he could into the man's sexual organ. Once it was in as far as it could go, Sly grabbed the head of the dick with his other hand.

"Just watching this hurts me."

Sly bent his wrist, and broke the thermometer in half. He heard a faint *snap* and knew that pieces of glass had been broken into shards, and those shards were now cutting into the inside of Victor's penis.

Sly laughed, and his laugh was even louder than Victor's screams.

Blood started to run out of his pecker, and Victor passed out from the pain.

Sly was bored with his unconscious houseguest. He grabbed a blade, and cut the man's throat. The warm blood ran down Victor's chest. Sly grabbed the garden hose and started rinsing the blood down the drain in the center of the floor.

The smell of copper in the air made Sly's stomach turn. He wondered which part of Victor he should save for himself to eat. He remembered that Betsy's (his beloved pig) favorite part was the thigh.

Sly used a hunting blade to carve a large piece of skin and muscle from Victor's thigh. He very carefully glided the blade with precision around Victor's muscles.

Sly chopped the rest of Victor's body into pieces for his pigs. They would be happy with their feast. It had been a few days since they had a feast. It wouldn't take them very long to devour the man's dead body.

Cindy would be arriving tomorrow. He wanted to cook Victor's thigh now, but instead he refrigerated it in a large freezer bag. He had to get the guesthouse cleaned up for Cindy.

He sprayed every last bit of blood down into the drain. After he rinsed the blood away, he always poured bleach on the floor to get rid of the rest of the evidence. Then he had to clean up the smell of bleach.

He got down on his hands and knees and scrubbed the concrete with good old fashioned soap and water. He always used too much bleach, and hoped that Cindy wouldn't be able to smell it in the upstairs of his guesthouse.

He wanted everything to be perfect for Cindy's stay.

CHAPTER 5:

Sly heard his alarm clock buzzing, and checked the time. He was still exhausted from carrying the pieces of Victor's body to the pigs. It took him most of the night to clean the basement of his guesthouse. He hoped that Cindy wouldn't move the rug. He didn't want her to find the hidden basement.

At least if she did, it would be clean. He even put the tools away in a toolbox. On the off chance that she stumbled across his dungeon, he could deny even knowing that it was down there.

Every muscle in his body ached as he put his feet on the floor. His stomach growled for the want of food. He still had plenty of Betsy left in the freezer. He motivated himself to brew a pot of coffee and start cooking some sausage.

As he dug around the freezer he saw the large slab of Victor's thigh. He decided to cut that into steak size fillets. Since he had never cooked human flesh before, he thought it would be best prepared on the grill. He wanted to flavor the flesh with charcoal.

Maybe he could convince Edward to come over later that evening. He had enough meat from Victor to grill out three steaks. One for each of them. Sly. Edward. And Cindy. A cookout could be her welcome home celebration.

Just as he turned off the stove, Cindy's car came into view from the window. He walked outside to greet her, hoping she would stop by the main house before driving the mile to the guesthouse.

Cindy parked her car, and got out, looking as beautiful as ever. She had cut off a few inches of her hair, and the way it framed her face was absolutely stunning. Her eyes shone in the sunlight. Then, when she smiled, Sly felt his heart melt.

She was the only woman that ever gave him butterflies in his stomach. She made him feel like a kid in high school. His tongue was always twisted around her, and he never knew the right things to say to her.

"Perfect timing. Breakfast is ready. Where's the moving truck?" Sly tried to keep his eyes in his head, and stared just past her. He didn't want her to think that he was checking her out. He didn't want her to feel uncomfortable around him.

"The moving van already unpacked, at the

storage shed. I have some luggage in the car. I figured I won't be here long enough to bring all my stuff. I was hoping that my friend, the realtor, could help me find a place soon. I don't wanna be a burden."

Sly wanted to tell her that she could never be a burden. But instead he bit his tongue. Instead, he could talk about business. "Well, you're in luck. The market is good for buyers right now. Sellers, not so much. But you're welcome to stay as long as you want." Part of Sly actually meant it.

Another part of Sly hoped she would leave soon. He didn't like the idea of not being able to use his guesthouse basement.

As they went into the house, Sly offered her some sausage.

"Edward said this is the best sausage ever. Oh yeah, I heard about Betsy. I'm sorry." Cindy took a bit of the human fed pig. "Oh. This is really good. What's your secret, Chef Sly?"

"If I told you, I'd have to kill you." Sly chuckled. Even though it was just a saying, his words rang true. He couldn't tell her what Betsy's special diet consisted of.

Cindy laughed it off, and went to the guesthouse to unpack. He watched her drive away until he couldn't see her car any longer.

He was glad she was there, but knew that he had to rack his brain for a new place to conduct his hobby.

That evening, Edward came over for the cookout. Victor's thigh, once cut up, looked like three perfectly cut steaks. Edward nor Cindy knew they were about to taste human flesh and muscle meat.

Sly manned the grill, and noticed how easily the chunks of Victor darkened as he cooked them. It smelled and looked just like grilling any other piece of meat.

After the food was ready, Edward made a toast to Cindy.

"Finally, my little sister is home. Here. In the country. Where she belongs. Cheers!"

The three turned up their beers. Cindy had already thanked Sly several times, but felt the need to thank him again.

"Thank you so much Sly. I'll be outta your hair before you know it."

Before Sly had a chance to respond, Edward spoke up.

"You could always stay with me. But I get it. He has a whole spare house. All I have is a spare room."

Then Sly had a thought. "I'd like to also give a toast to Betsy's memory. Edward, do you remember that time you let Betsy loose and she got in the swimming pool? It was so fun watching her swim. And she loved it. I was thinking about burying some of her at sea. Do you still have your boat?"

A boat, in the middle of a lake would be a perfect place for him to kill and dispose of a body. If only he could borrow Edward's boat.

"I have it. But the engine is blown. Sorry, pal."

"I guess I can buy one." He already planned on buying a little jon boat. Something that was all aluminum. No carpet. Something that would be easy to bleach free of any trace of blood.

Now, he didn't need his guesthouse basement. He would now do his killing on the water. Problem solved!

Sly laid out the plates on the picnic table for his guests. "Eat up, while it's hot!"

He watched as Cindy carefully cut off a portion of Victor's thigh, and then raised the fork to her sweet lips. As she chewed, Sly was wondering what she was thinking.

Cindy raised a napkin to her mouth so she could speak. "MMM. HMMMM. This is yummy, Sly. Did you use some special tenderizer? This is so tender and juicy. Is this pork? Is it some more of Betsy?"

"I second that. This is the best cookout ever." Edward washed down his bite of Victor with a gulp of ice cold beer.

Sly cut off a small piece of his own steak, and chewed on it. The juices ran along the sides of his tongue, and he agreed. It did taste like pork. "Yeah, it's some of Betsy. I wasn't sure how'd she taste on the grill. But I like it."

Sly laughed at his friends. How could they mistake the taste of human flesh for pork? The three ate their meal in silence, enjoying every bite that they took. Sly had to laugh at himself. If only his guests knew what they were eating.

CHAPTER 6:

The very next day, Sly bought a used boat. Luckily, he already had a truck on the farm to pull it with. The boat was sixteen feet long, and had metal benches that served as seats. There was a small room built on the boat. Four walls, a cover, and a door. It wasn't fancy, but it would suit his purpose perfectly.

There was no carpet that would hold blood stains. It was just metal, and he could use bleach on the metal to wash away the blood.

He knew a boat wouldn't be as safe as his guesthouse basement, and that he couldn't keep his victim for days. But if it was late, and dark outside, he could take someone out to the middle of the lake. Noise would be the problem. He would have to keep them gagged.

He wouldn't feel safe killing someone under the night's moon, but it was better than not participating in his hobby. His hobby kept him sane. He seemed to always be full of rage. Murdering people seemed to subside his rage.

Sly had a rough childhood growing up. As

a small child, he remembered how his parents fought all the time. Then, when his Father went to prison for killing his Mother, he spent the rest of his childhood in foster care.

Most of his foster families had abused him. As he got older, he realized that he was nothing but a paycheck for them. The government paid them to *care* for him. If you could call it caring for him.

They fed him most of the time, and kept a roof over his head. But mostly, they were mean to him, like maybe he was more of a bother than his paycheck was worth.

Sly grew up as an angry child. He acted out in school. When he was fifteen, he couldn't control his rage. Foster families kept moving him home from home, each home being worse than the last.

He remembered how it felt, when he was fifteen, and he committed his first murder. He had been in the woods, playing with his foster father's handgun. He knew that he wasn't supposed to be playing with it, but he did anyway.

He was only fifteen years old, and he was in the woods. He held the gun in his hands, realizing how much heavier it was in real life than it appeared on television. There was a hunter off in the distance, dressed in all orange.

Sly heard a rustle in the brush, and saw the most beautiful animal he had ever seen in his life. It was a deer, and he stayed completely still, so the animal would approach him.

The deer got close enough for Sly to pet it, it was a young deer, just like him. He reached out his hand, and then Sly heard the hunter shoot.

The small deer fell right in front of him, blood pouring out of its heart.

The hunter came to claim his prize, and hadn't even seen Sly on the other side of the tree. Sly just couldn't understand why someone would want to kill such a magnificent creature.

Sly raised the pistol towards that hunter and shot him square in the chest. The hunter fell to the ground, grasping his chest.

Sly stood over his body, and watched as he leaked blood all over the leaves around him.

In that moment, Sly felt at peace. It was the happiest he had ever felt in his entire life. He knew then, that his purpose in life was to kill worthless people.

Sly was never caught for that crime. Instead, it got pinned on his drunken foster father, since the gun was registered to him.

After that, when he was seventeen, Sly got a great foster family who he thought really loved him. His foster father at that time was a realtor, and didn't take him in for the money. He did it because his wife wanted a child.

That was when Sly decided to become a realtor. He never wanted to be poor. And ever since then, he knew that he wanted to kill worthless people.

When his foster family got pregnant with their own child, they forgot all about Sly. It didn't matter, though. He would be eighteen soon. And he started his own life.

Sly had thought about taking in foster children of his own, but knew it would conflict with his hobby. Instead, he would rid the world of bad people.

At the age of eighteen, he legally changed his name to Sly Verdict. He went to real estate school. He worked hard. By the age of twenty-four, he had several realtors working under him, and Verdict Realty was created.

His life was complete. He had a great job, and an even better hobby. Yet still something was missing.

Maybe Cindy was his missing piece. Maybe they could start their own family together. Then, perhaps, Sly would feel like a whole person, and not an empty shell of a person.

CHAPTER 7:

Sly drove to his guesthouse to check on his current houseguest. She was the only ever willing houseguest to stay there. He had a yearning and he had to see Cindy.

Remembering his childhood left him feeling broken and alone. He was torn between taking his next victim, or visiting Cindy. Since it was still daylight, and he only had the boat to perform his hobby, visiting Cindy won the toss up.

He knocked on the front door and waited patiently for her to answer.

A disheveled Cindy opened the door. Her hair was a mess, and she was holding a coffee cup. "I know. It's noon. I should be out looking for a job. But I was so tired from the move. It really drained me."

Sly just laughed. "I told you. Stay as long as you want. I'm not your master. I'm not telling you to go out looking for work." He flashed his smile of recently bleached white teeth at her. "I come in peace. As a friend."

She offered him a cup of coffee, and he eyed the rug that hid his dungeon door. It hadn't been moved.

"I bought a boat today. Thinking about taking part of Betsy out tonight. She'd like a burial at sea, even though I don't have all of her."

Cindy pulled her hair back into a ponytail. "You want me to go with you?"

Yes, Sly did want her to go with him, but he had other plans. He already had a victim lined up for that night. "It's kinda personal, I prefer to be alone."

Cindy's facial expression changed, and her heart ached for Sly.

"That came out wrong. I'd love to have you go with me, next time. How's that?"

Cindy placed her hand on Sly's shoulder. "Of course."

Sly felt the heat from her hand warm his heart. "I'm sorry. It's just been a bad day."

She pulled Sly in for a hug, and slightly placed her lips to his. But then quickly pulled away.

Sly's face turned red, and he realized he was blushing.

Sly didn't want to make it awkward, so he chose not to discuss their kiss. "You know. You could stay in the main house with me. There's no cable or internet out here. How in the world will you entertain yourself?"

"I was thinking that maybe my landlord

would let me use his pool?" She phrased her statement almost as a question.

Sly shook his head yes. "I'll meet you by the pool. I got plenty of beer, too."

Sly looked really tanned in his bright lime green swimming trunks. Cindy arrived wearing a pair of cut-off blue jeans and a bikini top that looked like a bra. He was already in the water.

He had brought out a cooler of ice, full of beer. Cindy helped herself to a drink, and removed her cut-off shorts. When Sly raised his head from the water, he swore that she looked better than any beer commercial, standing in her bikini holding a beer.

She was driving him crazy. She was looking too good. He made it a point to keep the lower half of his body hidden under the water, to hide his attraction. He didn't want her to see the bulge in his shorts.

They spent the afternoon drinking beer, swimming, and talking. Even though he was perfectly content spending time with Cindy, his mind wandered off thinking of his next victim.

Cindy didn't offer him as much comfort as he thought she would. Even though the butterflies in his stomach told him that she was the missing piece of his life, he still obsessed over his hobby. Nothing was as fulfilling as killing bad people.

Soon, night would fall, and he could take his boat out for a test drive.

CHAPTER 8:

One year ago, to the day, Sly had sold a home to a Ms. Marlene Weatherby. Ms. Weatherby was a widower, and at first, Sly felt bad for her.

Until he found out that she didn't report all of her income. She made a base income of $40,000 a year working at a bank, but she had $60,000 to put down on her new home. The numbers didn't add up.

Sly found this to be suspicious, and when he asked her about it, she gave him her business card. In the evenings, she moonlighted as an escort. An escort was just a fancy word for a hooker.

He never took her up on her services, but he knew that her prostitution could ruin marriages. He didn't like anyone who could ruin marriages. Marriage was sacred to Sly.

Luckily, he still had her business card, and called her (from a burner phone) and told her that he required her services.

He had told her to meet him at a hotel. His plan was to meet her in the hotel parking lot, and then drive her to the boat. He made sure to leave a copy of her business card in the parking lot, so that when she was reported missing, the police would find only her car, and a business card that basically stated her profession as prostitute.

Maybe then, the police wouldn't look too hard for her.

Sly made sure to park his car across the street from the hotel, and he waited on an outside stairwell, with a dark hat to hide his appearance. She said that she was driving a small maroon car, and it was barely light enough to make out the color of her vehicle.

Sly quickly walked over to her car to greet her. She was wearing a slinky black dress, that didn't leave much to the imagination. It was so short he could see her panty line. The neck line was cut so low he could practically see her nipples. She looked the part of a street walker.

He walked her across the street to his car, and asked her how she felt about a boat ride. She gladly accepted his offer, after he paid her. After paying her that much money she would have probably done anything that he asked of her.

He drove to his boat. It was already in the water on a large lake. She wasn't pleased with his boat and joked about how she was sure that he could afford something nicer.

As he started the engine, and drove the boat to the center of the large lake, the joke was on her. He knew that she would never return.

Marlene was not impressed with the boat, but she sure was impressed with Sly's cash. They only passed one smaller fishing boat on the lake, and Sly made sure to get as far away from them as he could.

After Sly turned off the engine, it was silent on the lake. There was no one around as far as the eye could see. There was nothing but water, and the nearest land was barely visible.

The moonlight cast enough light of what could have been a romantic setting, and Sly thought of Cindy. Even after spending a full day with her, he wanted more time with her. But his hobby came first. It was his duty to the world.

He didn't understand why, that when he was with Cindy, he obsessed over his next victim. Yet, when he was with his victim, his mind stayed on Cindy. He wanted the best of both worlds. If only he could combine Cindy with his hobby, then he would be a happy man.

The water was slapping the sides of the boat, rocking it gently.

Sly looked at the hooker. "We're all alone out here. What do ya think?"

Marlene pointed her nose in the air. "When was the last time you cleaned this boat? Did you at least bring a blanket?"

Sly had brought along a bag of tools, but no blanket. He opened the door to the small room. "Just in here. I have it set up perfectly for us in here."

Marlene walked through the door. "This room is tiny, what do you expect..."

Her words were cut off by Sly grabbing her from behind, his forearm around her throat.

Marlene reached in her purse, she needed her stun gun. She always carried one when she was on the job. She rummaged through the contents of her purse the best she could with his grip around her neck.

Sly tightened the grip on her neck, and Marlene panicked. She was gasping for air. Slowly her vision turned black. She felt the stun gun with the tips of her fingers. But it was too late. Her limp body collapsed on the floor of the small room.

Sly quickly pulled out the duct tape, and started taping her wrists together. He also put some tape over her mouth, just in case she decided to scream when she woke up.

Sly sat on the metal bench of the boat, and looked at the moon. It was truly a beautiful night. He enjoyed the serenity of the water lapping on the sides of his small boat. He was at peace.

While he waited for Marlene to wake up, he pulled out his fishing pole. He already planned on catching some fish. If he cleaned some fish on the boat, that would explain some of the blood, as long as he didn't overdo it, and make her gush blood.

Sly pierced the head of a minnow with a barbed hook, and dropped the fishing line into the water. It didn't take long for him to feel a slight tug on the end of his line. He yanked up on the pole, and began reeling.

He reeled in the catfish, and held it in the air. He used a fishing knife to cut off the fish head, and let the blood run down his arm, and drip on the floor of the boat.

Even though it was only a small bit of blood, he hoped that if anyone did stumble across his little boat on the water, they would think the blood was from fishing.

Marlene woke in the small, dark room. She couldn't see much of anything. Even though her wrists were taped together, she managed to bring her hands to her mouth, and she removed the tape from her mouth.

She instantly started screaming.

The door to the small room opened, allowing the moonlight in. Her eyes adjusted and she saw Sly, looking at her and laughing.

"Scream all you want. There's nobody around."

Marlene kicked at Sly, and he grabbed her

ankle with his right hand. He held onto it, until she fell backwards onto her back.

She looked up at her captor. He sat on her knees, pinning her legs down. Even though her wrists were taped together, she began beating him in the chest with both of her fists.

"Looks like I have a fighter on my hands. Every fisherman loves a fighter!" Sly laughed as she continued to struggle and hit him. He grabbed her fists, and pinned them to her chest with one hand.

"You were gonna use this on me? Not smart." He used his other hand to hold up her stun gun, and then zapped her with it. Her body gyrated. She looked like she was having a seizure.

Foam ran from her mouth. Once again, she lay unconscious.

Sly undid the tape from her hands, knowing that wasn't going to work. He put her arms to both sides of her body, and duct taped her arms to the upper part of her body. He wrapped the tape around several times, mummifying her.

As Sly used a curved fishing hook and some fishing line to sew her mouth closed, Marlene started to wake up.

Marlene tried to open her mouth, but she couldn't even part her lips. She opened her eyes, and saw Sly sitting on her chest. She felt a tug on her lips, and it took a second to process what her eyes were seeing.

She could see Sly sewing her lips together! She panicked. She tried to squirm, but she couldn't move anything but her legs.

"Be careful. I might miss my mark. You don't want me to jab your gums with the hook." Sly laughed. "This will teach you to scream. And you think this is bad? When I'm done, I'm gonna sew your money maker shut!"

Marlene's eyes got as large as silver dollars.

Sly shook his head yes. "I'm gonna sew you shut. Down there. The essence of your womanhood. You shouldn't be selling that!"

Marlene passed out from the pain.

The task was much easier with Marlene passed out. Sly raised up her skirt, and stared at her vagina. He grabbed all four lips (labium minus and labium majus), and squeezed them with his fingers. He noted how soft her genital lips were to his touch.

He threaded the fishing hook with some fishing line, and poked the outside of her coochie, piercing through the tender flesh. He made sure to push the hook through all four layers of her labia. He started at the bottom of her opening.

Marlene started to wake up, but with Sly sitting on her knees, she couldn't move. Since he had sewed her mouth shut, she couldn't even scream. Her sounds were just hollow cries for help. When she tried to open her mouth, she felt the pain of the fishing line that had sewed her mouth closed.

Her arms were pinned and taped to her sides. Marlene couldn't do anything except feel the pain the realtor was inflicting on her.

He threaded through her gash, pulling the fishing line so tight that it closed up her opening. After he had sewed the majority of her beef curtains closed, with seventeen stitches, he came to her clitoris.

It was like it was poking its little head out and begging for Sly to sew the fishing line through it.

He pierced through the little organ, tightly pulling the fishing line completely through the clitoris. The skin bunched up, resembling a wound with just a small protrusion.

Then Sly had to make a decision. He wanted to kill her in a bloody way, but didn't want to clean up the boat. And he had to decide if he wanted to dispose of her body in the lake. After doing his research, he found out that gas in the body makes dead bodies float in the water. Sure he could chain her to a concrete block, but that wouldn't feed his pigs.

After thinking long and hard, he decided to kill her in a not bloody way, and then wrap her in a tarp. He would take her home to his pigsty and see if they would devour a whole human body that hadn't been cut up.

Sly used a plastic shopping bag and wrapped it around her head. He taped the bag tightly to her neck, where no oxygen could get through. He watched as the bag moved in and out with each breath she took.

The bag expanded and then deflated. The harder Marlene struggled, the quicker her own oxygen evaporated. Sly laughed in her face as he watched her slowly dying. Her eyes told him that she was aware that she was dying.

CHAPTER 9:

After wrapping Marlene's dead body in a tarp, he made sure there was nobody around to see him carry her to his truck. He drove home feeling a natural high. He felt so daring driving down the road with a dead body in the vehicle.

He thought he would be more paranoid of police officers. Instead, it did the opposite and made him feel rebellious. His heart beat fast and his blood pumped even faster. There were no cars around, and he even howled at the moon.

It was late, and he hoped that Cindy would be sleeping. The pigsty was close to his guesthouse, and he certainly didn't want her to find him feeding his pigs a dead body.

When he got home, he parked his truck so it would block Cindy's view from the house. She wouldn't be able to see what he was doing at the pigsty. It was dark anyways, but the pigs made a ruckus, hungry for their food.

He unwrapped Marlene's body from the tarp, and threw it in the pigpen. The hungry pigs quickly made their way to her body. They made snarling noises at each other, each rushing for their piece of the body.

Sly saw the porch light of his guesthouse turn on, and he walked over to the porch. He couldn't risk Cindy seeing what his pigs were eating. He decided to distract her.

As soon as Cindy opened the front door, Sly looked her in her big eyes. He said no words. He wrapped his arms around her, and gave her a soft kiss on her lips.

Cindy responded by parting her lips, and sliding her tongue into Sly's mouth.

Then Sly got to thinking how sexual it was sewing Marlene's snatch closed. He was so turned on. It was too late, but it was then he realized that he hadn't saved a piece of Marlene for him to eat.

It was too late now. He was busy anyways. Cindy backed into the house, with Sly still attached to her mouth. Their bodies moved as one, as she led him down a hallway.

When they got to the bedroom, Cindy broke her lips free from his, long enough to fall backwards onto the bed. She started tugging on her pajamas, pulling them from her body, exposing her nakedness.

Sly wasted no time, undoing his belt, pulling his pants off, and exposing his hardened manhood.

Cindy's eyes widened when she saw blood on his arm. "Are you hurt?"

Sly shook his head no. "I skinned a fish. Let's move this to the shower."

The couple pawed at each other like wild animals, both releasing their built up lust. They made love in the shower and on the bed. Finally, Sly had made Cindy his woman.

She fell asleep on his arm, and in the quiet of the night, Sly could hear the pigs grunting outside, enjoying their feast. Tonight was a good night.

Sly woke with Cindy on his arm. He dreaded the fact that he had to go to the office today. He wanted to spend all day in bed loving on her. He gave her a peck on her forehead, and it woke her.

She reached out her arm towards him. "Do you have to leave?"

"It's work." Sly started putting his pants on. "I have to. But do you have plans tonight?"

She shook her head no, and they made plans for later that evening.

Cindy was worried what her big brother might think if he knew that his best friend and his sister hooked up. "Edward? What about Edward? What are we telling him?"

"I'll tell him. Leave that to me. I'll just call and tell him that you're my girlfriend."

Cindy blushed at the word 'girlfriend', but

she didn't protest.

He gave her a kiss goodbye.

As he walked past the pigsty, he saw no obvious signs of Marlene's dead body. He waved bye to his pigs as he drove away.

CHAPTER 10:

Today felt different for Sly. The hour drive to the office felt shorter. The sky looked more blue. The sun seemed to shine brighter. He was just in a better mood.

When he walked into his office, he didn't even glance at his eye candy secretary, Stacy. Stacy was adorned in her normal professional yet revealing garb, but his eye didn't wander in her direction.

"Good morning Mr. Verdict. You have a showing in one hour."

"Thanks, Stacy."

Sly strolled into his office, feeling like he was walking on air. He sat at his desk and started preparing the necessary paperwork. He saw a bird fly past his window, and he watched outside as the bird flew across the street to the coffee shop, looking for cookie crumbs the customers may have dropped.

Then, Sly saw *him*. Officer Williams was across the street, sitting in the outdoor seating area of the coffee shop. Despite the restraining order, he found a way to be 500 feet away, and still keep an eye on Sly.

Sly regretted the day he got sloppy in his hobby. When he abducted and killed Officer William's brother-in-law, he had no clue that it would lead to a police officer stalking him.

Life was going so good for him right now. Now, he still had the problem of Officer Williams. The man looked mad. From what Sly had heard, Officer Williams had eventually lost his job. It started as a suspension, and led to him being fired.

Sly picked up his briefcase, and walked out to his car. Officer Williams was still sitting at the outdoor table, holding a cup of coffee. Sly looked in his direction, and waved. He wanted the Officer to know that he knew he was watching him.

Officer Williams did not wave back. As Sly got in his car, Officer Williams got up from his chair. Sly sat in his car, letting the air conditioning cool him down. As Sly drove away, he saw Williams approaching his office.

Sly turned his car around, and Williams scampered away, seeing that he was closer than 500 feet from him, as requested of the restraining order. As the cop ran away, he dropped a flyer.

'DO NOT BUY A HOUSE FROM THIS MAN! HE'S A MURDERER!'

And there was a picture of Sly underneath the

words.

Sly had to take care of Officer Williams sooner than later.

"Mrs. Langsdon, I assure you, this is an excellent school district." Sly had already shown this woman four houses, and she wasn't pleased with any of them.

The woman pursed her lips as she looked at the exterior of the home."It's stone. I don't like stone. I want brick. Not large stone."

Sly wanted to strangle this woman, right then and right there. He needed to release his anger. He was full of rage from Officer Williams following him.

Unfortunately, this woman didn't appear to be a bad person. From what he had seen, she was a loving wife, and a great mother.

"But it's in your budget which is low for this neighborhood. Do you want to live in a nice area or not?" Sly tried once again to use his salesman skills to convince the woman to buy. He was trying to be nice, even though he didn't want to be.

Mrs. Langsdon stood her ground. "I don't like it. Show me another home."

It took every ounce of Sly's self-control to calm himself. He took ten deep breaths, and tried to think of Cindy. He tried to think of anything that would make him happy again.

"You haven't even been inside yet."

The bitter woman wasn't budging. "I hate it."

Sly tried to bite his tongue. He tried to not be rude. But he couldn't control himself any longer. "Of course. Let me call another agent for you. Perhaps, they could work a miracle for you and find you a home in a nice neighborhood on a low budget."

The woman looked appalled.

Sly knew what he had just said would not be good for business. He had to control himself. He just couldn't stop thinking about that stupid flyer. He wondered where else Officer Williams had put the slanderous pieces of paper.

He was contemplating calling a lawyer to settle his score with the cop, but decided against it. Instead he called one of his employees, so they could take care of Mrs. Langsdon. He needed to go home and be with Cindy.

CHAPTER 11:

Sly's drive home from work wasn't as pleasant as his drive to work. He wanted to scream. He wanted to punch something. He wanted to kill someone.

A small part of him wondered what normal people do when they're mad. None of the people he knew killed people as an anger outlet. He hoped that Cindy could help him. He needed something to make him feel better.

Sly didn't bother going to his main house. Instead he drove straight back to his guesthouse. He got out, and the pigs greeted him with their beastly sounds. He knocked on the door, and waited for Cindy to answer the door.

Cindy's hair was a mess, yet she was still beautiful. His mood started to change. Just seeing her was cheering him up.

She was biting her lip "Did you call Edward? I just got off the phone with him. He didn't say anything."

Of course, he couldn't just enjoy peace with his girlfriend. She was already on him about calling Edward.

He tried to put on his most innocent and apologetic face. "I'm sorry. I forgot."

Cindy was not pleased. "You forgot. I thought you said you'd take care of it!"

Sly was shocked by her little outburst. Nothing seemed to be going his way today.

"Calm down." Sly said it as more of a command than a suggestion. "We'll do it together. Tonight."

He paused, and she started to smile.

Finally, he sighed with relief. "I've had a bad day. Can't we just play nice."

Cindy's warm smile melted his heart. "I'm sorry. I'm just stressed out. I don't know what we're doing here."

Sly used his hand to brush the side of her cheek. "What do you mean doing here? I've loved you for so long."

"And you're a great guy, Sly. But just because last night was so easy, doesn't mean that we're in a relationship." Cindy stopped for a second to think. "We lost touch for years. And…"

Sly cut off her words. "That doesn't matter. I know I love you. What else is there?"

Cindy held up a finger. "Well, one thing is Edward. What's he gonna think?" She held up another finger. "Number two. What if you get to know me, and you don't like me?"

"Edward knew this was coming. And I have loved you for years, of course I like you."

Cindy shook her head no. "We should take this slow, before we tell him."

"I want you to move in with me. Into my main house. We belong together."

Cindy shook her head no, again. "I was thinking, we should just date. I'm gonna stay with Edward. And we should date. Let's not complicate this."

Sly didn't understand. "You belong with me."

"Let's just date. Then we'll take it from there."

Nothing was going right for Sly today. So much for his good mood.

At least he would have his guesthouse basement back.

CHAPTER 12:

Just like that, Cindy packed her bags and went to stay with her brother, Edward. It was Cindy's idea to have the three of them meet at the bar. And see how Edward really felt about the pair dating.

Sly showered and shaved and was smelling good and looking even better. His goal was to impress Cindy. If she wanted to date, then he would woo her.

He picked a beautiful rose from his very own rose bush. He didn't care what Edward would say. Surely, his best friend would tease him and call him soft. He didn't care.

Edward was sitting at the bar, on his usual stool, drinking his usual beer. He looked up as Sly entered the bar, wearing a suit. Nobody else dressed up at the hole-in-the-wall country bar. The next most dressed up person was Edward, and that was just because he was in his Sheriff uniform. Everyone else wore blue jeans and t-shirts.

Edward called across the room. "Hey fancy

pants! You're buying tonight, right?"

Sly's eyes scanned the room until he found Cindy. He walked right up to her sitting at a little table, and Sly bent down to give her a kiss on her cheek. He pulled the rose out from under his suit jacket, and presented it to her.

Edward watched, his mouth gaping open. He slammed his beer down on the bar, and marched over to Cindy's table.

Edward's eyes twitched, trying to figure out what was happening. "Who wants to tell me what's going on here? I think I'm drunk, 'cause I thought I saw fancy pants here being romantic with my sister."

Sly sternly looked at his friend. "So what if I am?"

Edward just looked at Sly. "When she called me, and said she wanted to stay with me, I didn't know why. Did you put the moves on my sister? Did you make her uncomfortable?" Edward puffed out his chest towards his best friend.

"Maybe I did. But I don't think I made her uncomfortable."

Edward tried to read his sister's face, but she buried her blushing face with a beer bottle.

Edward took a deep breath, and sighed very audibly. He snarled his upper lip, and grabbed Sly by the top of his arm.

Sly puffed up his chest, thinking Edward was gonna hit him.

Instead, Edward patted Sly on the back.

"Welcome to the family brother." Then he screamed loud enough for the whole bar to hear. "Drinks on the house. This man's paying. For a cheers to a new couple."

The four other people in the bar cheered.

Cindy smiled, and stood up and gave Sly a sloppy kiss on his mouth. The very small crowd in the bar cheered, and went to the bar to get their free drink.

Cindy finally spoke up. "Welcome to the family? Not yet. We're just dating."

That was all Sly needed. The 'okay' from his girlfriend's big brother. Life was getting better.

After a couple of cheers and congratulations, Sly sat next to Cindy and she held his hand. Her hand was warm and soft, and felt so good. Cindy excused herself to go to the restroom, and Sly saw a chance to talk to his friend about other matters.

He told Edward about how Officer Williams was still stalking him, but from 500 feet away. Edward, also being an officer of the law, told him that was within his rights, as long as he didn't come closer than that. Sly didn't mention the flyers of libel.

Sly didn't want Cindy to know about Officer Williams. Not too long ago, Officer Williams startled Cindy when he trespassed on Sly's farm. Luckily, Edward had been there to arrest him.

When the night was over, Sly asked Cindy to come home with him, and she agreed. Not to live with him, but just for an overnight visit with her new boyfriend.

While he drove home, her hand was on his thigh, and he knew what she had on her mind. He drove faster. He wanted to get his girlfriend home, so he could woo her some more.

CHAPTER 13:

Sly woke up, once again in a great mood. He kissed Cindy goodbye as he left for work. The morning sun felt good on his face, and he rode with the top down on his convertible for the hour drive to his office.

He had rescheduled to see Mrs. Langsdon again, hoping he had finally found her a suitable house. He wasn't going to let anything ruin his good mood. He had to make things right with the client he was rude to yesterday.

He stopped by the office, got the key to the house he was going to show Mrs. Langsdon, and checked the coffee shop for any sign of Officer Williams.

When he looked across the street, Officer Williams was there, but he didn't see the man holding any papers. At least today, he wasn't handing out any flyers trying to damage Sly's reputation.

At least the copper was staying 500 feet away. Sly hoped he would get closer. But he wouldn't call the police. He would handle things in his own way.

Sly ignored the cop, and drove on to meet Mrs. Langsdon.

When he arrived at the house, Mrs. Langsdon was already outside, admiring the outside of the house. Sly got out of his car, and walked up behind the lady and gave her a startle.

Sly turned on his salesman's smile. "Thank you for meeting me today. I'm sorry about yesterday, I apologize. I wasn't having a good day. But I've got a deal on this home, so I hope you can forgive me."

"I love the outside of the house. It's brick, like I wanted. But it's smaller than I like." Mrs. Langsdon semi-smiled back to Sly.

"Well, you can't see the basement. Which is large. And this house is actually under your budget." Sly was proud of himself for finding her this house, even though it was his secretary, Stacy, who told him about it.

It turned out that Mrs. Langsdon loved the house. When they got to the backyard, she loved how large it was.

"Fluffy will love it back here!" Mrs. Langsdon exclaimed. "This will be a great area for him!"

Sly was puzzled. He hadn't heard about Fluffy, even though he had shown her several homes. "Fluffy? Who's that? You haven't mentioned Fluffy before."

She went on to tell him that Fluffy was the

family dog. She hadn't mentioned him because he was strictly an outdoor dog that never came inside of the home. She said they only had the dog so the kids could play with him, but even the kids had lost interest in him.

Sly hated the thought of a dog outside all the time, lonely, and enduring the elements. It got hot in the summer, and cold in the winter. Mrs. Langsdon might have just earned her a spot on his next year's line up of Sly's houseguests. She might possibly be one of his special houseguests that never leaves.

After she agreed to buy the home, Sly made a mental note to keep a spare key to this home for easy access next year. But before she made the list, he would have to come back after she moved in. He would have to see exactly what the dog's living conditions were. He had a feeling the dog wasn't being properly taken care of.

Plus, with Betsy gone, Sly could use another pet in his own life. Maybe a dog wouldn't be a bad idea.

CHAPTER 14:

Sly was in his pool, floating on a lounging floater, when Cindy came over. She looked just as mesmerizing as ever. But seemed to be in a panic.

She had run from her car and was breathless by the time she reached the pool. "Huhuhuh." She was trying to catch her breath. "That man. Huh Huh. That man is parked up the street. That cop that Edward arrested for trespassing."

Sly laughed. "My driveway must be at least 500 feet. He's not bothering us. He's within his rights according to your brother."

"Well he got out of his car, and he started screaming something at me! But I drove faster, I didn't stop to listen to him." Cindy had finally caught her breath.

Sly climbed out of the pool, and put his arms around her. "It's okay now."

She pulled away from him. "You're wet! Let me change into my bathing suit, okay?"

Sly maintained his good mood. He wouldn't let the psycho-stalker ruin his good time.

Cindy came out wearing a bikini and looked

around and she didn't see Sly. He had hid around the corner, and waited for her. He ran up behind her and grabbed her by the waist. He held onto her tightly, and jumped into the pool.

He was just playing with her, but she screamed bloody loudly. It was a high-pitched feminine scream that echoed around the whole farm.

The couple fell into the pool, and Sly laughed at Cindy as she wiped her wet hair from her face. She ended up laughing and enjoying Sly's playfulness. She loved the way she felt like a kid again when she was with him.

Their playtime was cut short by a car speeding towards the house. They couldn't see it. The house blocked their view. But they could hear a car, and it sounded like it was driving at a high speed.

Sly and Cindy stood completely still, listening as they heard a car door slam shut.

Officer Williams dashed towards the pool in a rush, with his hand gun held at the ready. "Let her go! I've caught you now Bastard!"

Sly and Cindy put their hands in the air, so as to not alarm the lunatic.

Williams aimed his weapon towards Sly. "You're safe now, Ma'am. Call the police! I've saved you."

Sly felt his blood begin to boil. He was filled with rage. He wanted to smash Williams' head in.

Cindy was confused. She wondered if this man really thought that he was saving her.

Cindy took the opportunity to defend her man, and prayed that the cop wouldn't shoot him. "No. You've got this wrong. We're just playing in the pool. He's not hurting me!"

Even though Sly's hands were in the air, he balled up his fists. "You're supposed to be 500 feet from me. If the cops come, you're the one going to jail." He was consumed with rage.

Officer Williams motioned with his gun. "Girl! You get out of the pool. Move away from the suspect."

Cindy did as she was told. Williams kept his weapon trained on Sly. Cindy climbed out of the pool, and covered her exposed belly with her arms, obviously feeling uncomfortable.

She scanned Sly's face, for an idea or a hint of what she should do. She got nothing. She didn't even see fear in Sly's eyes even though he had a gun aimed at him.

"Ma'am. Did he hurt you? It's okay. I'm a police officer. Er. Well, I was until…"

As Officer Williams voice trailed off, Cindy charged towards Williams, hoping that she made the right choice. Her shoulder contacted with his chest, causing him to stumble backwards.

Sly saw an opportunity, and he took it. He leapt out of the pool, and jumped on Williams while he was unbalanced. The gun dropped from his hand and slid out of his reach.

Sly sat on top of the cop's chest and beat him in the face with his fists. The first punch looked like it broke Williams' nose because it started gushing blood. That wasn't enough for Sly. He wanted to hurt the man more.

Sly drew back his other fist, and came down with all his strength, hitting the cop in his eye. The officer tried to block his face with his hands, but Sly was much stronger than him.

Cindy grabbed the gun. "Sly. Stop. He's hurt. I have the gun. He can't hurt you now."

Sly stood up, and kicked Williams several times in his ribs. He turned around and saw Cindy holding the weapon. He grabbed the gun from her. And then shot Williams in the face.

CHAPTER 15:

Cindy stood. Paralyzed with shock. She was trying to rationalize what she just saw. She stared at the brains on the concrete. She knew that Sly had just murdered the man. Sure, she had feared the man, but she didn't want Sly to kill him.

Sly looked at Cindy. "We have to get rid of the body."

Cindy didn't respond. She thought she heard Sly say that they had to get rid of the body. But that couldn't be right. She knew that they had to call the police. They had to tell someone in law enforcement what just happened.

She wanted to call her brother. He was the sheriff. They could tell him how Williams broke the restraining order. How he waved a gun around threatening them. It was self defense. Well, for the most part it was self defense. Maybe Sly had overdone it by murdering him.

Sly realized that Cindy wasn't moving. She wasn't saying anything. He paused for a moment, trying to put himself in her shoes. She wasn't used to seeing people's blood and organs outside of their body like he was.

He realized that he had to say something to comfort her. "It's okay. It's over now. But now we have to act."

"Act? What? We need to call Edward."

Sly put his arms around her and spoke in a calm tone of voice. "Cindy, we can't. I killed a cop. I'll go to jail."

Cindy pulled away from him. "It was self defense, right?"

Sly shook his head no. "He's a cop. That's a no-no. Plus, this would make all the newspapers. I'm the face of Verdict Realty. A court trial would kill my business."

Cindy still didn't respond. He knew he had to spin it from a different angle to please her. "Your prints are on the gun, too. Do you really want to explain this to the cops?"

Cindy tried to think. She wanted to make sense of the situation, but she couldn't. Her mind was mush. She couldn't understand what Sly was saying. She walked over to a chair and just sat down.

"Cindy. Listen to me. This has to be our secret. We can't tell anyone. Not even Edward. Okay? Deal?"

Cindy just shook her head. "I don't know. Where would you hide a body? We can't hide this."

Sly wanted to comfort her by telling her that his pigs would eat every inch of evidence, but he didn't want her to know that he had done that before.

"I'll take care of it. You stay here. Let me handle it. But I have to do it now. You can burn his clothes, right? I'll leave them here with you." Sly began undressing the dead police officer. "Burn them. On the grill.Okay?"

After undressing him, Sly put Williams' dead body in Williams' car. He drove back to his pigsty. Luckily, it was too far away for Cindy to see him. He was at least a mile from her.

He threw the whole dead body in the pigpen, and the munchers were in hog heaven, tearing into the cop's flesh. He knew he had to get rid of the car. He wasn't sure how to do it. When he parked Chester's car (William's brother-in-law) in the woods on his property, some neighbor kids found it. Then he thought about the pond on his farm.

He drove the car to the pond, and drove it into the water, and watched it sink.

By the time he ran the couple miles back to the main house he was out of breath. With every step he took, he wondered if Cindy had done like he told her. He hoped that she hadn't done something stupid like called her brother.

She was still sitting in the same chair. It

looked like she hadn't moved.

He approached her, and spoke in almost a whisper. "Did you call Edward?"

She shook her head no.

He could see that she had been crying. "That's a good girl." He bent down to her level, and gave her a kiss on her forehead. "I'll burn the clothes. Then I need to clean up this mess." He looked at the blood and grey matter on the concrete.

The whole time he was cleaning up the mess, Cindy didn't move. He realized then that she was weak. He picked up the gun, and mentally noted that he could hide it in his guesthouse basement. He might need it one day. Afterall, it did have Cindy's fingerprints on it. He hoped it wouldn't come down to that, but he refused to go to prison.

Even if it meant blaming it on the love of his life.

CHAPTER 16:

It was a long night for Sly. Cindy didn't sleep. She didn't move, either. She just laid in bed, sobbing. Sly tried to comfort her, but she was inconsolable.

All he could do was keep his fingers crossed that she wouldn't tell anyone. At least she hadn't called Edward yet.

Sly stayed home from work the next day so he could spend time with Cindy. He called Stacy (his secretary) and had her change all of his appointments. Work could wait. He had more pressing matters to address.

Sly got out of bed, and started the coffee pot. He knew Cindy would need caffeine due to not sleeping. He started to prepare breakfast. He still had some of Betsy left. Human fed pork was yummy. And maybe it would cheer Cindy up.

Eventually, she made her way to the kitchen. In a robotic manner, she poured herself a cup of coffee, and sat at the table and watched Sly cook.

After a few minutes of sitting in silence, she began to speak. "I didn't sleep at all. I still think we should call Edward."

Sly convinced her that it was too late to call the police now. A full night had passed, and law enforcement wouldn't like it that they had tried to hide their offense.

Plus, the body was already gone and Williams' car was in the bottom of the pond. Cindy didn't bother to ask where the body was.

She still had an appetite, and that was a good sign. She ate all of Betsy that was on her plate, and even told him that it was the best sausage she had ever eaten.

The lovers spent the day lounging by the pool. Like they tried to do the previous evening, before the crazed cop had interrupted their evening.

Physical contact was minimal, even though Sly tried to be affectionate. She was very distant, but he understood. Right now, Cindy just needed some space.

They barely spoke. They just laid in the sun, baking their skin trying to get a tan. Cindy dozed off in the lounge chair. Exhaustion had finally taken hold of her. Sly knew that she needed sleep. Maybe it would make her feel better.

When Cindy woke after her three hour nap, Sly was by her side. He rubbed her shoulders, trying to comfort her. She still looked beautiful even though her eyes were red and puffy from crying.

Sly was trying anything to try and make his girlfriend feel better. "Do you want some coffee? It might make you feel better."

"I think I need some sleep. In a real bed. I think I'm going to Edward's. This is crazy! My life is crazy. I'm staying with my brother. I'm practically homeless. Then this happened. I have no job. I do have an interview in the city tomorrow. But I don't know if I can do it. I just need sleep."

Sly was hurt by her words. "As long as I'm around, you'll never be homeless. And I can pay your bills. You don't even have to work. Don't be stressed out."

Cindy started to cry again. "I watched you murder a man, and you're telling me not to be stressed out. I helped you cover it up. If I could go back and relive last night, I would."

Sly started to panic. "You're gonna tell Edward, aren't you?"

She shook her head no. "I can't. I'm an accessory."

At least that made Sly feel better. He only hoped that her conscience wouldn't get the best of her.

CHAPTER 17:

After Cindy left, Sly knew he had some errands to run. There had been a red circle on his calendar, that was a day or so overdue. The red circle symbolized a person that he deemed not worthy. They would be the next guest in his guesthouse basement.

A year ago, Sly had sold a house to a bachelor named Eric Rugden. Eric was a doctor with a drinking problem. When Sly had done his background check on the doctor, he saw that there were two complaints against him professionally. People who said that Dr. Rugden had misdiagnosed them.

Sly didn't know what happened in the lawsuits, he just assumed the doctor paid good lawyers to get him off from the charges. But Sly knew he was an alcoholic. He had been drunk each time Sly showed him a house. Sloppy, falling down drunk.

Sly had been patient, waiting one full year since he sold him the home. That way, hopefully the police would never tie the doctor's disappearance to his realtor.

Sly sat outside in his car, (with a fake license plate on it, so his car would be unidentifiable) watching for any signs of life from Eric Rugden's house. There was a small light coming from one of the windows that might be a tv.

It was dark outside, and Sly used the spare key from last year's sale to let himself into the doctor's house. He went in through the backdoor, which opened into the kitchen. There were two empty bottles of wine on the counter, and Sly only hoped that the doctor was drunk. This would be easier than he expected.

Sly quietly tip-toed down the hallway, following the sound of the television. He leered his head around the corner into the living room. Just as Sly had suspected, Eric was passed out on the couch, snoring.

This would be easier than Sly had suspected.

It wasn't hard to get the doctor to the car. The doctor was so drunk that he didn't even wake up as Sly threw him over his shoulder. Sly put him in the backseat of the car before the doctor started to wake up.

Sly quickly taped the doctor's ankles to each other, and then his wrists. Even if he fully woke up, Eric wouldn't be able to get away.

Sly drove straight to his guesthouse.

Sly spent all night in the basement with the doctor, waiting for him to wake up. Sly even dozed off a couple of times. He had made a pallet on the cold concrete floor. He didn't gag the doctor, because he wanted the doctor's screams to wake him up.

It was morning before Eric woke up. Sly was woken up by the man screaming. Even though Sly hadn't hurt him yet, he screamed like he was already in pain. But it was just panic. Pure panic from waking in a dank basement being chained to a chair.

"Good morning, Doctor. Welcome to casa de Verdict."

The doctor widened his eyes and looked at Sly. For a moment, he stopped screaming. "I must've been drunk last night. Do you wanna enlighten me? Where am I? Am I dreaming? How'd I get here?"

Sly stood from his place of slumber and laughed. Then, he bent down close to the doctor's face and laughed louder.

"I told you. You're at my guesthouse. Welcome."

When the doctor realized he was chained to a chair, he started screaming again. "Why am I dreaming about my realtor? I just wanna wake up. Can you pinch me?"

Eric's eyes scanned the room, and saw

the workbench with a variety of tools. Screwdrivers, knives, hammers, drills. What he couldn't see was his own scalpel. Sly had taken it from the doctor's house.

Sly picked up the scalpel. "This looks sharp. Perhaps I could cut you with it. Do you think you'd wake up then?"

The doctor looked terrified. "That's not a toy. Just pinch me."

"So, I know you're a doctor." Sly poked the tip of his own finger with the surgical tool, and a small drop of blood ran to the surface of his skin. "And I know you're an alcoholic. What I don't know is why there were medical complaints against you. Malpractice. Yeah, that's what it's called."

The doctor shook his head. "Is this some nightmare from my conscience? It feels so real. Wake up. Wake up. C'mon Eric! WAKE UP!"

Sly decided to play along with the doctor's delusion. "You'll wake up when your conscience is clear. What do you have to confess?"

"Confess?" The doctor fought back the tears that felt far too real. "My dream wants me to confess. Why to my realtor?"

Sly thought fast on his feet. "Because I'm the jury. I'm the judge. And I'm the torturer. Just confess. The sooner you confess, the sooner you'll wake up."

Eric looked relieved."I get it. Your last name is Verdict. And my verdicts in court were bribed. I got off. Thanks to my lawyer. This seems more like a nightmare than a dream."

"You bribed your innocence. That's your confession?"

The doctor was crying and he shook his head yes. "Yes. I was guilty. I was drinking too much on the job. I missed a malignant tumor. A patient died due to my drinking. Can I wake up now?"

Sly just laughed and waved the scalpel in front of the man's face. "Where was this tumor?"

Eric started talking, thinking this was just a dream. Dreams can't hurt, right?

"The tumor was in his head. The frontal lobe. I missed it." The doctor started crying even harder. "The patient died. But the courts didn't see it as malpractice. Isn't that what matters?"

Sly had heard everything that he needed to hear. It was time to start his own brain surgery.

Sly started by using the scalpel to cut a square out of the man's forehead. He assumed he could get to the brain that way.

The man screamed. Sly pressed extra hard into the man's skin, wondering if the scalpel would also cut through the bone. But it didn't. All Sly managed to do was cut a square piece of skin from Eric's forehead.

Blood ran down into the doctor's eyes. It felt like someone had just thrown salt into his eyes. Luckily, he was crying, and some of the tears cleared the blood from his vision.

Sly wasn't sure how to get to the man's frontal lobe. He remembered a scene from a movie where they used a handheld circular saw to cut away the skull to perform a makeshift brain surgery.

Sly glanced over at his tools, and he didn't have one. He tried to apply more pressure to the scalpel, but it just wouldn't cut through the skull.

The whole time, Eric screamed and begged for Sly to stop. He finally realized that he wasn't dreaming. It hurt too much for it to be a dream.

Since the scalpel wasn't working, Sly picked up his jigsaw. He turned it on, and listened to the small motor roar. The blade on it started moving up and down. He figured that might just get the job done.

He turned the small tool off, and pressed the tip of the blade into the spot on Eric's forehead that was missing the top layers of skin.

When he turned it on, the tip of the blade easily punctured through the skull bone. He had to guide it with both hands to cut out a square shaped piece of bone. Fluid was running from the incision. Not all of it was blood. It was a red fluid mixed with a clear fluid.

In Eric's head, the sound was too loud. He could hear the jigsaw, and feel the vibrations. He tried to scream, but he couldn't. It hurt so bad, then all of a sudden he couldn't feel anything. He was lucky to still be alive, but he couldn't move his face at all.

Sly powered down the small tool, and looked inside the man's forehead. Some of the brain had ended up on the end of the saw blade. Sly shook off the squishy substance. He had never seen a human brain in this state.

He looked at Eric. He was shocked to see that the man was still alive.

"You're still alive? This is one helluva dream, huh?"

Eric wanted to respond, but he couldn't. He was screaming in his head. His body just wouldn't respond.

Sly used his fingers to poke around the opening. The inner layers of the doctor's brain were warm and softer than Sly had imagined. He knew that monkey brains are considered a delicacy in some countries, and wondered what a human brain would taste like.

He carved out a portion of the man's brain with the scalpel and set it aside. It's what he would have for dinner. He figured it wouldn't be too hard to fry. He wanted to eat the brains crunchy.

The doctor blinked. But that was the only movement that Sly could get from the man. He must have been braindead. Sly didn't know much about anatomy, and which part of the brain did what, but he honestly expected the man to be dead.

He got out the garden hose, and sprayed the man to cleanse him of all the blood and bodily fluids. He thought it would be fun to keep this man for a couple of days. He could try eating different body parts.

He put the hose in the man's mouth, hoping he was drinking at least a little bit of water. He needed him hydrated if he intended to keep him alive for a couple more days.

CHAPTER 18:

Sly held the piece of Eric's brain in the palm of his hand. It wasn't a large piece, but it was just enough for a snack. Since he loved fried foods, he figured frying it would be best.

He even considered baking it, but he wouldn't know which temperature to bake it on or for how long. It's not like he could look in a cookbook and get a recipe for baked brains. Maybe he should start writing his own cookbooks.

He could see his book on bookshelves in homes all around the world. 'How To Eat Fried Brains'. Even the title would be more interesting than any other cookbook ever written.

Sly cracked an egg, and soaked the brain in the slimy substance. After letting it soak for just a moment, he breaded it with some flour. He even added some salt and pepper, hoping that would enhance the taste.

He poured the grease in his skillet, and let it warm up. He didn't want to get his grease too hot, but just warm enough.

He carefully placed the brain in the skillet, and the grease responded by splashing and popping all over the stove. Sly carefully took a spatula and centered the brain. He watched as it cooked, and the grease turned a dark color. Maybe he was cooking out some sort of brain fluid. He wasn't sure.

He flipped his snack, and saw that it had started to brown. Being a fan of crispy fried foods, he knew that he had to fry it longer to get his desired texture.

After it was sufficiently dark, he pulled the breaded brain from the pan. He placed it on a plate, and stared at his food. Part of him was excited that he was eating brain. Another part of him was anxious and just a tad nervous. It's not like he had a spare brain lying around in case this one wasn't prepared correctly.

Just in case he would need it, he pulled out a bottle of hot sauce from the refrigerator. Hot sauce made everything taste better. He just wasn't sure if that would be the case in this scenario.

He carefully cut off a rounded piece with his steak knife, and examined his food. It almost resembled a thick pork chop that had too much fat and sinew.

He stabbed to cut off a portion with his fork, closed his eyes, and put it in his mouth. Before chewing, he let the flavor marinate on his tongue. It actually tasted good.

He took a bite, and fluids filled the crevices of his mouth. It tasted even better than the thigh steaks he prepared. It tasted even better than Betsy.

He put the hot sauce aside, knowing that he wouldn't need it. Sly enjoyed his snack, and made a mental note that he should treat himself to brain snack more often.

CHAPTER 19:

Sly woke up and checked his phone. He had been trying to call Cindy the night before, but she didn't answer. He hoped that she was only sleeping. He prayed that she wasn't avoiding him. Her conscience was too good to be involved in a murder.

He hoped that she didn't see him differently after witnessing him murdering Officer Williams. The man had it coming. Williams had no right to come on his property waving a gun at him and Cindy. He wished that Cindy felt better about the whole situation. Maybe her goodness was what he loved so much about her.

He didn't have any missed calls. She hadn't tried to call. He knew that she had an interview today, but he wasn't sure what time. He would try calling her again, later.

For now, he had to go into the office. He had to finalize the paperwork on Mrs. Langsdon's house.

Closing on a house was always exciting. The buyers were always anxious to get into their new home. His job was truly rewarding.

Plus, the sooner that Mrs. Langsdon got into her new home, the sooner he could check on Fluffy, her dog.

Sly loved having to drive an hour to the city. The countryside was a beautiful sight. The skies were so blue. The pastures were so green.

He loved letting the top down on his convertible. Feeling the wind on his bare head was always a great way to start the day. The drive was the perfect remedy to keep his mind from worrying about Cindy.

Not knowing how she was handling the situation was the worst part. At least he hadn't heard from Edward. That must have meant that she hadn't told him.

Mrs. Langsdon was already at the office, awaiting Sly's arrival. Sly walked into his office, and Stacy, his secretary, greeted him.

"Good morning, Mr. Verdict. Mrs. Langsdon is waiting for you. The closing papers are on your desk. The broker is already here, too. They're waiting for you in conference room one."

Sly grabbed the papers, and went to the conference room. He loved seeing excited new homeowners. He also loved the money that he made. Selling houses was very lucrative.

After all the necessary papers were signed, Sly gave Mrs. Langsdon the key to her new home. Of course, he had kept one for himself. Soon, he could check on Fluffy's living standards. If they were poor, she would make the red circle list for a brief stay in his guesthouse basement.

He made small talk, and asked when she planned to officially be moved in.

In a few days, he could go and check on the dog. As he was speaking with the new homeowner, Stacy buzzed over the intercom, telling him that he was needed in the reception area. Sly very politely excused himself.

He heard screaming from the hallway. All he could hear was a female's voice, and he wondered what was going on. When he stepped out, he saw Sara Harris. Chester Harris' wife. Officer Williams' sister.

Sara Harris was upset. "My brother didn't come home last night. He had something to do with it." She pointed her index finger sharply in Sly's direction.

Stacy asked her boss if he wanted her to call the police, but Sly advised against it. Instead, he welcomed Sara into his office. He hoped they could speak like rational adults.

"Mrs. Harris, I'm sure you know I had a restraining order against your brother. I haven't seen him. It would be illegal for me to see him."

Sara was not pleased. Her face turned red. "He lost his job because of you. He's convinced you did something with Chester. Now, I know you did something to him. He told me he was going to spy on you. Then he didn't come home."

Sly let her scream and get the rage out of her system. He listened attentively, and tried to look as innocent as he could.

He tried his best to control his temper, but his will wasn't that strong. "I assure you that I haven't seen your brother. Do I have to get a restraining order against you, too? You need to leave now! Never return to my office! I'm conducting business here. The police cleared me in your husband's disappearance. Kindly leave now!"

As Sara turned for the door, she turned around, and pointed her finger at Sly again. "You haven't seen the last of me. I'm on to you."

Sly sighed. So much for his good mood. Why couldn't people just leave him alone?

CHAPTER 20:

He tried calling Cindy several times that day with no answer. As he got home, he saw the Sheriff's truck in his driveway. His heart sank, wondering if his best friend was there to arrest him.

If Cindy told Edward, would he arrest him? They were best friends after all. Maybe Edward would talk to him first. If Edward knew, would he help him keep it a secret?

He had no way of knowing if Edward knew. He considered turning the car around and driving away. But he didn't. He parked his car, and walked around back to the pool. He just sat down, and watched the sun reflect off the water. He knocked on his backdoor to get Edward's attention.

Edward came out, and his mouth was full of food. "I don't know what that was in the baggy, but it sure was good."

His best friend came over to raid his refrigerator. And he ate the rest of Eric's brain. Sly was saving that for another snack. He laughed.

Here he was worried that his friend was going to arrest him. He couldn't have been more wrong.

"Pork. It was Betsy pork."

Edward agreed. "I see. That's why it was so good then." Edward was still chewing.

Sly couldn't help but laugh. His Sheriff best friend was a cannibal and didn't even know it.

Edward finished chewing. "What happened with Cindy? She slept all day yesterday. She didn't even go to her job interview today. What'd you do to her, man?"

Sly tried to play dumb. He couldn't tell Edward that she watched him murder Officer Williams. He just kept his mouth shut. And he smiled.

Edward wasn't a dummy. He thought he knew what that smile meant. "Did you keep her up all night?" He put both his hands in the air. "She's my sister. I don't wanna hear it. Keep it to yourself, man."

Sly laughed. He was so relieved that Cindy hadn't told Edward anything about their situation. Thankfully, she could keep a secret.

Edward and Sly spent the evening listening to music and goofing off in the pool, just like kids. Sly kept checking his phone, but Cindy still hadn't called him back.

After Edward left, Sly went to check on his houseguest. Of course, Dr. Eric Rugden was waiting for him. The doctor sat, unmoving, making no noise. The only sign of life was the drool running from his mouth.

Sly figured he was braindead. He was missing part of his brain. It was now in Sly's and Edward's bellies.

Sly put the water hose to the man's mouth, yet he didn't drink. He just sat. This was no fun for Sly. He liked it when they struggled and when they screamed for help. He loved the moment that they realized they were gonna die. The look in their eyes gave him an adrenaline rush.

Eric wasn't capable. Sly tried everything. He drove a nail through the man's foot, and he didn't flinch. He pulled one of Eric's teeth. He pulled out a fingernail.

The man didn't make a sound. And he didn't move. Not an inch.

Sly looked at the man. He was nothing more than a slump of meat. His chest barely moved when he breathed. But he was breathing.

There was one thing that Sly always wanted to try, but never had the nerve to act on it. He wasn't gay. He was just curious what it would feel like to put his dick in a man's asshole.

He never acted on it. Always afraid that someone would call him gay. He had nothing against gay people, it's just that most people in the country where he lived discriminated against gay people.

He would not have to worry about what the doctor thought of him. It appeared that the doctor wasn't capable of having thoughts right now.

Sly used the key to unlatch the handcuffs, and stood back. Waiting to see if the doctor was feigning being brain dead. The man didn't attempt to move. Sly almost expected him to jump out of the chair and grab a weapon. But he didn't.

Sly slid his pants from his legs, and used the hose to rinse Eric's rump. It didn't look any different from a woman's rear. But Sly had always wondered if it felt different.

Sly used his mind to picture Cindy naked. He stroked himself, until his penis stood at attention. He laid Eric facedown on the concrete.

Sly got down on his knees, straddling Eric. He spit on his hand, and wiped it on his cock. It was better than not using any lube.

Sly slid his dick into the doctor's tight anus. It was warm and tight. But it wasn't juicy like a vagina. He missed the way a pussy felt wrapped around his cock.

But since he had already started, he figured that he might as well finish. It's not like it didn't not feel good. Sly thrust a few super hard pumps until he blew his load.

He then looked at the unmoving, unfeeling,

unthinking man. He wondered if he could feed a live person whole to the pigs. Would they eat it? There was only one way to find out.

Sly firemanned carried the brain dead man up the ladder. He carried him all the way to the pigsty, and Sly felt something tap him on his back.

Sly dropped the man, and turned around. Eric raised his hand towards his captor, and said something that might have been 'help'.

He wasn't as brain dead as Sly thought. The man didn't move much. He didn't try to run away. He didn't cry for help.

Finally, Sly was gonna get to have some fun. He picked up the half dead man, and threw him (alive) in the pigsty.

Sly watched as the pigs tore their teeth into the still breathing man's flesh. The pigs pulled Eric's flesh from his bones. The pigs were happy.

Sly watched as they devoured the man whole, until nothing was left. Then Sly could have kicked himself. He didn't save any piece for himself, to eat.

CHAPTER 21:

The next day, Sly called off from work. Cindy hadn't called him back, and he thought it would be more important to check on her than to make some money. He made a percentage anyways from all the realtors who worked under him.

Sly loved his life. He made a great income. He had a wonderful hobby that suited him fine. And he had great people in his life. Now, he wished that he hadn't alienated Cindy. How was he to know she would react so negatively to him murdering Officer Williams?

He went to Edward's house (where Cindy was staying), and found Cindy still in bed. He had brought along a dozen roses to try and cheer her up. He tickled her face with the rose petals.

He tried to kiss her, and she just rolled over. She was pulling away from him. He had to do something to get her back to her usual self.

"Wake up sleepy head. It's a beautiful day outside."

Cindy turned over.

"Please. Wake up. This isn't healthy. Besides, I wanna give you something to be happy about."

She turned back to face Sly. "What? Happy? How can we be happy right now."

Sly got down on one knee, where just his chest and head was poking up from the side of the bed. He pulled a small box out of his pocket.

"Cindy Haskins, I love you. I always have and I always will. I want to make you my life. I want to provide for you, emotionally and physically. I promise to take good care of you. Will you do me the honor? Will you marry me? We could run away to Spain and elope. Or do you prefer Vegas? We could go anywhere you want."

For a split second, Sly saw a flash of happiness in her eyes. He knew that she loved him, too. Even though it was complicated now, this could change everything.

The flash of happiness disappeared. She spoke in a whisper. "I watched you murder a man, and you want me to marry you?"

Sly didn't know what to say. Momentarily he was at a loss for words. "I did it to protect you. He had a gun on us."

Then she lashed out in anger. "But we covered it up! What's wrong with us?"

Sly knew it would be wise to apologize. "We weren't thinking straight. We were in shock. But it's over now. Make me the happiest man in the world. Marry me?"

Cindy half-heartedly smile. She looked at the large, shining diamond ring. "If you would've asked me a couple days ago. I would've said yes. But now, I don't know."

"Let me take you out today. And you can think about it. For now, wear it on your necklace, close to your heart."

Cindy agreed. She knew it wasn't good for her to just lay in bed. She took a quick shower, and got dressed. She wondered what Sly had in mind for her.

Cindy still seemed distant, but she did wear the ring on her necklace. So it wasn't a no yet. At least she was thinking it over. Of course, Sly had his own ulterior motive.

A husband and a wife can't be forced to testify against each other in a court of law. He did love her, too. The legal aspect was just icing on the cake. An extra benefit. A perk.

He put the top down on the car, and let Cindy feel the wind in her hair. She looked like she was enjoying the sun on her face.

He took her to the lake where his boat was docked. He had packed a picnic. He thought she might enjoy a day of boating. His main goal was to get her out of bed and out of the house. But he didn't want to force her to be around people just yet.

She was open to the idea of a quiet day

spent with her lover. She didn't like the boat too much. He realized that it wasn't in the best of shape, but she would have appreciated a real chair. The hard metal bench hurt her butt.

She even pointed out a bit of blood on the side of the boat. It was legitimately fish blood. And he was glad that he had the idea to skin a fish on the boat.

Cindy had no clue that Sly had used the boat as a safe haven to murder that hooker, not too long ago.

They were alone, and after they ate the sandwiches that Sly had packed, he tried to put the moves on her. He put his arm around her shoulders, and she didn't pull away. Finally, she was letting him touch her.

"I'm serious, Cindy. I have loved you for so long. I want to marry you. If you married me, you would never have anything to worry about. Ever. I'd take care of you." Sly meant what he just said. His words truly came from his heart.

"I do love you, Sly. But I see you as a murderer. "

Sly was glad that she wasn't aware of his hobby. She would really think he was a murderer. Because he was.

"I did it to protect you. If anything, it should show you how much I love you." It made sense to Sly, but his wasn't of popular opinion.

Cindy cried, and he gently wiped the tears away from her face. "I just need time. I need time to think it over."

Sly would have to be patient. He knew that in time, she would agree to marry him.

CHAPTER 22:

After dropping Cindy off at Edward's house, Sly noted how the night had started to fall. It was getting late, and he decided to go check on Mrs. Langsdon's dog, Fluffy.

He drove to her recently purchased home, and he didn't see any lights on in the home. There weren't even any cars in the driveway. Maybe they hadn't finished their move yet.

Sly wore dark clothes and a dark baseball cap as he quietly crept into the backyard. He heard a dog yapping. The family must have moved in some of their things, because their dog was already there.

It was a small white dog, but it was dark. Sly couldn't tell exactly what kind of dog it was. His eyes adjusted to the darkness and saw that it was a poodle.

The dog was on a short chain, and didn't have any food or water. Sly's heart ached for the dog. This was no way for an animal to live its life.

Luckily, he had packed some sandwich meat, and threw a piece of bologna to the dog.

The dog stopped barking, and quickly ate it. After it ate the meat, the dog looked at Sly. He figured that Fluffy wanted more.

He took the collar off the dog, releasing it from the chain. The dog sat by his feet, begging with its eyes for more food. Sly petted the dog, and it sat on his feet. Sly needed a dog around the farm. Fluffy followed him to his car, and jumped into the passenger seat.

The dog would be a nice addition to the farm.

Sly stopped by the store to buy some dog food. He wondered if the dog would eat human meat just like Betsy did. The dog was skinny so he figured that it would eat almost anything. If only Sly had a victim. Currently, his guesthouse basement was empty. And there were no red circles on his calendar of victims for another few days.

He contemplated breaking his own rules. He wanted a new victim. He craved the idea of another kill, another chance to try eating another part of a human being.

Picking a random person to kill was against all of his rules. He wouldn't know what their sins were. But this whole ordeal with Cindy had made him nervous. The best cure for the case of bad nerves (for him), was to kill someone.

It was dark, and it was late. He could go pick

up a hooker. He would know what their sin was. But he had just killed an escort, and wanted a variety of victims.

He would have to wait. It was just a few days. He just didn't know what he would do with himself in the meanwhile. He could spend his time with Cindy. He needed to get her out of the funk that she was in.

Plus, he needed time to train Fluffy. He assumed that Fluffy wasn't house broken. And his dog would be in the house. He wasn't so mean that he would make an animal spend all of its time outside.

When he got home, Fluffy followed him in his house. Sly laid down in the bed and Fluffy jumped up in bed with him. He was going to like having a dog.

Sly tried to sleep, but his mind was heavy with worry. He worried mostly about Cindy. He wished that she would have just said yes to his proposal. He didn't like the way that she was sinking into a deep depression.

He couldn't understand why she was so upset. For him, murder was no big deal, and it was hard to arrange his mind to understand the concept that murder was bad.

That was why he loved her so much. She was his opposite that would keep him grounded. She was everything good and pure. He needed some good and pure in his life.

His hobby was a stress reliever, but it also

came with a lot of stress. Sometimes, his hobby made him paranoid. Especially after Williams stalking him. Now he had to worry about Williams' sister.

Sleep didn't come easy, and he enjoyed the warmth of the dog's body snuggling up against him. Eventually, he fell asleep.

CHAPTER 23:

Sly woke to a very warm feeling on his leg. It felt like someone was pouring warm water on his leg. He opened his eyes, and realized that Fluffy was urinating on him.

He quickly woke up, jumped out of bed and told the dog 'No'. He carried Fluffy outside, hoping that was the way to teach the dog to pee outside.

It was a fresh morning. He hoped that Cindy would wake up feeling the same way. He called her and asked her to come over. He wanted her to meet Fluffy.

It took a few hours, but Cindy showed up. He didn't tell her about the dog over the phone. He wanted it to be a surprise for her.

As soon as she got out of the car, Fluffy yapped at her. The dog stood by the door, barking. At least the dog would let him know if there was anyone on his property.

Sly went to greet Cindy with a hug, but his heart fell when he realized she wasn't wearing the engagement ring on her necklace.

Cindy stood a distance away from him. "I'm only here to give you this." She produced the ring from her pocket.

Sly stood still. Saying nothing.

She continued. "This is so hard. I don't think I can see you anymore."

Sly felt his blood start to boil. This couldn't be happening. "But I had a surprise for you. Just come inside, and we'll talk."

"I'm not coming in Sly. I'm leaving."

She turned to get in her car. "Oh yeah, I forgot." She tried to hand him the ring, but he wouldn't accept it.

She threw the ring on the ground. Fluffy scampered over to the ring, and started to chew on it.

She was definitely surprised to see the dog.

Sly tried to scoot the dog away from the ring, but it was too late. Fluffy put the ring in his mouth, and swallowed it.

Sly sighed. "Great, that's gonna be a trip to the vet."

"No it's not." Cindy smiled for the first time all day. "I had a dog when I was a kid. Trust me when I say it will pass through his bowels."

Sly cringed at the thought of picking through dog poo for a diamond ring.

Cindy bent down to pet the dog.

Sly saw an opportunity to talk her out of leaving. "But I love you. Please, just talk to me."

Cindy opened her car door. "I can't. I see you as a murderer. What you did... What WE did was wrong."

In that split second, a million thoughts rushed through Sly's mind. Would she tell Edward what he had done? Could she keep the murder a secret? Why didn't she love him?

Sly didn't think. He just acted. He grabbed Cindy by the hair, and slammed her face into her car door. Her body collapsed to the ground.

Cindy woke up a few minutes later, chained to a metal chair. She looked around. She was in a concrete room. She was cold. She turned her head, and saw Sly standing over a workbench of tools.

Her face hurt, and she had a taste of blood in her mouth. She wondered if her nose was broken.

She wiggled her wrists against the handcuffs. "What's going on here?"

Panic enveloped her. Sly didn't look like himself. He was Sly, but he looked like a complete stranger due to his facial expression.

"Sly! Talk to me!"

He had rehearsed in his mind what he would say to her, but he had a hard time producing any words. He wanted to tell her everything. He wanted to open up to her. He wanted to see if she would accept him for who he truly was.

"Sly. It's me." Cindy searched her mind for the right things to say. "I haven't told anyone about Officer Williams. It's our secret. What are you doing?"

Sly looked Cindy in her eyes. He wanted to see if her eyes showed fear. If her eyes showed fear, that meant she was scared of him. It meant that she saw him as a murderer.

He saw fear in her eyes. "Why was this so hard on you? Officer Williams was waving a gun around."

Cindy tried to be logical. "I've never seen someone's brains outside of their head. Why was it so easy for you?"

This was Sly's opportunity to tell her about his secret hobby. Maybe she would still love him. Maybe she would accept him for who he was.

He spoke in a tone just an octave higher than a whisper. "I've killed before."

Cindy shook her head, and her eyes welled up with tears. She thought that her boyfriend just confessed to being a murderer. "What? Say it again. Louder. I didn't hear you right."

This time Sly screamed. "I like to kill people! It's my life's purpose!"

Cindy couldn't fight back her tears. Her murderous boyfriend had now chained her to a chair in some type of a dungeon. She thought that maybe she could talk her way out of this.

"It's okay. I understand. We can get you some help. I love you, Sly."

Sly heard her. She said she understood. She said she loved him. But her eyes said otherwise. Her eyes showed fear. And she wanted him to get help. He didn't need help. He was serving a purpose. Ridding the world of bad people.

He hoped he could make her understand. "I only kill bad people. I'm doing the world a service."

Cindy flinched at the word people. He just confessed to killing more than one person. The plural of person. People. "Bad people? What do you mean? Like other murderers?"

"I mean thieves. People who are cruel to animals. Cheaters. People who sin."

Cindy wondered how many people he had killed. She was afraid to ask. "Sly, I love you. Will you please undo my handcuffs?"

The word love rang through Sly's body. Did she actually love him? She didn't even accept his marriage proposal. She was just breaking up with him a few minutes ago. Now she was claiming that she loved him.

His own parents didn't even love him. He didn't believe her.

Sly stood in silence, reading the fear in her beautiful eyes.

A single tear fell down his cheek. "I'm sorry. It's too late."

Cindy begged and she pleaded. "It's not too late. Let's get married."

This wasn't Sly's first rodeo. He knew that people chained to his chair of doom would say anything. Even lies.

Sly picked up a butcher knife. Cindy cried and continued begging as he plunged the tip of the blade into her chest. He slowly guided the full-length of the blade deeper, puncturing her heart.

Sly cried as he held Cindy. At least he had given her a quick death. She died in his arms.

CHAPTER 24:

Sly undid Cindy's handcuffs, and laid her dead body on the cold concrete floor. He admired her beautiful body as he slowly undressed her. As he looked at her nude breasts, he felt a tickle in his pants.

Sly pawed at his crotch, and his penis was very quickly at full attention. He felt an ache. He desired one last chance to be with her in the biblical sense.

He lowered her panties and felt of her vagina. He tried to stick his cock inside of her, but her female area was dry and not pleasant.

He looked at the hole in her chest. It was still kinda warm, and there was plenty of blood to lubricate the entry of his penis. He stuck his fully erect dick into the hole in her chest.

It was the best feeling he had ever experienced. The hole was tight. He pumped himself inside of her chest until he came all over her heart.

This would prove to be his most favorite

memory of Cindy.

Cindy was special to him, so he was very careful as he cut up her dead body. He wanted to save most of her body for himself. He would throw her chest to the pigs. He didn't want to eat his own cum.

He saved the arms and legs for himself, skinning most of the meat from her bones and sticking it into his freezer. He cut off her head with the butcher knife. He threw her torso and her head into the pigsty. He watched as the pigs fought for their place by the dead body.

He gave Fluffy a hand to chew on, and the dog nibbled on the flesh until he got to the bones of the hand. He then chomped on the bones, dissolving them into tiny unrecognizable pieces.

Sly stared in his freezer. Perhaps he could make a stew out of the meat of Cindy's flesh. Surely it would be good boiled.

Sly grabbed his largest pot, and chopped the meat into small chunks. He cut up some carrots and potatoes, and threw them in the pot. He filled the pot with water and started to boil it.

He flavored the stew with some beef bouillon. He put the flame on high until the water started to boil. Then he lowered the heat and let it simmer for a couple of hours.

When it was finished, he poured some of the stew into a bowl. He took his fork and stabbed a carrot and a piece of Cindy's meat. The carrot was crunchy, and the meat was chewy.

It was a perfect combination. It was the best soup he had ever eaten. He poured a bowl for Fluffy, who ate every last bit of it.

Sly was pleased. He somehow managed to turn a bad situation into something good.

CHAPTER 25:

Sly needed a day to himself. He called off from work, and was basking in the morning sun by his pool. He took off his shirt, noting how he needed a tan on his chest.

He was still waking up, sipping from the coffee cup in his hand. Sly was in his own little world, when Fluffy started yapping.

Fluffy ran to the front of the house and Sly followed. Fluffy was good to have around. He would alert Sly whenever someone was on his property.

It was just Edward, rolling up in his Sheriff vehicle.

Sly started to sweat. He hadn't put a single thought into how he would explain Cindy's disappearance to his best friend.

Edward got out of his truck, and Sly felt like he was moving in slow motion. He needed a moment to get his story straight. At least he had already sunk Cindy's car in the pond.

"Mornin' Sly. I'm looking for my sister. That interview place keeps calling for her. Is she here?"

He tried to read Edward's face. Did Edward know that his sister was coming over yesterday to break up with him? Edward's face was solemn, and unreadable.

"I haven't seen her in a couple days. Not since the day we went out on the boat."

Sly felt like Edward was studying his face. Sly got paranoid. The tension could have been cut with a knife it was so thick. But Sly stood his ground.

"I took her out on my boat. I even proposed to her. Haven't heard from her since."

"I saw the ring. Is that why she had been acting so strange lately?"

Sly didn't know what to say. He couldn't tell his best friend that she had acted strange because she watched him murder a cop.

Sly said nothing. He just looked down at his bare feet.

"I already know, man. She told me that she wasn't gonna marry you. She told me she was coming over yesterday to break up with you. It's just that I haven't heard from her since."

Sly knew that he was busted in his lie. He had to say something. "No. I haven't heard from her. Not even a phone call." Sly remembered how he took the sim card out of her phone and broke it in half, and threw it in the bottom of the pond. "I figured by the way she acted on the boat that it would be a no. I figured she didn't wanna marry me."

"So she never came over yesterday?"

Sly felt like he was being questioned by the Sheriff, and not his best friend. Sly shook his head no.

"Sly, I've got a feeling something's wrong."

Sly sternly looked at his friend. "Something is wrong. She didn't have the heart to break my heart. No, I'll bet, she ran away."

"Ran away? And didn't tell me? I'm her brother. She would've at least said bye. She didn't even pack up her stuff."

"I dunno, man. I dunno what to say."

Edward climbed back up in his truck. "I'm gonna go to the station. I'm gonna put out an All Points Bulletin on her car. I'm worried. But don't you worry. I'm gonna find her."

And just like that, Edward drove away. Sly hoped that his best friend would never find out the truth.

Sly spent a serene day floating in his pool. At lunchtime, he made himself a bowl of Cindy stew. He chewed up the meat and remembered all the good times he had with her. If only she had been open to his hobby, then life would have been good.

He wanted a wife. He needed someone in his life that knew who he really was. But where would he find a woman like that?

CHAPTER 26:

Sly needed to keep his mind busy. A part of him regretted killing Cindy. But he knew he had done the right thing. He couldn't chance her telling anyone that he murdered Officer Williams.

He didn't want to go to prison more than he loved her. He had to kill her. It was the only way to keep her quiet. She wasn't cut out to be his wife.

She couldn't handle one murder, nevertheless the fact that he had murdered dozens of people.

Work was the perfect way to occupy his mind. He checked his calendar from last year for this year's victim, and saw that he was due to pick up a Mr. Albert Grisham.

He had suspected Albert of beating his kids. When he showed him a house last year, the man publicly spanked his three year old for acting out. The very next day, the boy showed up with a large bruise on his arm.

He didn't show Albert anymore houses after that. He hoped the guy hadn't found another realtor and already moved.

Sly made it through his day at the office. He had spent the day balancing accounts and making out the paychecks for his employees. He hated being behind a desk, but it was part of being the boss.

He would much rather enjoy working with the public. His reward was stalking Albert Grisham.

He waited until nightfall, and changed the license plate on his car. He had stolen another license plate off a car that was identical to his, just in case anyone ever saw him partaking in his hobby. The license plates would be traced to whoever he had stolen the license plate from.

His least favorite part of his hobby was doing recon. There had been times that he spent hours in his car, stalking his prey. He had to learn their patterns and their schedule.

He was sitting, watching Albert's house, and noted there were two cars in the driveway. He wasn't sure which vehicle belonged to his victim. He sat outside the house for so long that he had fallen asleep.

Exhaustion had gotten the better of him. When he woke up, he noticed that it was six in the morning. He had spent an entire night asleep in his car.

He started his car, and was going to drive

away. But then he saw Albert walking to his car. The man was holding a briefcase. Sly suspected that he was on his way to work.

He slowly drove behind the man, and when the man stopped at a stop sign, Sly barely tapped the rear bumper of his car with his own. The man got out of his vehicle.

Sly rolled down his window so he could hear Albert.

"Did you just hit my car? I hope you have good insurance."

Sly stepped out of his own car and looked around. They were in the suburbs and there were no other cars around. He didn't see anyone outside.

"I'm so sorry I have my insurance card right here, in my glove box."

Sly opened his passenger door, and pretended to rummage through his glove box. Albert approached him, and Sly used his stun gun to tase the guy once he was close enough.

The man's body fell to the ground, and Sly quickly put him in his car. He drove away as fast as he could, abandoning Albert's car at the stop sign.

Sly sped home, tasing Albert each time that he woke up. It was fun driving down the street and electrocuting the man. It was the kind of fun that he needed to get his adrenaline pumping.

He lugged Albert's body over his shoulder, throwing the man down the ladder into his basement. He got some of his victim's drool on his shoulder and it disgusted him.

He climbed down the ladder and kicked the man in his ribs for drooling on him. Sly handcuffed the man's ankles together. He chained Albert up in a standing position, with his toes barely touching the ground.

Albert woke up, and he was hanging from chains. His calves hurt from standing on his tiptoes. Every muscle in his back ached. He was in a very uncomfortable position.

Sly was there to greet him when he woke.

"You like to beat kids, aye?"

Albert couldn't make sense of anything. The last thing he remembered was on his way to work. Then it started coming back to him. His realtor had abducted him.

Sly left his victim alone. He wanted to give him time alone to think. Anyways, it was time for breakfast. He still had some left over Cindy stew to eat.

CHAPTER 27:

Sly was heating up his stew, and Fluffy started barking at the door. Sly looked out his window and saw his best friend. Sly tried to swallow his guilt. His conscience wouldn't allow him to look Edward in his eyes.

Edward didn't even bother knocking. He walked right in.

"I'm worried. Have you heard from Cindy?"

Sly shook his head no. "I'm worried sick, man. She broke my heart. Now she's gone. I've tried calling her, but it goes straight to voicemail. I thought maybe she was just avoiding me."

"It's not just you. What smells good in here?"

Sly offered his friend some of the stew. Edward took a bite.

"That's the best stew ever! You have the best food, Sly. What's your secret?"

Sly's conscience once again got the best of him. He just shook his head.

Fluffy started yapping, and Sly let him out.

Edward watched the dog from the window.

"Where'd you get the dog, Sly?"

"He's a stray. I fed him, now he sticks around. I dunno where he came from."

The dog started howling like he was in pain. Edward watched as the dog relieved his bowels. It was like the dog was straining.

Edward pointed outside. "I think he's sick. He's having a hard time out there."

Sly looked out. "He's just going number two. At least he went outside to do it."

"No. Look. It's hurting him." Edward opened the patio door and walked out back.

He bent down to pet the dog, but Fluffy pulled away. The dog was straining. Trying to go to the bathroom.

Sly followed him outside. "Wanna go out on the boat today? We could do some fishing or something. Ya know, to keep our minds off Cindy."

While the men were talking, Fluffy howled in pain.

Edward watched the dog. "Maybe you should take the dog to the veterinarian. What's he been eating anyways? He's shitting and it looks shiny from here."

Sly remembered that the dog had eaten Cindy's engagement ring. Sly started sweating, hoping Edward wouldn't check out the dog poop.

"Yeah. You're right. I gotta take Fluffy to the doctor. How 'bout a rain check on that fishing trip."

"Is that jewelry?" Edward picked up a stick and shifted through the dog poop.

"Dude, that's gross. Stop. Like I said he's a stray."

Edward hooked the ring to the stick and pulled it away. "Is this Cindy's?"

Sly wiped some sweat from his brow. "It can't be. Nope. That's not the ring I gave her."

"It looks like it."

"You're just worried. It's not hers."

Edward started thinking like a detective. "Maybe she left it here and the dog found it."

"If she did, I didn't know it. Maybe I was feedin' the pigs or something."

"I don't like this Sly. Maybe something bad happened."

Sly patted his friend on the back. "You worry too much. C'mon. I'll buy the beer. Let's go fishing."

CHAPTER 28:

Albert had stood in the same position for nearly fifteen hours. His toes could barely touch the ground, and his arms were chained above his head. His whole body hurt.

He was hungry and thirsty. Plus it was cold and dark in the basement. He screamed all day to no avail. All the yelling did was dry out his throat. No matter how hard he tugged at his chains, they didn't budge.

He was relieved when he saw some light. Apparently someone had opened the hatch, letting the light in. Albert wasn't sure if he should be relieved or scared.

Sly came climbing down the ladder. "Did you have time to think?"

Albert thought it was a trick question. Of course he had time to think. He couldn't move, nevertheless do anything other than think.

Albert thought it would be wise to call his captor by his proper name. It was a sign of respect. "Mr. Verdict, what am I doing here?" His voice was shaking. He could barely speak.

Sly just laughed. He could have answered

that question in so many ways. He chose the simplest answer. "You're being tortured. Then murdered. Because you beat your kids."

The word murder upset Albert. "My kid is a brat. He deserved everything he got. Do you have kids? If not, you wouldn't understand."

Sly understood everything that he needed to understand. "I understand that I am going to beat you, just like you beat your kid. Simple as that."

Albert started to beg and cry, just like his child had done with him. Sly put a gag in Albert's mouth. Albert tried kicking at his captor but he didn't have the strength to raise his leg. The chains around his wrists were supporting his full body weight.

Every muscle in Albert's body hurt. He didn't know how much more torture he could endure.

Sly brought along a special toy for Albert.

"Does this look familiar?" Sly pointed to the contraption. It looked like a tripod with something setting on top of it. "Kids use them. Maybe you didn't play baseball with your kids. This is a pitching machine. It throws baseballs at speeds up to 80 miles per hour."

Albert tried to scream through his gag while Sly set up the machine and loaded it with baseballs. He aimed the machine at Albert.

He set the baseball pitcher a few feet from the dangling man. With the push of a button, it threw six baseballs within a fast recession. Each ball hit Albert at a high speed, and the man grunted each time he was hit.

Instantly, welts and bruises appeared on the man's skin. Sly laughed as the baseballs hit him. Most balls hit him in the lower abdomen, but one made contact with the family jewels. Albert squelched through his gag in a high pitch manor.

When the machine ran out of balls, Sly picked up an axe. He used the blunt side of the weapon to hit Albert across his face. The man spat out most of his teeth with an array of blood.

Then Sly used the sharp side of the axe to chop off Albert's head. Sly laughed at the look in the man's eyes as he knew that death had come swinging towards him.

Sly watched as Albert's head rolled to the ground. Blood ran down his entire body, soaking his body in the crimson substance. Sly laughed. He now had a huge mess to clean up.

At least he would have a feast for Fluffy and his pigs.

CHAPTER 29:

After feeding the pigs and cleaning up the bloody mess in his guesthouse basement, Sly felt empty.

He pulled out a picture of Cindy and remembered all the good times they had together. How he wished that she hadn't forced him to murder her.

If only she had been more open-minded. Then they could have lived happily ever after, but it wasn't in the cards.

He watched as Fluffy chewed on one of Albert's bones. He patted the dog, and realized he was a nice addition to his farm.

Sly's phone rang. It was Edward.

Edward didn't even say hello. He got right down to the purpose of his phone call. "I got a trace on Cindy's phone. The last place it tracked was at your farm."

"Like I said, I didn't see her. Maybe I wasn't home. I dunno. I wish I'd have seen her. I would've begged her to marry me."

"What I don't get is why did she turn her

phone off *after* she left your house."

Sly thought for a moment. "Maybe her battery was low. I don't know."

He only hoped that Edward wouldn't start making sense of Cindy's disappearance. He made plans to spend some time with him. He only hoped that it never came down to him having to murder his best friend.

CHAPTER 30: ONE LAST KILL

Sly was angry at the world. Cindy was gone, and his best friend was now asking too many questions. He knew that he looked guilty, but there was nothing he could do about it now.

Sly broke every rule in his own handbook when he abducted a homeless man. He wasn't killing for the victim's sin. He wasn't killing because someone knew of his hobby and could tell the police.

He was killing for pure sport. Just because he wanted to kill. He wanted to feel powerful. He wanted to see another human being in pain just because it made him feel better about himself being in pain.

The homeless man didn't even see Sly coming at him. Rupert laid in his cardboard box under the viaduct, minding his own business. All he knew was that one second he was super sleepy and was on the verge of getting a good night's rest. Then the next moment, his cardboard box caved in, and the man whose pictures were on the advertisements at the bus stops was screaming at him.

He felt electricity flow through his body as the man used a taser on him. Rupert was rendered helpless, and his world went black.

Sly looked over his shoulder. Sara Harris had made him very paranoid. He hated the way she came to his office. He hadn't seen any sign of her since. But if she was anything like her brother, Officer Williams, she wouldn't give up quite so easily.

When Rupert woke up, he felt a throbbing in his head. It wasn't quite a headache. The pain he felt was way worse than a headache. He could taste blood in his mouth. Perhaps the realtor had hit him and busted his lip open.

The copper taste in his mouth was strong and pungent. He opened his eyes slowly, and gave them time to adjust to how dim the room was. He looked at his feet that were taped together. He tried to move his hands, but he saw that they were handcuffed to the metal chair.

Rupert caught a chill, and tried to shake off his quivering. But his body naturally responded by slightly shaking. The concrete walls and floor were very bare. He was trying to figure out where he was, when the realtor entered the small space.

"Am I dreaming? You're the guy on all those ads?" Rupert wasn't sure if he was forming questions or making statements. He just couldn't think straight.

The realtor stood in front of him wearing nothing but his birthday suit. The man seemed to be proud of his nakedness. He didn't even try to hide his half erect manhood.

Sly felt powerful in this moment. Here and now, he had a human being in front of him. Whether this homeless man lived or died was Sly's choice. What other decision could ever be as important as this decision?

Sly didn't know what to say. All his mind could focus on was the loss of Cindy. "My girl. My fiance. She's dead."

The homeless man spit some blood from his mouth, into a tiny pool on the concrete floor. "Dude, I'm sorry about that. Do I know her or something?"

Sly loved it that he had found someone he could talk to about killing Cindy. He couldn't tell anyone else. They would turn him in to the police. With Rupert, Sly had no worries.

Sly knew that the homeless man would never see the light of day ever again.

Sly appreciated the fact that the homeless man wasn't screaming like some lunatic, like most of his victims do.

Sly shook his head no. "No, you didn't know

her. But I had to tell someone. I thought it would make me feel better."

Rupert nonchalantly gestured his head to his wrists. "Well, now you've told someone. You ready to untie me? I gotta go now."

Rupert watched as Sly's eyes changed from being filled with sadness, to being full of pure hatred.

Sly, once again, shook his head no. "You don't get it old man. I killed her."

Rupert understood. He knew that he was dealing with a psychopath. "You? You killed the girl? Why?"

"She witnessed me murdering a cop. I had to kill her."

Rupert was now shaking his head. "I don't get it. How do I fit in the equation?"

"Because I want to hurt someone. I want to make someone hurt as bad as I hurt."

It was in that moment that Rupert realized he was living his last day on Earth.

Sly didn't bother to gag Rupert. He wanted to hear his screams. He wanted Rupert's pain to be audible. He also wanted Rupert to watch what he was doing, but the homeless man kept shutting his eyes.

Sly used a barbed fish hook, and pierced through one of Rupert's eyelids. Even though it's a thin piece of meat, the eyelid is rather durable.

Sly had to push extra hard to get the hook to pierce completely through.

Then, Sly tugged on the hook, and pulled Rupert's eyelid upward. He pushed the hook through some fatty flesh by his eyebrows. The barb caught in place, and Rupert's eye was now stuck in an open position.

"You're gonna watch this. It's just how it goes." Sly laughed maniacally. "Not too long ago, I killed a child rapist. I used glass in his dick. I regret that. I could've used something else."

Rupert tried to cry, but that just hurt his open eye even more. "Help me! I'm downstairs! Please help."

Sly knew there was no one up there to hear the homeless man's cries. Sly grabbed his trusty drill. His regret was not using the drill on Victor.

After dropping Rupert's pants to his ankles, Sly cut away his boxer shorts. Sly held Rupert's penis in his hand, and slid the small drill bit into the urethra. The opening in the head of the dick was just big enough to receive the drill bit.

Sly looked away before squeezing the trigger on the drill. Rupert begged and pleaded, telling the man that he wasn't a rapist.

"Please, stop. I'm begging! Nobody deserves this kind of treatment!"

Rupert's words fell on deaf ears. Sly loved hearing the man beg.

The drill bit started to spin, and it started carving away the inner layers of skin. The soft cock started twisting with the spins of the drill. After Sly turned the drill off, Rupert's sexual organ was not even recognizable.

It looked more like a blown out tire than a penis. Rupert was losing a lot of blood, and Sly feared that the homeless man might die. He wanted to keep this houseguest for a few days so he would have a way to keep himself occupied.

Sly held the dick, and tried to squeeze what was left of it. He needed to apply pressure to stop the bleeding. He used Rupert's shirt to make a makeshift tourniquet, but the blood wouldn't stop.

Rupert started looking pale from the blood loss. Sly knew that it was too late to try and save the man. He watched as the homeless man bled to death.

Then, Sly hosed down the dead man's body. He played eenie- meenie- miney -mole to see which part of Rupert's body he would dine on. Sly laughed as he pointed at various body parts, excited to see what he would eat.

He picked the liver. Or at least what he thought was the liver.

Sly wasn't a doctor and couldn't be sure, but he cut Rupert open down his chest and stomach. He spread the ribs and the skin away from the man's body, and looked at various organs.

He loved chicken livers so he only hoped he was correct that the organ he cut away was Rupert's liver. A liver was a part of the body that he knew how to prepare. A human liver wouldn't be any different than a chicken liver. It would just be larger.

After saving the liver for himself, Sly started hacking away at the rest of Rupert's body, making it easier to carry the various body parts to the pigs.

His faithful pigs were waiting at the fence on the edge of the sty. They saw the bloody body and knew that it was time for their feast. Sly didn't forget about Fluffy. He gave Fluffy a rib bone to chew on. The dog scurried away with his new found treasure in his mouth.

Sly looked around at all his animals, and realized that life was good. He didn't need Cindy to be happy, he had his farm. He wiped a tear from his face in her memory, and went to make himself another bowl of Cindy stew.

See ya next read.

Thanks so much for reading this book. Find me on Facebook (Sea Caummisar) or on Twitter (@seacaummisar). I love hearing from my readers.

Turn the page for Verdict Realty 3. Guilty. Extreme Horror.

I like reviews, too. No pressure, but they

really help out authors and give them encouragement to write more.

VERDICT REALTY #3

Guilty. Extreme Horror.

By Sea Caummisar

Sea Caummisar

Copyright © 2019 by Sea Caummisar

All rights reserved. No portion of this book may be reproduced in any form without permission from the publisher, except as permitted by U.S. copyright law. For permissions contact sharoncheatham81@gmail.com

This is entirely a work of fiction, pulled out of my own imagination. All characters and events are not real (fictitious). If there are any similarities to real persons, living or dead, it is purely coincidental.

Remember this is a book based on a fictional realty company.

SLY'S JOURNAL OF RULES (INCOMPLETE)

(in no particular order)

Rule #34: Wait at least one year.

After doing business with a person, wait at least one year before abducting them. That makes it harder for police to trace their suspicions to Sly, or his real estate company.

Rule # 19: Cover your tracks.

Try to make it look like the person is missing, not dead. Try to throw the police off Sly's trail.

Rule #8: No hair. Not on head. Not on body. (Except eyebrows and eyelashes).

Many serial killers have been caught by their DNA linked at a crime scene. Hair leaves behind too much DNA.

Rule #12: Wife beaters must die.

Coming from a broken home, and Sly's own Father killing his Mother, this rule is very important.

Rule #4: Dispose of bodies properly.

Without a dead body, there is no crime committed. The person is just assumed to be missing, not dead.

Rule #1: Married people shouldn't cheat.

Marriage is very sacred to Sly. Anyone who breaks their vows are not worthy of being married.

Rule #32: Leave nice people alone.

Nice people make the world a better place. Don't kill them.

Rule #27: Wear gloves when in someone's home or car.

Fingerprints can be traced to a person's identity. Leave nothing behind that can be traced to Sly.

Rule #24: Ignore your dick.

At all times, think with your brain. Not your manhood. Semen also leaves behind DNA in the event that a body is found.

Rule #17: Tell nobody. Ever.

The hobby is a secret. Many serial killers

have been caught by telling someone their secrets. Even if you feel close to a person and think you can trust them, you can't.

Rule #23: Don't break the rules.

Just a reminder to never break the rules. The rules are in place for a reason. They are not meant to be broken.

Rule #30: Don't get sloppy.

When you get sloppy, and don't think things through, you can get caught. Follow the rules, and keep your guard up at all times.

Rule #6: Get as much information as possible.

Know your enemy. Find out as much about them as possible. This makes it easier to abduct them.

Rule #13: Hide in plain sight.

Even though Edward is Sly's best friend, he is an enforcer of the law. Nobody would ever suspect that a serial killer would have such a close relationship with a police officer.

Rule #2: Deny. Deny. Deny.

Even if you have been caught, deny any allegations against you. They need evidence and proof before you can be found guilty. Following the rules ensures they will find no proof.

Rule #16: The hobby is for anger.

When angry, kill/torture someone. It is

very therapeutic. There is no better stress reliever.

Rule #11: Clean up is important.

Leave behind no traces of blood, or anything that can be linked to a missing person. Let the pigs dispose of bodies. Burn their personal items, such as clothes. Clean up blood with bleach.

Rule #20: No witnesses. Ever.

Witnesses are bad news. They could identify the criminal. When committing *any* crime, be sure to get rid of witnesses, even if it means breaking the rules.

Rule #7: Thieves must die.

Thieves should not be or exist. They should not breathe. The punishment for theft is death.

Rule #26: Disguises are good.

Sly is well known for his real estate company (Verdict Realty) commercials. When necessary, use hats and sunglasses or anything else to mask face.

Rule #33: Punishment should fit the offender.

Thieves do not need hands. Rapists do not deserve sexual organs. Abusers should be beaten. Etc…

Rule #9: Keep friends close, enemies closer.

Know your enemy. Get to know them. Kill

them (not literally) with kindness.

Rule #22: Show them the errors of their ways.

Make sure the victim knows why they were chosen.

Rule #3: Always be alert.

Even in personal life, be alert for enemies. Also, always keep an eye open for possible victims.

Rule #38: Professional. Personal. Hobby. Keep life organized in sections.

Do not let the different compartments of life blur and intersect. Know your role at the appropriate times.

Rule #15: Lay low if there's any doubt.

Even if it is just a small chance that you are being watched or followed, retreat.

Rule #31: Keep in shape. Especially for tough opponents.

Physical fitness is not only important for a healthy lifestyle, but also to abduct victims.

Rule #28: Know your opponent.

Know everything about your victim. That makes it easier to abduct them.

Rule #10: Use your brain, not your body.
Outsmarting the victim will help greatly.

Rule #29: Maintain a good reputation.

Being a public figure (real estate agent), it's important for the business to be represented by someone with an impeccable reputation. Do not do anything stupid. Don't get caught breaking any law, no matter how minor it may be. Do good things for the community.

Rule #18: Take care of guest to make it last.

It is impossible to get a new victim everyday. Make sure guest stays hydrated so there's always a guest to torture.

Rule #35: Use job to have the advantage.

Hang on to the spare keys of a future victim's house. Use the credit check to know their habits. Use spare key to snoop through their personal items.

Rule #5: Don't let the hobby consume you.

Make time for work. Money is important. Make time for personal life. Do not think about the hobby constantly. The mind needs a break from time to time.

Rule #21: Bully a bully.

Bullies are bad. Be their bully. Show them how it feels.

Rule #14: Be humane when possible.

It's important, especially in business and personal life, to be humane. Not every situation is an outlet for anger.

CHAPTER 1

Sly ran the blade of the knife along the weeping man's face. He wasn't pressing the blade into his skin, he was just scaring him. He wanted to see the fear in the man's eyes.

Matt pondered how short his life had been. Now he was staring at death by the hand of his crazed realtor. He hadn't seen him in a year. Then last night, Sly randomly showed up with a stun gun and abducted him.

The next thing Matt knew, he woke up in some sort of a basement, handcuffed to a metal chair.

When Sly had sold him the home, he couldn't help but notice that Matt had a larger cash down payment than his income working as a janitor at a high school would allow. While Matt had been at work, the realtor used his spare house key to snoop around his house. He found cocaine and drug paraphernalia.

Sly came to the conclusion that Matt had been selling drugs, perhaps even to teenagers. He didn't like the idea of someone corrupting the future generations.

Sly set the blade aside, and held a syringe in the air.

"I found this in your home. There were a bunch of them in a drawer."

Matt just stared at the paraphernalia. He couldn't make sense of what was happening to him. "You were in my house? When? Why?"

Sly put his finger up to Matt's lips to shush him. "Shh! Why do you have this?"

Tears fell down Matt's face. He had hidden his secret profession so well. Then, of all people, his realtor had found out that he was a drug dealer. It was just for the extra income. He didn't make much money as a janitor.

"So what? I made a little money! What's it to you?"

Sly had gotten the confession that he wanted. Well, at least half of it. He wanted to know if the janitor had been selling dope to teenagers.

Sly picked the blade up again, and slowly ran the tip down the inside of Matt's arm, leaving a thin trace of blood behind.

"Who did you sell to?"

Matt shook his head. The small cut on his arm was painful. And for whatever reason, his realtor wanted to have a conversation about his illegal activities. His mind told him to be logical. To give the man the talk he wanted.

"I sold to people who wanted to get high."

That was not the answer Sly was looking for. He pressed harder on the blade, digging deeper into the skin on Matt's arm. He drug the knife through his skin, from his elbow to his wrist. A thin wound opened, instantly blood ran down the sides of Matt's arm.

Matt tried to stop his tears, but he couldn't. He tried to move his arms from harm's way, but he was shackled too tight. "Okay. Stop! That hurts! What do you want from me?"

Sly gave the man clues as to the answer he was looking for. But he was having too much fun playing with Matt's fear. He didn't want the correct answer just yet.

"You worked at a high school."

Matt knew that he worked at the high school. This conversation was going nowhere. "I didn't sell to the kids if that's what you think. I'm not a monster."

The realtor knew better. He knew that Matt was lying to him. Even if he was telling the truth, it was too late now. Sly had plans for Matt. He was going to slowly torture him, for days. Then he, his pigs, and his dog were going to eat him.

Sly filled the syringe with bleach. He stuck the needle in a protruding vein in Matt's arm. Matt tried to squirm, but he couldn't move. The realtor pressed down on the plunger and let the chemical flow through his victim's blood.

He knew the bleach wouldn't kill him, but it would make him very sick. He left his victim alone to suffer through his sickness. This would teach Matt a lesson. He should know what it feels like to have poison coursing through his blood.

CHAPTER 2

As Sly was making plans in his head for the perfect torture for Matt, he was sitting on his back deck looking at his pool. The water was so peaceful. But it also reminded him of his pond, and how he had killed his girlfriend, Cindy, and sank her car in it.

He regretted killing Cindy. He missed her more and more everyday. He knew that he had to do it, but still it was a regret.

Also, his best friend Edward (the sheriff) was still looking for his sister. The only thing he knew was that the last place Cindy's phone registered was on Sly's property. Then he used his pull in law enforcement to put out a search for her car. Unfortunately, they hadn't found her.

Sly knew that was because her car was in the bottom of his pond. And he also knew that they would never find her body, because he ate her.

None of this stopped him from missing her. Things had been great between them. Until she watched him murder a police officer and hide his body. She had kept his secret for a few days, but after he proposed to her, she rejected him. He had a feeling that she wouldn't keep his secret for much longer. So he had to kill her.

He was staring at the sun reflecting off the top of his pool, when his dog Fluffy started barking. He loved having the poodle around. The dog had a knack for letting him know whenever he had a guest.

Of course, the visitor was Edward. He usually stopped by in the mornings for a cup of coffee or some breakfast before they both started their days at work.

"Hey you! Do you have any Besty pork left?" Referring to the pig that they had been eating on for a while.

She had been the best tasting pork ever, due to her special diet of human dead bodies. But the sheriff had no clue what her diet consisted of.

Sly shook his head no. "Fresh out. We ate her up pretty fast. But she sure was good." Sly decided to play coy. "Any word on Cindy yet? I've been worried sick about her."

Edward looked at his friend. He had black circles under his eyes. "You look bad, man. Have you been sleeping? But no word on her yet. I even tried her old job, and they haven't heard from her. I don't know where she could be." The sheriff stared at his shoes, and tried not to tear up. "I'll find her. I promise you that."

Sly hoped that his friend would never find

out the truth. He didn't want his best friend to hate him. Or even worse, arrest him.

Sly slapped his best friend on his back. "C'mon inside. I'll make some coffee. Maybe we can put our heads together on where she might have gone."

Sly pretended to be upset about Cindy being missing. He wanted to play the role of a distraught, heart-broken boyfriend. "When she didn't accept my proposal, I was beside myself. But I knew that it hurt her, too. She was just so good hearted. Maybe she just wants space away from me."

Edward shook his head. "That explains you. Why wouldn't she contact me? It doesn't make sense. I'm her brother."

"I don't know. Maybe because you're my best friend. Maybe she doesn't want any lectures from you. I just don't know."

Sly hoped his logic would be enough to keep Edward from learning the truth.

CHAPTER 3

After Edward left, Sly should have gone to work. But he didn't. His mind was jumbled with the mess he had created. He hadn't been himself since he killed Cindy.

He was angry with himself. When he was angry, all he wanted to do was hurt other people. Instead of going to the office, he decided to check on Matt to see how sick he was.

He drove back to his guesthouse, and climbed down the hatch to his hidden basement. Before he got all the way down the ladder, he could smell the rotten stench of vomit.

Matt was a mess covered in his own puke. Sly grabbed the hose to spray the man down, and Matt started vomiting again. The thick, yellow fluid flowed down his chin. Matt lunged forward in his chair to try not to mess on himself, but he couldn't move much being chained to the chair.

His clothes were soaked with the putrid ooze. Sly continued spraying him with water, all the while Matt foaming at the mouth.

"How's it feel to inject poison? You

shouldn't have ever given those kids dope. This'll teach you a lesson."

Tears were falling down Matt's face, mixing with his puke. His arms were shaking and he looked defeated. But the fun had just begun. He was far from being finished with the drug pusher.

Sly took the bottle of bleach, and poured it over the vomit covered man. The bleach stung Matt's eyes. His eyes watered even more, trying to flush out the chemical.

The bleach entered the knife wounds on his arms, but Matt tried to ignore the pain. He was more concerned with how sick he was. He couldn't stop throwing up, and at this point he knew he was spitting up his stomach lining.

As white foam bubbled out of Matt's mouth, Sly gagged. Between the bleach and the sick, the smell was just too much for his stomach. Matt's eyes begged for help, he knew he needed medical attention.

Instead, Sly just kept hosing him down until he was dry heaving. Once Matt stopped vomiting, his body convulsed. Sly just laughed at the sick man.

The realtor grabbed his hand cultivator. It was a small handheld looking claw, used in a garden to loosen the ground. It had three sharp points on it, forming a claw.

Sly waved the tool in the air for his victim to see. "If you wanna give those kids track marks, I'm gonna give you track marks!"

His victim's eyes filled with fear. He tried to speak, he wanted to beg for mercy. But he had no strength. No voice. His lips moved, yet he produced no sound.

His captor pressed the tool into the delicate flesh of his bicep. He pressed it hard into his skin, cracking it open. Then he slowly drug the tool down his arm. Three lines of blood followed in its path.

Matt couldn't even scream. He just had to endure the pain. He hung his head over in exhaustion, trying to figure a way out of this situation. He feared that death would come soon.

The madman laughed as he pressed the tool into Matt's leg. He pressed it firmly into his thigh, instantly ripping his skin open. After raking the tool down to his knee, he raised the weapon. He swiftly slammed it down on Matt's knee cap, and the pain radiated down to his foot.

Sly took the sharp points of the claw, and dug around the knee cap, peeling back the skin. He completed a full circle around the knee until he could peel the skin off exposing the bone.

With a maniacal look in his eye, Sly used his fingers to dig into the flesh, pushing it aside as if it had never been there. Matt looked at his bloody knee and felt like he was going to vomit again.

The realtor laughed loudly and the sound echoed off the concrete walls. He turned around to grab something from the workbench.

Matt feared whatever the madman would do next. He couldn't stand the pain too much longer. He knew that he was going to pass out soon. When he saw what the realtor was holding, his eyes begged for mercy and pleaded no.

Sly unscrewed the cap from the rubbing alcohol. He stuck his nose to the bottle of the astringent and smelled how strong it was. It smelled like it could hurt an open wound.

First, he tipped the bottle over Matt's arm, letting the clear liquid run into the claw marks and the knife wounds. Matt felt every nerve in his open wounds react . The alcohol seeped into his skin, burning deep down to his bones.

But when Sly poured a good amount of alcohol onto his exposed knee cap, Matt thought that his leg would burn completely off. He found the strength to grit his teeth through the pain.

Matt found a very soft, defeated voice. "Please. Stop. I can't take anymore." He hoped that his words would mean something to his captor.

Sly just laughed. He was just beginning. Not out of kindness, only of his own selfish accord to keep Matt alive for longer, he got the hose. He pressed the running water to his victim's mouth so he could hydrate. He wasn't done with Matt yet.

Matt lapped the water, knowing that he had no fluids left in his system from being so sick. He drank as much water as the man offered. Then

Sly turned the water off and left Matt wishing that he had gotten to drink more.

Sly knew Matt had enough for tonight, but he wanted to get a snack for Fluffy. He picked up the blade, and started hacking on Matt's pinky finger. He chopped until the small finger fell on the floor. The amount of blood alarmed him, and to stop the bleeding, Sly used a lighter to burn the skin. After the finger was properly cauterized, he picked up the dog treat and went up the ladder.

Matt was left alone in the dark, with nothing but his sickness and his pain. Barely alive, but he was still breathing.

CHAPTER 4

After a restful night of sleep, and a quick morning cup of java with his best friend, Sly was off to work. He had an hour drive to think about Edward. His best friend had been worried sick about Cindy lately.

Edward hadn't shaved and he also had big black bags under his eyes. He apparently wasn't sleeping well. A pang of guilt struck Sly.

He tried to keep his eyes on the road and concentrate on his driving. But his mind was on Cindy. Edward was a constant reminder of what he had done. Nothing more than a reminder that he had killed Cindy. Of course, he missed her.

But his hands had been tied. She had broken his heart, and she knew too much about him. He knew that he had done the right thing by eliminating her, but that didn't make the situation any easier.

He focused on the day ahead of him. All he had to do was get through a day at the office. Plus, he had some snooping to do on a potential future victim. Then he still had Matt in his basement. At least he had something to look forward to.

As he entered his office, Sly's eyes wandered to his eye candy secretary Stacy. She was wearing a low-cut royal blue dress. The color of the dress really brought out the color in her blue eyes.

Then he remembered Cindy's eyes as he stabbed her in the heart with a blade. He had been looking her straight in the face as he killed her.

Sly shook his head. He had to get Cindy off his mind. He had to focus on his job. Stacy greeted him, but he walked right past her into his office. He shut the door behind him and stared at the stacks of papers that required his attention.

His job needed him right now. He was the head of the office, and he had employees that relied on him. If he didn't do the payroll accounts, then they wouldn't get paid. It was crucial that he kept a clear head about him.

As he sifted through the papers, adding up the numbers on his calculator, he cleared his head of all the bad memories. The world around him was still spinning and his life still had to go on.

He had killed many times, but never someone that had a personal importance to him. He had no clue that Cindy's death would shake him so badly.

He signed his name on the payroll checks and balanced all the accounts. Before he knew it, the better part of the morning had gotten away from him. It was finally lunch time.

The past couple of weeks he had been working with a newly married couple, showing them houses. At first, they seemed like the perfect couple and deeply in love. But the last time he had met up with them, she had her arm in a sling and wore dark sunglasses. When he had asked them what happened, they said it was a car accident, and quickly dismissed the question.

Sly suspected that maybe he was a wife beater. If there was anything in this world that Sly hated, it was a man that beat on a woman. Sly remembered the day he watched his Father smack his Mother around.

"At least not in front of the boy!" His Mother begged and pleaded with his Father.

Still, his Father backhanded her in the face. Her small body couldn't take the blow of the shock. She dropped to the ground with her hands on her head, as if it was some tornado drill.

But there was no tornado. Only an angry, drunken man.

The drunk sloshed his way across the kitchen floor and kicked the kneeling woman in the ribs. Finally, he kicked her in the face, and she was forced to roll over on her back.

She didn't even try to fight back. She knew that she was no match for her strong husband.

Sly, being only a young boy, lunged at his father. He wanted to stop the attack. His Father took an elbow and rammed it into Sly's head, and he fell backwards.

His Mother tried to get up and help him, but she wasn't quick enough. Her angry husband knelt down on top of her and grabbed her by the neck. He repeatedly slammed her head into the hard kitchen floor tile.

Sly ran for help. He went to the neighbor's house. They called the police. However, Sly's mother was dead before they even arrived.

Sly shook off the bad memory. He didn't want to relive his past. Instead, he wanted to help other women that were being beaten on by a man.

Sly grabbed the spare key to the house that he was supposed to be showing. He told the young married couple that he had an interested buyer. It was just an excuse to get into their home.

He wasn't going to show anyone their home. He just wanted to be in their house alone and snoop through their belongings. If she was getting beat on, then he would find some evidence.

The realtor pulled up in front of the home, and straightened his tie before getting out of his car. Here he was, in broad daylight, practically breaking into a home. People actually trusted them with their home key.

He loved his job.

Sly slid his key into the front door of the home and appreciated how clean they kept the house. Naturally, most people kept their home cleaner when it was for sale. It was a common sense sales tactic.

He didn't have to worry about the neighbors seeing him slip inside. He was a realtor. He didn't have to worry about the occupants coming home. They knew he was there, he knew they were at work.

He scanned the living room, and didn't see anything beneficial. He started in the bedroom. He was looking for personal papers. Hospital bills. Perhaps court documents. Arrest slips. Anything to prove the husband's guilt.

In the top of the closet, he found a small lockbox. The fireproof kind. Easy to lockpick. He picked the lock. But there wasn't anything except birth certificates, social security cards, and passports. Not what he was looking for.

Then he went into the room they used as an office. There was a stack of bills on the desk, nothing from the hospital. Even though he hadn't proved any guilt yet, he hadn't proved innocence either.

Sly was ready to give up on his search. One last room. The kitchen. That's where he saw it. Magnetted on the refrigerator. A reminder to call the car insurance company.

Along with the post-it note, was a folded up piece of paper. Sly unfolded the piece of paper. An estimate from a body shop, assessing the costs of repairs for a wrecked car.

Turns out they weren't lying about the car accident. Sly was disappointed. He very much looked forward to adding a new victim to his list.

Instead, he pulled out his phone, and left a voicemail for the homeowners saying that the people wanting to buy their home was a no-show.

Sly locked the door behind him on his way out. He whistled on the way to his car, and gave a friendly wave to a neighbor trimming their shrubs.

As soon as he sat in his car, his phone rang. He looked on his screen and saw that his office was calling. Perhaps it would be a new client, a potential new victim.

"Sly here. Speak."

"Hey Sly, it's me." Instantly he recognized the voice as his secretary, Stacy. "I've screened five calls today from a Sara Harris. She is very persistent in trying to reach you."

Sly politely asked for her phone number, knowing that he had zero intention of calling her back. Sara Harris. The sister and wife of two of his victims. He would definitely be avoiding her.

CHAPTER 5

Sly looked forward to spending his evening with Matt. He drove home singing along with the radio. His mind almost got the best of him wondering why Sara Harris would be calling him.

He had already disposed of her husband's and brother's bodies. She would never find anything. He tried to convince himself that he had zero worries.

For a split second, he thought about returning Sara Harris' phone call, but decided against it. What was the big deal if she suspected him of foul play? With no proof, her suspicions meant nothing.

Plus, if he called her, it would do nothing but ruin his good mood. He had a houseguest waiting for him, and he didn't want to be a rude host.

Sly walked into his guesthouse, and quickly

disrobed. He didn't care if his victims saw him naked. It was a lot cleaner to kill this way. He rolled up the rug, uncovering the hatch door to his basement.

He whistled as he climbed down the ladder. He smelled the sick before he saw it. He turned on the light to see Matt covered in some more vomit.

Apparently injecting him with bleach did not agree with him. Matt didn't look too good. He barely opened his eyes. His lips moved, but no sound came out.

Sly quickly hosed him down, washing the throw up down the drain. He offered water for his victim to drink, but he was pretty much unresponsive.

He had hoped to keep this one for a few days. He wanted to play host to Matt for as long as he could, but it looked like his stay would be coming to an end.

Sly looked at the freshly rinsed off man, contemplating what would be the best way to reward his own good mood. He knew that he wanted to eat a piece, or perhaps pieces of the man. But also knew that he had to feed his pigs. They were hungry, too.

Sly wanted to avoid his arm that he shot the bleach into. He didn't want to chance getting sick. So he chose to eat the legs himself, and give the rest to the pigs. Fluffy would get all the fingers.

Sly started with his fingers, cutting each one off individually. As he placed the pruning shears around Matt's thumb, his eyes begged for mercy. He was just too defeated to scream out of pain.

Even though the victim was still breathing, he was dead inside. He knew that he was on the brink of death. All he could do was groan in pain.

Sly snipped off his thumbs, and let the blood flow freely onto the floor. It would be easily hosed down the drain before the night was over. He inspected the fattest of the digits and wondered if Fluffy would be happy with just the thumbs.

He knew that Fluffy loved to chew, so he proceeded to snip off his other eight fingers, making a nice pile for Fluffy.

Matt was still alive as he inspected which part of his legs he wanted for his own meal. He took a hunting blade and carved around the calf. He carefully cut along the muscle, avoiding the bone, pulling off the thickest part of the bottom of the leg with his hand.

Sly was happy with his chosen meal. The meat seemed flexible and he hoped that translated to tender. He noticed that Matt's groans had stopped. He figured that he had bled to death.

He continued cutting up the rest of Matt's body. He had to cut it into small sections to carry it up the ladder to the pigs. He liked using the blade instead of an electric knife to cut up the bodies. Sly liked working with his hands and it just felt more personal. He felt closer to his victims this way.

He cut off the legs at the bend in the hip area. Then he worked his way to the arms, slicing through the shoulder area. Then he came to the head. His favorite piece to cut off.

Even though Matt was dead, the blood still flowed freely from his neck. He took his time sawing through the front of the neck. When he got to the spinal cord area, the knife hit resistance, and he had to put some more elbow grease into it.

After feeling that the parts were now easy to transport up the ladder, he made several trips to the pigsty. Sly was still naked and covered in blood. He loved the fact that his farm was so private that he could roam around in his nudity, looking like the madman that he was.

Fluffy greeted him with a small yelp, and he threw the fingers to him. The dog scurried away with a few of the treasures, he could only carry so much in his mouth at one time. Sly only hoped the dog wouldn't bury them. He needed the body properly disposed of.

The fingers that the dog couldn't carry, Sly picked up and threw to the pigs. He didn't have to worry about the pigs burying anything. They ate every last bit that he gave them.

The pigs grunted and snarled and thanked

him for his hard work. He watched the pigs eat their meat, procrastinating the cleanup in the basement. Sly checked his watch, and knew that it was going to be a long night. But he didn't mind. It was all worthwhile.

As he rinsed the blood from the chair and the concrete floor, he felt like he was washing away Matt's sins. He watched as the blood ran through the drain in the floor. Eventually, the crimson red ran clear. Sly felt fulfilled. He knew that he was doing the world a service by ridding it of the drug peddler.

He scrubbed the chair and the floor with bleach, fully removing the sin from the room. Then he rinsed his own body with the cold tap water. His duty was done.

CHAPTER 6

Sly had such a great evening. He was proud of his well-rounded butchering of the muscle. After getting out the slow cooker, he cut the muscles into smaller bite sized chunks. He added potatoes and carrots and filled it with water. He added beef bouillon for flavor, and set the simmer to low.

This time tomorrow, he would have what he hoped to be a tasty meal.

He climbed in bed naked, feeling his silk sheets press against his skin. Sly loved the small luxuries of life. He rested his head on his perfectly plump pillow, and closed his eyes to go to sleep.

As soon as his eyes closed, he saw a flash of Cindy's face. He outstretched his arm across the empty bed, and remembered what her warm body felt like beside him.

He kept reaching, only to feel the silk glide across the palm of his empty hand. Pushing her memory aside, he closed his eyes tight and tried to get some rest.

Eventually, sleep fell upon him. But his mind did not rest. Dreams of Cindy got the best of him. No matter how hard he tried, he couldn't wake. His mind was forcing him to relive the moment that he killed his lover.

The scene was a little bit different in his dream. It started with them making love, in his bed, their naked bodies pressing into each other, unable to get close enough. She nibbled on his ear as she whispered how much she loved him.

He gently stroked her face. Then all of a sudden, they were transported to his basement/dungeon of doom. They were making love on the cold concrete floors and their moans echoed off the bare walls.

She acted very primal, reaching for his body pressing him deeper into her. Her teeth tore into his skin. Their bodies were intertwined, then they weren't.

She was sitting naked in the metal chair, her eyes staring into his. Like she was begging for him to kill her.

When he looked at his hand, he held the same blade that he had plunged deep into her heart. He tried to pull the blade away in his dream, but he couldn't. He ran the blade along her plump breasts, and she begged for more.

He squeezed her nipple with his thumb, squeezing it against the blade until her small peach nipple fell into the blade of his hand. He sucked the blood from her injured nipple, enjoying every last drop of hurt that her body was willing to give him.

"Sly. Kill me. Make me your victim. Bind me to your soul."

He shook his head no. He didn't want to kill her. But he couldn't control the actions in his dreams. He was forced to watch as he shoved the blade into her vagina. Her groans were haunting.

Moving his head down to her wound, he licked the blood from her thighs. As the blood trickled from her opening, he couldn't lick fast enough. He shoved his tongue into her gash, needing more of the coppery fluid in his mouth.

She begged for him to be inside of him. After sticking his erection into her, she groaned for more. Her blood was the best lubrication he had ever felt in his life.

She grabbed his face with both hands and forced him to look at her as she spoke to him.

"Do it. Finish it! Bind me to you."

She raised his body until he was standing, and his dick was level with her mouth. She wrapped her lips around him, trying to suck his fluids from him. Her blood that was on his cock made a messy ring around her mouth.

She took his hand that was holding the blade and guided it to her neck. Sly tried to pull away, but some force had come over him.

She sucked him deep into her mouth, deep into her throat. He knew that she must be suffocating. After unsuccessfully trying to pull away, she guided his blade hand across her throat, instantly spilling her blood.

After all the blood drained from her neck, he felt the air hit the tip of his dick. He took his fingers and shoved them into the hole in her neck. He could feel his dick protruding through the gash in her neck.

He tried to pull out of her mouth, but a force had made him paralyzed. He was stuck with his cock threaded through her mouth and hanging out of her slit throat.

After he could move, he forced his fingers deeper into the slit, trying to push his erection out of her neck. Even though she was dead, her throat made gurgling sounds. She seemed to be sucking harder.

She was sucking so hard, and it felt so good. When he ejaculated, the sperm flowed down her chest covering her breasts. She ran her hands through the cum and blood covering her nipples.

After trying many times, Sly finally woke up. His body was covered with sweat and he checked the clock. It was morning, yet he didn't feel rested at all. His face was damp, and he wiped his eyes. Apparently, he had been crying in his sleep.

Sly wasn't one to cry. He couldn't remember the last time he actually had a good cry. Was it when his Father murdered his Mother?

He couldn't stop his tears. Sitting on the

edge of his bed, holding his face in his hands, the flood gate opened. Tears feel for Cindy, for his parents, and most of all for himself.

Who had he become? What used to be a hobby was now something that was consuming him and haunting his dreams. He blamed Cindy. If only she had been accepting of him, but she wasn't.

He couldn't go backwards and change the past. All he could do was move forward with his own life.

A smell from the kitchen distracted him and he remembered that he had been simmering Matt in the slow cooker. He had something to look forward to today.

Fluffy jumped up on the bed, almost like the dog could sense his sadness. The dog licked his owners hands as he petted him and rubbed him between the ears. Sly was thankful that he wasn't alone.

CHAPTER 7

Like clockwork, Edward showed up for his morning coffee. He had some papers with him, and he rushed into Sly's house.

"I finally got it! Cindy's phone bill came in. It listed all the numbers she called the past month. Some kind of detailed billing." Edward paused for a moment and took a deep breath through his nose. "What smells so good?"

Sly just laughed. "I'm cooking up some sort of special roast. I've been slow cooking it all night with carrots and potatoes. It will be extra tender this evening." He couldn't help but laugh at the fact that he had turned his best friend into a cannibal.

Everytime Sly had cooked someone, Edward ended up eating some of it. And he loved it. He had turned into some sort of people eating fiend, even loving the smell of people being cooked.

"Anyways. Back to what I was saying. The bill even lists numbers with the old area code of when she lived in the city. Maybe, she's hiding out at one of their houses."

Sly raised his eyebrows. He knew that none of Cindy's friends knew where she was. He was the only person that knew she would never be found. But he couldn't tell Edward that.

"Maybe you're one step closer to finding her. There has to be someone that knows where she is." Sly paused for emphasis. "But even if they know where she is, maybe she told them to keep it a secret. Maybe they'll lie. They still might not tell you where she is."

Edward looked like he was deep in thought. Here he was thinking that he had struck gold only for his best friend to burst his bubble. He scratched his forehead and stuck his chin high in the air. "I dunno. But we still have to try, don't we?"

Sly slid a cup of coffee in front of his guest, and glanced at the eight pages of phone numbers. "You're gonna need this. Looks like it's gonna be a long day. But I'm on board. Give me a page of that bill."

After hours of fruitlessly making phone calls but still no answers, Sly tried to appear persistent in the search for Cindy. A lot of the phone numbers they called were businesses, apparently where she had been looking for work. Then there were also the moving companies she must have called to get quotes from when she moved.

Very few of the phone numbers were actual people. So then they started calling just the phone numbers that she had sent texts to. The reasoning was that you only text your friends.

Most of her actual friends they got a hold of were concerned. Saying that they hadn't heard from her since she moved. Sly kept dialing the numbers and talking to strangers even though he knew it wouldn't do any good.

Edward tried to use interrogation tactics to get information from her friends. Afterall, he was a trained law enforcer.

Sly listened in on one of Edward's phone calls.

Edward's forehead wrinkled up as he listened to whatever the person on the other end of the phone was saying.

"But I'm her brother. I'm just worried. So if you, or anyone you know might know her whereabouts…"

Edward scribbled a silly picture of a tree as he listened to the other person speak. "But she broke my best friend's heart. I believe you might be hiding her because she asked you to."

Edward pulled the phone from his ear as the person screamed something at him. Apparently, he had pushed it too far. People didn't like to be called by a stranger and being told that they were liars. The person hung up, and Edward placed his phone on the counter. He shook his head and tried to fight back a tear. He noticed that Sly had been watching him.

"I'm not getting anywhere with this. Someone out there has to know something."

Sly had an odd feeling in the pit of his gut. Perhaps it was guilt. He was torn between comforting his friend or pretending to cry for his own heartbreak.

He chose to do both. As he teared up, he placed his hand on Edward's shoulder. This was a perfect time to apologize. "I'm so sorry." Sly left it at that. He stopped himself from saying too much.

Edward studied the worry in his face. "It's not your fault. She broke your heart. You didn't tell her to run away. I just don't get it though. This is the last place her phone was pinged. Why did she turn her phone off?"

Sly offered the best answer that he could. "It's obvious. She doesn't want to hear from me. It hurt her to hurt me. She's just too good a person."

Still determined with his goal in mind, Edward dialed the next number on the long list. He wasn't going to give up. He had to find his sister.

Tired of calling people all morning and almost all afternoon, Sly removed the cover of the slow cooker. The aroma filled his nose and made his stomach grumble. It was lunch time. Time to eat Matt.

He got out a couple of plates. It wasn't until

he started scooping the meat and potatoes that Edward finally set his phone down. He handed Edward a fork, and waited for him to take a bite.

As he placed the first piece of Matt's calf in his mouth, he smiled.

"Are you sure you aren't some sort of secret chef? You make the best food I have ever eaten. Maybe you're in the wrong business. You should open a restaurant."

Sly's mind drifted for a moment, thinking of feeding people to unsuspecting patrons. He wondered if everyone would actually love the taste of human flesh.

"Well, I own a cookbook or two." Sly chuckled, knowing there were no cookbooks with his recipe. "The secret is in the seasoning. It's actually pretty easy."

Sly tasted it for himself, and realized that he was onto something good using a slow cooker to prepare his victims. Matt's muscle was more tender than the Betsy pork they had eaten.

He just watched as his best friend devoured every last bite on his plate. When Edward asked for seconds, he couldn't help but to oblige. He loaded his plate up with more food. Then, he had seconds himself.

CHAPTER 8

After a long day of dialing his fingers to the bone, Sly told his friend goodbye. Sly had abandoned his search for Cindy, but Edward wasn't willing to give up just yet. Edward went to his office to figure out another way to find his sister.

Sly, on the other hand, was being eaten alive by guilt and anger. He thought his whole situation was doomed. How would he deal with seeing his best friend on a daily basis? With Edward being so distraught, and Sly knowing that he was responsible, filled him with rage.

He had checked his calendar for his next possible victim, and there wasn't one for another week. Since his guesthouse was empty, he had the opportunity to take some time to spy on his next victim. Of course, he would be cautious and be extra careful. Between Edward and Sara Harris, he couldn't handle anymore heat on him at this time.

Sly dressed in all black, and changed the license plate on his car. He waited until nightfall, and went to spy on his soon-to-be victim. His next victim would be Carl Rait.

Carl Rait was a successful business man, an accountant. He lived a very nice life with a beautiful wife in a very nice home. But after Sly snooped on him, he found out that he was a sexual deviant. He had drawers full of sex toys and cabinets full of porn. A year ago, he had 'searched' the home he was selling after showing it to potential buyers.

The sex toys and the porn wasn't enough to know which person in the household was a sexual deviant. Luckily, he had access to their computers. Carl's computer was full of porn, and weird searches for kinky women, even prostitutes. His wife's computer was full of self-help groups for women with cheating husbands. She was even a member of an online group for rape victims.

This was a victim that Sly had very much looked forward to making a houseguest. He could save Carl's wife from a life of misery. He hated the thought of such a beautiful woman having to endure a long life with a man like Carl.

The goal was to learn Carl's habits over the course of the next week. He wanted to know when he got home, where he went, what he did. He needed to know the best way to abduct him.

Sly parked down the street from their lovely home, with his taser in his pocket just in case he needed it. His only intention was to see what the married couple was doing.

He slinked in the blackness into the couple's backyard and luckily they didn't have any lighting on the back of their home. He just wanted to look into a window. He just wanted to stalk his prey.

As he walked towards the only light in the backyard, which was emanating from a window, he saw a shadow. Possibly the figure of another person.

Fearful that he wasn't alone, Sly walked on his tiptoes, creeping around in the night. He kept his distance from the window, and hid behind the base of a large tree.

A quick glance towards the figure showed him the stature of a thin male, also wearing black. He must be up to good.

It was hard from the angle he was standing, but Sly could barely see into the window. The mini blinds were barely opened, but he could see Mrs. Rait walking around the bedroom in very revealing lingerie.

The other man dressed in black must be a peeping tom! Sly wrapped his hand around the taser and aimed to shoot the peeper. He waited until the bedroom light turned off. Mrs. Rait must have left the room.

He kept his distance and waited until the peeper was leaving. The man stuck to the shadows as he made his way towards the street.

Luckily, his new found victim was actually walking in the direction of Sly's car.

He quietly kept a safe following distance, walking behind his prey. When the man was in a dark shadow, Sly aimed his taser and shot his victim. The man fell to the ground, jerking around. He didn't even know what hit him.

Approaching the man, he saw that his frame was smaller than he expected. Sly realized he was much younger than he thought. He looked like a teenager.

Sly knew that it was his duty to scoop this young boy up, and make him his next houseguest. He had to rid the world of this peeping tom.

It was actually very easy getting the young man down into the basement of his guesthouse. The volts of electricity must had been too much for such a lightweight. He was unconscious for almost the entire ride back to his house.

When he did wake up, he tased him again, shooting electricity into his body rendering him unconscious and drooling on himself. He even wet his pants in the passenger seat of Sly's car. He knew he would have to clean that up pronto.

Carrying the teen down to his guesthouse basement was actually very easy. This victim weighed far less than any other victim.

Sly had never killed a minor before, but his

mind was telling him it was the right thing to do. The boy would only grow into a worse citizen. Sly knew in his mind that someday peeping wouldn't be enough. Maybe one day he would evolve into a rapist. Sly couldn't have that.

Sly undressed the unconscious boy, he preferred for his victims to be naked. It just made his ways of teaching them, torturing them, easier.

He sat the boy up in the chair, and handcuffed both of his wrists to the arms of the chair. Then he used thick tape around his ankles to secure them to the legs of the chair.

He made several wrappings with the tape. When he was sure that the boy was secure and sufficiently tied up, he undressed himself, and waited for his victim to wake.

CHAPTER 9

The boy was groggy when he woke up. As he slowly opened his eyes, Sly studied his face. He couldn't be much more than sixteen years old. His boyishness showing through the fuzzy hair on his upper lip. It looked like he didn't even shave yet.

Even though he wasn't shaving yet, Sly knew he was old enough to have gone through puberty. Why else would he peeping in on Mrs. Rait? He just wanted to catch a glimpse of the half naked, beautiful woman. Then probably go home and masturbate.

Sly was proud of himself for foiling the young man's plans. He had definitely done his good deed for the day. His own reward after looking for Cindy all day.

The peeper opened his eyes, and slowly rolled his head, looking around the room. His mind panicked as he saw how dim it was. He shivered from being cold. He couldn't make sense of what was happening to him.

Sly tried being polite to the boy. "Welcome.

You're my newest houseguest."

The young boy shook his head. "Where am I? I have to get home. My mom is gonna kill me."

Sly laughed to himself. Here it was, the young boy feared his mother killing him, not Sly. In time, the boy's fate would reveal itself. He didn't want to ruin it for him too soon.

Sly wanted to keep it short and simple, and just get the information that he wanted. "How old are you?"

"What's that have to do with anything? Have I been arrested or something? I'm too young to be arrested. I'm only sixteen."

Sly had been right about the boy's age. Also, he was stupid to think he had been arrested. Sly had been standing naked in front of him. What kind of cop gets naked during an arrest?

Still, he had to go forward with eliminating the boy. Society depended on him. "Arrested? So you know you did wrong?"

The young boy started crying. Tears fell down his face. "I know I shouldn't have looked, but I couldn't help myself. But I didn't hurt anyone. Can I just go home?"

Sly shook his head no. He knew that the boy would never go home, but he didn't want to tell him that. "You know you did wrong. That's all that matters."

That was when he proceeded to put the gag in the boy's mouth. He didn't need to speak to him anymore. The boy twisted his head and screamed, and tried his best to refuse the gag.

Sly was just too strong. He fasted the leather to his face, and forced the ball into his mouth. Now he had a young man that could do nothing but stare at him and cry.

Sly was used to the tears. Every victim cried. But he wasn't used to the tears falling from such young eyes that were full of inexperience. This boy had barely lived his life, but that wasn't Sly's fault. The boy had chosen to live wrong.

Sly started out easy on the boy. A very appropriate punishment. He whipped the boy with a leather strap across his chest. His skin cracked open and blood ran down and collected in his belly button. Slights screams of pain tried to escape his gag.

Young kids deserved whoopings. Sly's dad whooped him when he was a child.

This boy had committed a sin with his eyes. It would have to be his eyes that were punished.

Sly lit the wick of a candle. He waited for the flame to grow. He held the flame close to the boy's eye. He tried to turn his head, but Sly held his face in place by grabbing him by the chin.

As the flame got closer to his eyeball, the peeper closed his eye. That was no worry to Sly. The flame quickly destroyed his eyelid, exposing his eyeball.

Sly held the flame to the boy's eyeball, and watched while the liquid around the orb started to boil. The boys muffled screams were louder than any other victim in the past.

The realtor was surprised when the eyeball 'popped'. It was almost like it exploded. From the inside out, the sight organ exploded, revealing a trace of slimy mucus and goo. It was almost like watching wax melt, but it wasn't wax. It was an eye.

Then, when the eyeball caught fire, Sly was surprised. He withdrew the candle and watched as the small flame grew larger. Redness quickly overtook the boy's skin of his orbital socket. His eyebrow started to melt.

Sly let the flame grow, and when it covered most of his forehead, Sly let his hair catch fire. The smell of burning hair was really nasty. After a full minute of letting the boy burn, Sly grabbed the water hose to extinguish the fire.

That full minute felt like an eternity to the boy.

The cold water hurt just as much as the flame, but the peeper was glad that the fire had been put out. The whole side of his head hurt.

Sly saw that the boy's skin was gone, it had disintegrated in the fire. What was left behind was an unrecognizable mess of red spots and blisters forming.

As soon as a blister formed, Sly took his finger and popped it, letting the clear liquid run into the boy's wounds. The boy didn't look so young now. Now he looked like the monster he was with half of his face charred and his hair burnt off.

Taking the palm of his hand, Sly laid his hand flat on the damaged side of the peeper's head. Even though the fire was gone, he could still feel the heat radiating from the injuries.

The peeper now had only one eye. He used his good eye to watch Sly, flinching every time he moved. The boy couldn't believe how much pain he was in. He wondered what he looked like. He was sure that the fire had done a ton of damage.

He tried to speak, but all Sly heard were hum-like sounds. He couldn't produce words, only sound. And Sly didn't care. He had no desire to hear the boy beg for his life.

Sly examined his subject. He, hopefully, had now learned his lesson. It was getting late, and Sly decided to call it a night and try to get some rest.

As he was leaving, he couldn't help but notice how skinny the boy was. He knew that he wouldn't be good for eating. At the very best, he would just be a snack for his pigs. Halfway disappointed that he wouldn't partake in the consumption of the boy, he reminded himself to be grateful to have a houseguest after the bad day he had.

In his nakedness he strolled past his pig pen to his car. They growled and snorted, begging for a human to eat. He loved the fact that he had turned them into his own little monsters.

He threw them some normal pig feed, and watched as they smelled it, not sure if they wanted to eat it or not. It was great that he had the fortune of spoiling his pigs with his hobby. Soon, he would be able to give them what they wanted.

CHAPTER 10

Sly went to bed, hoping that it wouldn't be a repeat of the night before. He didn't know how she was doing it, but Cindy had found a way to haunt him.

She had to be the one that planted the dream of her in his head. He had killed many people before and never dreamed of any of them. What was so special about her?

Was it because he loved her? Was it because he wanted to spend the rest of his life with her?

Nope. She ended up not being the woman he wanted her to be. She couldn't even handle a murder that happened due to self-defense. He couldn't have ever spent his life with her.

She just didn't understand him. So, then why had he dreamt of her? It didn't make sense to him.

Maybe it was Edward. Perhaps it was Edward's fault. Seeing him full of worry to the point that he was practically sick. Any of his other victims never had someone in his life that was around to make him feel guilty.

But what could he do about Edward? Should he distance himself from him? He was his best friend. He usually loved spending time with him. There was no easy answer to this problem. Sly would just have to play it by ear.

He would take life as it came to him. He could decide how to handle situations as he went along.

He closed his eyes, and a vision of Cindy flashed in front of his eyes. She even had the stab wound in her chest that he had given her. She looked exactly as she did when he chopped her up for his stew.

He smiled as he remembered the Cindy stew. It was pretty tasty. He saved most of the Cindy meat for himself to eat. He only gave the pigs a small portion of her to eat. He wanted her for himself.

There had to be a way to sleep without thinking of her. He took a couple of some over the counter sleeping pills, hoping they would offer him the rest that he very much needed.

Tonight, in his dream, Cindy was the one in 'control'. She grabbed him by his head, and sat him down in the metal chair in his basement. She licked her lips, and ran her tongue along his bald head.

She very seductively handcuffed him into the chair as if it were some bdsm scene. She slowly undressed in front of him, wiggling her hips in a teasing manner.

His eyes scanned her curves, admiring how sexy her body was. She swayed back and forth, running her hands across her bare breasts. She squeezed the mounds together and shoved his face in between them. He kissed her soft skin, tasting the salt in her sweat.

She ran her tongue down the side of his neck, all the way down to his firm abs. She stopped just before reaching his erect pleasure zone.

She raised her eyes to meet his, and he shook his head yes.

She wrapped her lips around his manhood and very lightly tickled his balls with her soft fingers. Even though it was a dream, it felt so real. It honestly felt like his dick was being sucked.

Suddenly, she bit down on his cock. That also felt very much real. The pain radiated down his legs. He looked down and saw blood dripping from her pretty mouth.

She took her fingernails and dug them deep into the tender flesh of his ball sack. She grinded her hand painfully into his balls, smashing them into each other.

But she wasn't done yet. She walked over to the workbench, grabbing a knife. Sly looked down at his ruined cock and wished the bleeding would stop.

He couldn't move. For some reason he was once again paralyzed in his dream. He was forced to watch as she cut a slit across his scrotum. Cindy reached inside the wound, pulling out a small circular object.

He couldn't wrap his mind around what he was seeing. Sly was staring at his testicle in Cindy's palm, outside of his body. She shoved it in his mouth, and for some dumb reason, he willingly accepted it. He chewed on it until it was smashed into pieces small enough to swallow.

She walked around to the backside of the chair, and shoved the long knife through his back. The blade was sticking out the front side of his chest.

She undid his handcuffs, and told him to lay down on the cold concrete ground. He willingly obliged, how he wasn't dead yet, he didn't know.

Sly laid on the floor, with the blade sticking out of him. She climbed on top of him, straddling the blade with her crotch. She slowly slid the blade into her woman hoe, and began humping it. She was screwing the blade sticking out of his chest.

She was ruining her vagina, but she was moaning in ecstasy as if it felt good. Cindy just kept on sliding up and down on the knife, blood running out of her gash onto Sly's chest.

Then, in his dream, Sly raised his arms, grabbing Cindy by her hips. He raised her into the air, pulling her chest down onto his. The blade struck her through her heart, then they both laid on the cold concrete floor and died together.

Sly woke up, grabbing his balls, making sure he still had both of them attached to his body. He peeked under the covers, and his dick was still intact. Running his hands across his chest, he also realized that there was no stab wound.

He woke up and took a cold shower. It was time to start his day.

CHAPTER 11

Sly checked the clock. It would be time for Edward to show up. He couldn't face his best friend today. Even though he must have slept because he obviously dreamt, he didn't feel well rested.

Instead of having to face his friend he sent him a text message.

Something came up at the office. Have to go into work early.

It was a lie, but it was better than having to see the worry in Edward's face. He got a reply from his friend acknowledging the text.

Then Sly sat and thought for a moment. He knew he needed caffeine. Maybe that could get him motivated for the day.

But after a cup of liquid caffeine he still felt horrible. He contemplated going into work, but decided against it. He didn't want anyone to see him in the fragile state that he was in.

After making a quick phone call to Stacy,

his secretary, Sly was relieved when she understood that he was sick. He was off the hook. He had a full day ahead of him with nothing to do.

He knew what he wanted to do. He wanted to check in with his current houseguest. He had a peeping tom waiting for him.

While he was driving the mile to his guesthouse, Sly realized that he didn't know his houseguest's name. It's not like it mattered. He would be evicted soon. Still, he wanted to humanize his victim.

He wanted to add his name to the long list of degenerates he had removed from society.

As the hatch opened, the young boy could see the light with his good eye. He had spent an entire night all alone, in pain, in darkness, chained to a chair.

He had no way of knowing how long he had been down there. Hours. Maybe days. It was long enough for him to urinate on himself a couple of times.

The young man's stomach grumbled for the want of food. It was pure torture. Being all alone, unable to move. For many hours. He couldn't even go to the restroom.

Plus, his head hurt so bad. He didn't sleep at all. He was almost relieved when he saw his captor. At least something was happening. The boy wished that the man would release him. A small part of him knew that wasn't a possibility. That part of him wished that the man would just put him out of his misery.

Sly was once again naked. But he didn't look the same. His face was unshaven and scruffy. The bald man hadn't even shaved his head in some time, and baby hairs sprouted atop his head.

The boy just watched the realtor's every move. He even tried to speak, but he only made indistinguishable noises through the gag.

Sly placed his hand on the leather around the boy's head. "I'll remove your gag. Please, don't scream. Nobody can hear you anyways. If you do, I'll cut your tongue out. Are we clear?"

Having no other choice, the boy shook his head yes. It would feel good to actually be able to close his mouth. He recognized the pain in his jaws from having an object lodged in his mouth for many hours.

His captor removed the gag, trying to keep his hand away from the strings of saliva.

The boy did not scream. He tried to speak, but his throat was too dry. At least some of the pain in his jaws was relieved.

Sly offered the water hose for the boy to drink. As the cold water fell in his lap, he caught an even deeper chill.

"Drink. You need your fluids. Then we're gonna talk."

The peeper willingly gulped the cold water. After drinking too much, he felt like his stomach would explode.

Sly set the garden hose aside. "What's your name?"

The boy could barely think straight. But that was right. He had a name. Why would this man who didn't even know him put him through such hell? After clearing his throat, he could speak. "Jonathon."

Then the man tried to put the gag around his head again.

The boy couldn't stand that thing in his mouth again. "No!" The boy screamed. "Please I beg you."

Sly set the gag aside. He already told the boy what he would do if he screamed, and he screamed. The realtor said nothing as he grabbed the pruning shears. He placed the handheld tool against the boy's face, and held him by the chin.

Jonathon knew he was trying to cut off his tongue. Holding his mouth closed, he felt the cold metal part his lips. He kept his teeth closed, but his captor didn't care. He banged the metal against his teeth, sending nerve pain throughout the boy's mouth.

Sly pried the boy's teeth apart, and finally got a hold of a snippet of the boy's tongue.

Jonathon tasted a rush of blood. With his mouth closed he had no other choice than to swallow some of the copper tasting fluid.

Sly watched as the rest of the fluid leaked from his mouth, running down his chin.

Sly spoke in a calm manner. "You'll bleed to death, unless I cauterize the wound. If you're smart, you'll open your mouth."

Jonathon debated with himself. Should he just die now? Should he allow himself to bleed to death, or should he cling to hope. He opened his mouth, and stuck his cut tongue out.

Sly took the opportunity to cut into the soft muscular organ. He snipped the end off, and laughed while the blood flowed.

Having done this before, Sly knew that he had time before the boy bled out. He went to his workbench and lit the candle. He returned with the flame and held it to Jonathon's damaged mouth.

Jonathon couldn't stand the pain. He quickly slipped his tongue back in his mouth and he felt like he was drowning in his own blood. Sly was burning his lips and watched as blisters instantly formed around his mouth.

Jonathon stuck his tongue back out, and endured the pain while Sly held the candle to it.

After the wound was sealed, Sly laughed. "I bet you don't scream again."

Once again, he left the peeping tom alone with his pain to keep him company.

CHAPTER 12

A tired Sly spent the day lounging in the sun beside his pool. He swam a few laps, physical upkeep was important to him. Then he just laid in the lounger until he fell asleep.

Luckily, dreams didn't come to him. He had a nice restful sleep. Something he hadn't had in days

He was woken by Fluffy barking. Sly looked around, trying to get his senses about him. He was outside, and had been laying in the sun. He didn't know for how long, but it was long enough for his skin to start turning red.

Sly looked up to see Edward standing before him.

"Can you at least please stand where you give me some shade. I'm baking here."

Edward checked his watch. "The sun will go in soon. It's getting late in the evening." He moved over to cast a shadow on his friend."I was out making my rounds, and saw your car. Anyways, I have some news for you."

Sly scratched his head and felt the hair he

had allowed to grow. He knew that with his hobby, having hair was against his own rules. Hair could be linked to DNA and could lead to his arrest. He made a mental note to have his head shaved soon.

Sly sat up and looked at his friend, and had to squint his eyes because the sun was behind him. "Okay. So, what's up?"

"I got a fax today. From the state boys. Long story short, Sara Harris, Chester Harris' wife, tried to get a search warrant for your farm." Edward, tired of standing, sat down in the lounger next to his friend.

Sly recognized danger. "Let's go inside. I need a beer."

The men sat sipping on their brews. The cold beer was quite refreshing after sleeping all day out in the sun. "They already searched my place. They found nothing. It doesn't make sense."

Edward took a huge gulp of his beverage. "This time, it's about her brother. Apparently, Officer Williams has gone missing. The last place his phone registered, was here."

Sly remembered shooting the cop in his face. Cindy watched. She couldn't handle it. That's why he had to kill her, too. Sly said nothing.

Edward stared at his friend in the eyes.

"What is this place? The bermuda triangle? That's two phones, last pinged on your farm. Cindy and Officer Williams. Something here is strange." He scratched his head, hoping for a response from his friend. He didn't get one.

"So when should I expect a search." Sly tried to act unalarmed, but he was sweating inside. He couldn't chance the cops searching his pond. They would find two cars of missing persons in his pond. And not to mention, Jonathon was currently in his guesthouse.

"That's the thing. The one judge her brother was friends with is out of town. It's on the court docket for next week. This is crazy, huh? If I didn't know you myself, I'd almost think you were guilty."

Sly just laughed and tipped his beer bottle towards his friend. "Well good thing you know me. Otherwise, you might have to arrest me."

Edward laughed with his friend. "That's absurd right?"

The men drank their beers in silence.

Sly was thinking about all the possibilities. He hadn't gotten enough sleep and couldn't think clearly. What was his next move? Should he just wait, knowing they wouldn't ever find the bodies? Or should he run now while he had the chance? There had to be some tropical country where he could hide. He had plenty of cash in his bank account.

Should he drain his bank account now? Or

would that make him look guilty? Should he just wait to see what happens?

Edward finally broke the silence. "I know you're innocent. You don't have anything to worry about."

Sly tried to cover up his worry. "Yeah, but the last search they left my house in a mess. I really don't wanna clean that up again."

"The judge hasn't signed off on it yet. Maybe it won't come to that."

Sly crossed his fingers and held them in the air. Paranoia crept in on him. He tried to read Edward's eyes. Could the sheriff really be this stupid? How could his friend not know the truth?

Sly was really good at covering his tracks. Was it possible that he could get the cars out of the pond? But how? And then what would he do with the two cars?

The only thing he could do was hope that the judge wouldn't sign off on the search warrant.

Sly looked to Edward. "Can you do me a favor?"

His best friend shook his head yes.

"At least tell me if the search warrant goes through. I at least wanna be here while they tear up all my stuff."

He clinked his beer bottle to his best friend's. "You're a great friend, Edward."

CHAPTER 13

Full of worry, Sly needed a way to rid himself of his stress. Night had fallen, yet he had slept the day away. He couldn't possibly sleep with this kind of worry on his mind.

For a brief moment, he thought about going to get his next victim. It was almost time to go pick up Carl Rait. But he still had Jonathon waiting for him.

The boy had served his purpose. It was time to evict him. Plus, his pigs were bound to be hungry for their special meal.

Sly climbed down the ladder. This time he had even forgotten to remove his clothes. His mind wasn't working the way that it usually did. He wasn't being careful. This was the time he needed to be extra careful. The heat was on him.

His mind just wasn't registering like that. His mind only had one goal. He had to eliminate the bad people from the world. He had to hurt people. It was only fair. He was hurting, too.

He climbed down the ladder. Jonathon looked like a mess with the burns on the side of his face. The blisters on his lips were huge. If he hadn't known any better, it would have looked like Jonathon had been involved in a house fire.

Slowly, Sly poked his fingers in the blisters, letting clear juice run into the boy's ruined mouth. Underneath the blisters was nothing but the under layers of skin. Fresh, painful sores.

Sly laughed at the boy's pain. He, himself was in pain. He wanted to hurt the world as much as he hurt. He couldn't hurt the whole world, but he could hurt Jonathon as much as his heart desired.

He inspected Jonathon's burn wounds. The top of his head and around his eye was a delicate pink color of fresh under layers of flesh. He poured rubbing alcohol into his burns and laughed.

Jonathon had no choice but to endure the pain. He couldn't even scream. His missing piece of tongue that was now cauterized hurt him dearly. His whole mouth and head hurt.

His mentality hurt him the worst. The hours he had endured alone in the dark, in pain, had worn him down. Even though he had never experienced them before, he had suffered panic attacks while he was alone. His lungs felt like they were oxygen deprived as he struggled to breath.

He had silently been praying for death. Jonathon wanted death to come to him. He didn't know how he was still alive.

Sly looked at the boy, and was proud of his work. Jonathon could maybe be his masterpiece. He didn't know if he had ever hurt someone so badly. Maybe he had topped his own personal best.

Sly's mind was telling him to burn the boy in his delicate parts. Afterall, he was a sexual deviant. So his penis should be tortured.

Jonathon was already naked, and his crotch was bare. Urine had soaked his legs. It wasn't like he had access to a toilet toilet. Sly put a lighter to the wick of the candle.

Watching as the flame flickered, Sly got distracted for a second. There was something soothing about the flame that made him feel at peace. It took a moment, but then he remembered that he planned to burn Jonathon's privates.

Sly held the candle in his hand with the flame growing with each passing second. He held it close to the head of Jonathon's dick, and the delicate skin turned red.

Jonathon let out a slight groan. He had already given up on life. He thought that he had experienced the worst pain imaginable, but he was wrong.

Sly slowly moved the candle and its flame. He ran it up and down the shaft of the young boy's penis. Even though he was circumcised, by the time that Sly was done, the penis looked like a swollen mess of blisters and raw skin.

Jonathon prayed for death. It was a shame that his captor just wouldn't kill him. He wriggled his wrists the best he could. The handcuffs made noise against the metal arm of the chair.

The boy turned his wrists upward and mustered a single word. "Please."

The jingling of the handcuffs had caught Sly's attention. He looked up and saw the boy exposing the underneath of his wrists. When the boy begged for death, Sly knew that his duty was done.

The realtor grabbed the hunting blade. He had already decided that he wasn't gonna make it easy. As he flatly ran the blade against the skin of Joathon's wrists, the blade devoured the top layer of skin. Joanthon's veins were exposed, the veins the boy so desperately wanted to be cut.

Jonathon tried to jerk his arm away from the pain but he didn't have enough energy. His arm was limply on display. He tried to look at it with his remaining eye. He saw the bloody mess that was now his arm.

Sly had a small debate with himself. He felt as if the boy burned on his head and genitals had suffered enough. The skinning of the arm was just symbolic of his begging for death.

Sly pierced the boys veins with the tip of the blade. Pushing it deep into Jonathon's arm, he slowly glided it towards the bend in his elbow. Then, he just stood back and watched.

The blood escaped the young boy's body. It would take a few minutes to lose enough blood, but death would come soon.

The realtor stared the young boy in his good eye until he couldn't hold it open any longer. Just like that, death had put the boy out of his misery. Sly washed away the puddle of blood and watched it swoosh down the drain.

Then it was time for what Sly thought was the fun part. Preparing the body for the pigs. The boy was too skinny for him to eat, he wanted the entirety of this body for the pigs.

He began cutting the body into small pieces. Even though the boy was thin, it would be plenty to make his pigs happy.

CHAPTER 14

Sly was having so much fun with Jonathon, he hadn't realized that it was well into the night before he finished cleaning up. His body ached of exhaustion. Even though the boy hadn't weighed much, it still took a toll on him physically when he carried him to the pigs.

A day of sleeping in the lounge chair didn't offer him the rest that his body needed. He eyed his bed, only for it to taunt him. He didn't want to have anymore dreams of Cindy. His mind was on the verge of collapse.

His mind drifted as he sat on the bed. As soon as he was in a lying position, he heard a voice.

The voice belonged to Cindy. "Go to sleep. Spend the night with me. I miss you, Sly."

Sly looked around the room. Of course, he was alone. Nobody was in his home. It was just his mind playing tricks on him. There was no possible way that Cindy could be speaking to him. She was dead.

"You know you want me, Sly. Go to sleep. Be

with me once again."

Sly pressed his hands to his ears, but he couldn't block the noise. The voice was still audible.

"Please, lover. I beg you."

He tried shaking his head. He kept his eyes open, looking for a ghost. Did ghosts even exist? Were they real? He had never seen one before, but that didn't mean it wasn't possible.

After searching every room of his home, and realizing that he was alone, Sly tried laying down on his couch. Maybe her ghost powers only worked in the bedroom. He hoped he was free from her haunting him.

He situated a pillow under his head and pulled a cover over his body. Sleep had nearly come to him, when the voice started speaking again.

"Sly, you can't get away from me. You did this to me. I can find you anywhere."

The realtor sat up quickly, his whole body covered in sweat. He wiped his eyes. Maybe he just wasn't seeing clearly. Cindy was in the house somewhere. There was an ache in his body telling him that he had to find her. Maybe he could save her.

Then, he realized this must be what having a conscience felt like. Was it his own guilt that was haunting him. That would be the only logical explanation.

Guilt was not an emotion that he was familiar with. Feeling this way was brand new to him. He was terrified of how he felt. There had to be something he could do to get some sleep.

He tried to push his guilt aside. He needed sleep. He knew there were no ghosts. She was only in his head. The best possible solution was gaining control over his mind.

He wasn't weak. There had to be a way to claim what was his. His sanity.

Alcohol. That was what he needed. Just a drink. Maybe a few drinks. Perhaps if he drank until he passed out, then he wouldn't have dreams.

The dreams didn't worry him as much as hearing Cindy's ghost while he was awake. Sly took his bottle of bourbon, and figured he could escape her in the guesthouse. There was a bed there. Maybe he could find solace there.

He poured the bourbon straight into a glass. After taking a huge gulp, his body started to warm. Clearly, a natural reaction to the potent drink. There hadn't been any ghosts in the guesthouse. At least none that had spoken to him yet.

Sly downed the stout liquid. Liquid courage. Then maybe he could deal with Cindy's ghost.

He enjoyed the silence of the home. After realizing that he never spent much time in the upstairs of his guest home, he could appreciate it for what it was.

It was his safe haven. The place where his hobby was ruler of the domain. Sure, the home was just for appearances. Noone would ever know what took place in the basement, except his victims.

And they never lived long enough to tell a soul.

Finally, he laid his head down on the soft pillow. The bed was actually quite comfortable. His mind told him that Cindy had spent time in this bed. They had even made love in this bed.

But memories were okay. Memories weren't haunting him. Her ghost, an apparition of his guilt, was haunting him.

This bed was a safe haven. No ghosts here. Closing his eyes, he prayed for the much needed rest his body needed.

CHAPTER 15

In his dreams, Cindy still found him. Even though he had tried to wake up, he couldn't. The dream was forcing him to relive the last decent night that he had with Cindy. But some of the events had been changed. In his dream.

In the dream, he was taken back to the evening where he was swimming in his pool. Cindy showed up, out of breath. Warning him that Officer Williams was on the road, screaming something at her.

Just like he had done in real life, he grabbed Cindy by her petite waist, and jumped in the pool with her, causing her to scream. The dreaded scream that caught Officer William's attention. Sly wished that scream had never happened.

Perhaps things would have turned out differently.

Sly was forced to dream and watch while Officer Williams waved the gun at them. Just like it had happened in real life, Cindy got out of the pool while the cop kept the gun trained on

Sly.

Cindy rushed him and the gun fell. Sly took his opportunity, jumping out of the pool, attacking Officer Williams. He beat him in the face. Then, things started to change. Now, the dream began altering from what had really happened.

Cindy was the one who picked up the gun. She pointed the gun at Sly.

"Get off him! Sly! Stop!"

She pointed the gun at him. He had no choice. She had a deadly weapon pointed in his direction. If things had really happened like this in real life, he could have spoken to her. But in his dream, he was mute. No words came to him.

"Take him to the basement. Show me who you are. Do to him what you wanted to do to him. You wanted to torture him, right? A bullet to the face didn't teach him a lesson. I want you to teach him a lesson."

She held him at gunpoint, making him reveal himself to her. She followed as he drug the cop down the ladder into the basement. How did she even know that the dungeon existed? He had never told her about it.

Cindy didn't take the gun off him once. She watched as her boyfriend shackled the cop to the chair. The workbench had caught her attention. There were a variety of tools and weapons on display.

Cindy made a command. "Do to him what

you want."

Sly stood, pondering if she would still love him after seeing what he did to bad people. The only problem was that Officer Williams wasn't a bad person. His only mistake was stalking Sly.

He usually didn't kill stalkers, but she was forcing him to do it. He didn't know whether or not he liked the dream version of Cindy. She was grittier. Downright bad. Evil.

Real life Cindy didn't have an evil bone in her body. That's why he loved her so much. She was good. He needed someone good in his life to keep him balanced.

But here was dream version of Cindy, forcing him to reveal his true self to her. Dream Cindy picked up a hammer.

She handed the tool to him. "What do you do with this?"

Once again, in his dream, Sly couldn't speak. He could think, though. His thoughts were that he could inflict pain with the weapon. He could hurt people. He usually desired to hurt people, but it was different this time with Cindy watching.

Officer Williams sin was stalking. The punishment must fit the crime. Sly held the hammer, with the claw side facing Officer Williams.

Since Officer Williams had been watching him, it was only fair to damage his eyes. This way he could never see to stalk someone again.

Sly plunged the claw into the man's orbital

region. He positioned it between the bone and the actual eyeball. The concave shape of the claw wasn't only good at removing nails. It was also good for removing eyeballs.

A quick flick of the wrist, and the circular eye popped out. It dangled by thin strings, perhaps nerves. Sly grabbed the eyeball and yanked on it, ripping it from the strands that were attached to it.

Dream Cindy laughed. Real life Cindy would have never thought of that as amusing. Maybe he had turned her ghost into some sort of monster.

Sly looked to Cindy for affirmation, and she shook her head yes. He knew that meant to proceed with the torture. She wanted to see more.

Sly raised the hammer over his head, aiming it toward Officer William's good eye. The hammer came down with great force, and Sly felt a squish as he made contact with the soft eyeball. Sly proceeded to beat the bones around the man's eyes.

Blood spewed from the man's face, speckling Sly's face. Cindy laughed as she watched, giving Sly the approval that he very much needed. Sly pounded the metal tool into the man's face until his bones gave and sunk inward.

The man was no longer recognizable.

Then, Sly remembered the flyers the cop had made. Accusing Sly of being a bad man. Officer Williams' goal was to damage Sly's realty company.

The cop had to make the flyers with his hands. The punishment should fit the crime.

The man's arms were shackled to the metal arm of a chair. His fingers were on display, laid out before him.

Sly raised the hammer, bringing the ball shaped metal down on the frail bones in the cop's fingers. The skin instantly smashed, and blood seeped from his body. Sly was having fun with this now. He smashed every finger with the hammer.

The weirdest part of the dream was that Officer Williams did not react. He didn't scream, he didn't struggle. He just sat and took his torture.

Cindy laughed at the man's sunken face. Every bone in his face was broken and the skin was gone. There was nothing but blood and the underlayers of pink flesh.

Cindy pointed at the man's hands, all of his fingers broken. Dream Cindy had a shrill laugh that gave Sly chills up and down his body.

Then no words were needed. She handed him the gun. He knew that meant that she wanted him to kill the cop. In reality, killing the cop was why he lost Cindy. In his dream, she begged for Officer William's death.

Sly held the gun inches from the man's broken face. He pulled the trigger, and the noise was so loud in the basement. The thunderous boom echoed off the bare concrete walls, hurting Sly's ears.

Dream Cindy just kept laughing her shrill laugh as she watched him murder the man. Sly put two more bullets in the man's brain for good measure.

Dream Cindy stopped laughing for a brief moment. Just long enough to speak. "Now, show me what you do with the bodies."

Cindy watched as Sly started cutting the man into small travel-size pieces. He used a large hunting knife. He sawed off the arms at the shoulder joints. It was a slow process, but dream Cindy still seemed amused. She just stared and laughed.

He then started hacking into the man's legs at his hips. After he removed the first leg, Cindy took the limb from him and held it.

Dream Cindy ran her hand up and down the detached leg. "We'll eat this. The rest goes to Fluffy and the pigs."

Sly was shocked! How did she know that he fed bodies to the pigs? Even worse, how did she know that he ate some of his victims? Dream Cindy had special powers and knew more about Sly than he imagined.

After cutting off the next leg, the last leg, she helped him transport the body up the stairs. She gave an arm to Fluffy, and watched as the dog chomped down into the dead cop's flesh. Then, she threw the other arm to the pigs.

She watched as the pigs fought over who

would get to eat the arm. Several pigs gathered around the limb, their teeth tearing easily into the muscle. Their faces were bloody, and dream Cindy seemed to enjoy watching the bloody mess.

She paid no attention to Sly as he brought the rest of the dead body to the pigsty. Her focus was on the pigs. They made her laugh. Even they seemed to dislike how shrill she sounded.

After the body was disposed of, she looked at her murderous boyfriend. "Let's go inside. You're making me dinner."

CHAPTER 16

Even though Sly tried to wake up, he couldn't. It felt like this dream was lasting forever. He kept telling his body to get out of bed, but it just wouldn't respond.

He sat in the kitchen and watched as Cindy prepared the leg.

She turned on the water faucet, and tried to wash away all the blood. She took a butcher knife, and started cutting into the thigh.

He remembered that the thigh had always been Betsy's favorite part to eat. Did dream Cindy know that?

She peeled away the skin with a vegetable peeler. Then she used the butcher knife to cut the thigh muscles into bite size chunks. At one point, she even put a raw bite-size chunk of leg in Sly's mouth. He had never eaten a person without cooking them in real life. Why was she making him do it now?

Sly bit into the chunk and blood flowed across his tongue. The liquid filled his mouth as he kept on chewing on it until it was swallowable. When he finally did swallow, she patted him on the head like he was a dog obeying her every command.

She filled a pot with water, and seasoned it with beef bouillon. "You made a stew out of me, right? Did you flavor it with bouillon?"

She went to the ice box and got out some vegetables. Dream Cindy was slicing carrots and potatoes just like a normal housewife would prepare dinner. But normal housewives didn't use dead people in their stew.

In his dream, it didn't take long for the stew to boil and simmer. It felt like it was instantaneous. Before he knew what was happening, she brought him a bowl.

Sly used his spoon to poke around the food. But he didn't eat. He didn't know if he should take a bite or not. He had a feeling that maybe she poisoned it. He didn't know if he could die from something that happened in his dream. It did feel very real.

Dream Cindy saw that he wasn't eating. She poked a fork into a chunk of meat and force fed it to him. Even though he tried to keep his mouth closed, she somehow made him open his mouth with some unseeable force.

She slid the piece of Officer Williams' leg into his mouth. She had some sort of control over him because he chewed and swallowed. His mind was telling his body not to eat it, but her force was too strong. Sly was no match for dream

Cindy's powers.

"Is this what you wanted? You wanted me to be okay with your hobby. How does it feel?"

Sly still couldn't speak, but he sure could think. He was thinking that this wasn't what he wanted. He wanted to keep her innocent and pure. All he had wanted was for her to accept him for who he was.

Now she was too accepting.

She smiled at him. For a brief moment he felt peace and happiness. Dream Cindy felt as familiar and comforting as real life Cindy. Was it because she had accepted him for the monster that he was?

They ate the meal together in silence. As Sly was finishing, he took his plate to the counter. He turned around, and dream Cindy was gone. He looked under the table, maybe she had hidden from him. She wasn't there.

Sly went from room to room looking for his comforting lover. Just when he got comfortable with her, she vanished. Even his dreams weren't fair to him. They only gave him what he wanted so that it could be taken away from him.

His dreams wanted him to feel lonely. After searching and finding nothing, he heard a voice, coming from the kitchen.

"Lover, I'm in here."

Sly ran to the kitchen, wanting to see her once again. As he turned the corner and entered the room, Cindy stood still, waiting for him. She held the butcher knife in her hand.

Even though he saw it, he was running too fast. He ran right into the blade. It pierced him through his chest, finding its way to his heart. The blade must have punctured an artery because the blood ran rapidly to the floor.

He looked at the hole in his chest. It was the same exact wound that he had given Cindy. The same size and the same location.

Dream Cindy laughed in her shrill tone as he collapsed to the ground.

Sly woke up in a cold sweat laying in his guesthouse. He looked around and saw no ghosts. The ghost must have been content haunting him in his dream.

The sunlight had started to come through the window curtains. It was time to start a new day.

CHAPTER 17

Before leaving for work, Sly checked his reflection in the mirror. He had stubble-like baby hair on his head. He needed to get his head shaved soon. The black bags under his eyes were large. His eyes were red.

Frankly, he looked like crap.

Sly tried to cover his bad appearance by wearing a nice-fitting suit that hung on him perfectly. Well, it used to hang on him perfectly. Today he noticed that he had even started to lose weight. The realtor didn't want to lose weight, he was content with his size.

It must have been his nerves. They were really taking a toll on him. He had to find a way to forget about Cindy. He had to devise a plan to dodge her ghost.

He left extra early for work to avoid seeing Edward. He couldn't stand seeing the worry in his face. A small voice inside of him, his conscience, was telling him that if he told Edward the truth about Cindy, then maybe she would stop haunting him.

His brain told him that was a stupid idea. He had no desire to go to jail. Plus, he has all the Sara Harris stress. It was only a matter of time before a judge might sign off on a search warrant for his property. He didn't know what he would do if it came down to that.

The hour drive to work wasn't as enjoyable as it usually was. Sure, the sun was shining and the grass was still a beautiful green. It was his mind. It was riddled with guilt, giving him no peace.

He arrived at the office and Stacy promptly greeted him. She had been a good secretary over the years, and Sly had a feeling that he hadn't shown her the appreciation that she deserved.

He didn't know why all of a sudden his conscience was bothering him. He never knew what guilt felt like until now. And now, it was smothering him alive from the inside.

Sly sat down at his desk, looking through all the bookkeeping he had to catch up on. There are a few memos reminding him to call Sara Harris. Why would he call her? What could she possibly have to say to him?

Curiosity got the best of him. He mustered up some courage and picked up his phone. He slowly dialed the numbers, and hesitated when it was time to hit the last digit.

He thought for a moment. Would he want to hear what she had to say? Edward had already told him that she was pressing the issue of getting a search warrant.

The realtor decided against dialing the last digit. He sat the phone down and decided to throw himself into his work. Maybe all he needed to do was keep his mind busy.

Work was a perfect outlet to keep his mind busy. He balanced all the accounts and checked all the office expenses, making sure everything was as it should be.

Before he had known it, the day had slipped away from him. Sly checked his calendar for any important upcoming events. There was a red circle, signifying a new houseguest coming up in the next couple of days.

With the Sara Harris situation, he was afraid that he didn't have a few days. He decided to go pick up Carl Rait. It had been close enough to a year.

Sly worked until it started getting dark outside. He even went to the bank on his lunch break. He made a rather healthy withdrawal, just in case he needed the cash. He feared that soon he would be on the run from the law.

Cash would very much help if that were to be the situation.

He drove back to Carl Rait's house. It seemed familiar. He remembered the night that he picked up Jonathon, the peeping tom. Now he would have to be smart and figure out how to get

Carl Rait.

Tonight there was only one car in the driveway. The other night there had been two. He wondered who was home, and who was gone.

Sly threw caution to the wind. He was ignoring every one of his own rules. He parked his car on the street. Marched up to the front door, and knocked.

Luckily, Mr. Rait had answered the door. He was home. Now, all Sly needed to do was find out if he were alone.

Sly walked right past the man, entering the house like he owned the place. "Good evening, Mr. Rait. How's the new home treating you?"

A shocked Carl recognized the realtor, but couldn't understand why he would be visiting. Being a no nonsense kind of man, he blocked Sly from entering the house any further. "It's fine. What's this about? Can I help you?"

Sly looked innocent as he got down to business. "Your wife. I need to speak to her. Is she home?"

The man shook his head no. "What could you possibly have to talk to her about?"

Sly said no words. Instead, he reached into his pocket, pulling out the stun gun. Before Mr. Rait even knew what was happening, Sly placed the weapon next to his throat and pressed the buttons.

The electricity surged through the man's body and he fell down to the floor, and it almost looked like he was having a seizure. Sly just laughed and listened to the stillness of the house. Sly had taken a chance just barging in like this and just got lucky that Mr. Rait was home alone.

Sly shocked the man again for good measure until he was unconscious. He picked the man's limp body up, and carried him out to the car. It was dark, yet he still glanced around to see if there were any nosy neighbors seeing him commit this crime.

There wasn't anyone around, and Sly went about his business, putting the man in the passenger seat of his car. He used some tape to tie the man's arms to his side. He also wrapped the tape around his ankles, locking them together.

It felt good and Sly felt free not following his rules. Why had he restricted himself? It felt great to freestyle and just do whatever he wanted to do.

He decided that in the future he wanted to be freer with his hobby.

CHAPTER 18

During the drive back to his farm, Sly stunned his victim each time that he woke up. Drool ran from Carl's lips and it disgusted Sly. He was used to cleaning up blood, vomit, urine, and sometimes feces. But drool was something his stomach couldn't handle.

Sly fought the urge to vomit, he just wouldn't look at the bubbles and streams of drool coming from Carl's mouth. The man had even snotted on himself. His upper lip was full of drool and snot.

Sly got lucky that Carl didn't put up a fight. The man was larger than his last victim, the teenage boy. Sly's mind was trying to tell him that he was being too reckless, but a part of him just didn't care.

He was too interested in just doing what he wanted to do. He would deal with the consequences as they came.

It was difficult getting the man into the basement. Not as difficult as some of the other victims. He had taken larger prey before. It was just that Sly noticed a difference in his body since his nerves had started haunting him.

His muscle mass had been deteriorating. He used to be in excellent shape. But he was also used to getting restful sleep. Oh, how times had changed.

Being the new free Sly, he wanted to push his own boundaries. He wanted to see if he could cause this man more pain than he had ever caused anyone. He wanted to slowly torture the man.

He wanted to hurt him as much mentally as he did physically.

Sly laid his victim flat down, on his back, on a pallet of wood. Sly grabbed his hammer. He wanted to use his hammer because dream Cindy had been so fond of it in his dream.

He grabbed some long nails, and began with the man's palms. He had already driven a nail through the man's right palm, into the pallet of wood beneath him, before he woke up. As Carl woke up he screamed.

Luckily, the man's feet were still tied together, but he had full use of his left hand. Carl lunged at Sly with his free hand, and Sly backed out of the way. The man wasn't in good shape after being stunned.

Sly swatted the man's left arm with the hammer and he heard a crunch when it contacted with his elbow. The man's arm went limp, and Sly took the opportunity to sit on his broken arm.

Carl tried to struggle and wiggle Sly off of him, but Sly was determined to nail the man's left hand to the wood.

Sly swiftly swung the hammer, driving the nail deep into the man's flesh. It wasn't hard, it only took a few swings. Then the nail was nestled securely into the wood, binding the man in a sprawled out flat position.

Carl tried to raise his arms up. He thought maybe he could pull his hands free from the nail. He was wrong. The pain was too much to bear.

Sly got longer nails, and sat on the man's legs. He positioned the nail into the top of the man's knee cap. He swung the hammer until the nail had fully penetrated through his knee. Sly lifted up on the man's leg, and it didn't budge. It was secure and fastened to the wood.

Carl was screaming out in pain, but his realtor didn't care. He actually enjoyed the man's sounds. He preferred screaming over silence.

As if he wasn't injured enough, Sly put another nail through Carl's other knee cap. One time he missed the head of the nail, and the metal of the hammer crushed the bones of the man's knee. Sly even heard the crunch.

After the man was held in place, Sly examined his subject. He had a broken elbow, a broken knee, and four nails that had completely penetrated through his body. Sly knew that Carl wasn't going anywhere.

Since he wanted to keep his houseguest for the next few days, Sly decided to be kind. He turned on the water hose and offered the clear liquid to the man. Sly wasn't sure how much water the man actually drank. He was acting like he was trying not to drown with the water running in his face.

Then Sly realized that the man was overdressed in his boxer shorts and t-shirt. Sly grabbed a knife, and Carl saw it.

Carl pleaded with his captor. "Please! Stop! Do you want money? I have money."

Sly ignored the man's cries. But for some reason, when the man spoke, he didn't feel alone. He liked listening to a real live person talking. It was better than listening to ghosts. It was also better than the silence that his guilt used to haunt him.

Sly used the knife to cut away the man's clothing. He wanted the man naked. He had plans for him, and it would be easier without his clothes.

Exhaustion struck Sly, and he decided to call it a night. Carl would be waiting for him tomorrow.

CHAPTER 19

Sly stepped outside and took a moment to appreciate the simple things of life. Like night air. There was something about the way the darkness of the night felt.

Fluffy greeted Sly outside, almost like he was expecting a treat. Sly wished he had at least would have thought to cut off a finger for the dog. But he just patted the dog on his head and told him to be patient.

Then, Sly came to his pig pen. The creatures rushed to the fence he was standing by, pointing their noses in the air. He knew that they were trying to smell people meat.

He apologized to them, and threw them normal pig feed. They acted like they didn't like it much, but it was better than them starving to death. As much as his animals wanted to eat a person, Sly knew that it just wasn't possible to give them what they wanted everyday.

Sly wished he had a new victim everyday, but he didn't. That's why he enjoyed taking his time with the ones that he had. His hobby was what kept him sane, and he wanted his time with his houseguests to last.

Sly didn't feel so alone when he was with his pigs and Fluffy. He dreaded going inside and trying to sleep. He knew that Cindy would be waiting for him.

He sat down with his back up against the fence. Fluffy licked him in his face. He rubbed the poodle's curled fur and appreciated the company.

He closed his eyes, and drifted off to sleep under the night stars. He hoped that dream Cindy wouldn't find him here.

"Sly. I miss you. Come be with me."

Sly opened his eyes. He couldn't tell if he was dreaming, or if he was awake. All of his dreams had seemed so real. He decided to pinch himself. He felt pain. Did that mean he was awake?

Cindy's voice beckoned to him once again. It was coming from the pig pen. He turned around, but he didn't see her. He looked around, and he didn't see anything but his pigs and Fluffy.

He looked up at the night moon, and cried. Was he going crazy? He didn't like feeling like this. He got up, and decided to go inside.

Cindy called out to him again. "Sly. Here. With the pigs. Where you left me."

Sly turned around, and it looked like the pigs were eating something. Sly got closer. All he could see was that it was a large chunk of something. It wasn't the pig feed that he had given them earlier.

He squinted his eyes and waited for his eyes to adjust to the night. All of a sudden, Cindy's partial body raised above the pigs. She had no arms or legs, and she still had the knife wound through her chest.

The pigs chased her partial body. He remembered throwing the chest portion of her body to the pigs because he had sex with her. He wanted the pigs to eat his semen. He wasn't gonna eat it.

As the torso of her body was approaching him, he realized that he must be dreaming. There was no way that he was so crazy that he was seeing Cindy's ruined torso coming towards him.

He tried to run away from her, but she sped up. He tried to get away from her, but she was just too fast. It was like she was floating or maybe even flying through the air.

She caught up with him, and dream Cindy used her special powers to take hold of Sly. He felt an invisible force grab his body, and force him down on the ground. He was laying on his back staring at the night stars.

Then he heard a zipping noise, and realized that the invisible force was unzipping his suit pants. He watched, with his mouth open, and something pulled his pants and boxers down, revealing his penis.

Cindy's torso and head floated above him. He tried to speak. He tried to scream. But his mouth was forced closed.

He couldn't move. Sly was being forced to watch and wait and let dream Cindy do whatever she wanted to do to him. She began by licking him in his man parts, until his dick stood at full attention.

He tried to not get erect, but he had zero control over his body. He tried to close his eyes but he couldn't. He just kept repeating in his head that he should wake up.

But his body wouldn't respond.

Blood dripped from dream Cindy's stab wound as if it were a fresh wound. Dream Cindy placed her torso on top of Sly, and guided his dick into the wound of her heart. Just like he did when he killed her.

Now he regretted sexually mutilating her body after death. She was getting her revenge on him.

She floated up and down, stroking his dick every time she moved. He didn't want it to feel good, but it did.

Her torso humped him, thrusting him into the hole in her heart, until he came inside of her body cavity. The semen mixed with the blood. She floated above his face and let the mixture of the fluids drip all over him.

His cum made the blood even thicker. He didn't do it on purpose, a force made him do it, but he parted his lips allowing the cum and blood to flow into his mouth.

Then she drifted away. Sly tried to get up, but once again he was paralyzed. He wanted to wipe the mess from his face, but his hands were pinned to his sides.

Then, once again the invisible force took hold of him. It lifted him into the air, and sent him flying through the air,

The force held him until he floated above the pig pen. Then he thumped down into the pigsty, surrounded by his own pets. They smelled the blood in his mouth and showed their teeth. They were obviously hungry.

He felt their teeth rip into his flesh. Each pig was trying to carry his body in all different directions. Their hungry teeth had a death grip on his bones, refusing to let go of their meal. As they scurried away in all different directions he could feel his limbs being torn from his body.

The pain felt so real. He wished he would wake up soon. He couldn't handle being trapped in his mind being forced to endure this kind of pain.

He woke up in a sweat and saw that the sun had started to rise.

CHAPTER 20

Sly was washing his face, scrubbing it extra hard after his dream, when he heard his front door open. He knew that it was probably Edward, but all the same it startled him. He hoped it wasn't dream Cindy back to haunt him some more.

Sly crept through his house, practically on his tiptoes, trying to be extra quiet. He was relieved when he saw Edward pouring himself a cup of coffee. Finally, a visitor that was a real person. Not a real person that he wanted to see, but still a real live breathing person. He was sick of ghosts.

Sly wiped the sweat from his forehead. "Good morning. Why don't you help yourself to a cup of coffee?"

Edward chuckled. Then he looked at his friend. He paused and just stared.

Edward didn't remove his eyes from his friend. "What's wrong with you? You look like shit."

Sly didn't know how to respond. He

couldn't tell him that ever since he killed Cindy she was haunting him in his dreams every night.

He offered another logical explanation. "Worry. This whole Cindy situation is driving me insane!" He realized that he raised his tone, and tried to calm himself. And it wasn't a complete lie. Cindy's ghost was driving him crazy.

Edward took a sip of the coffee and realized that it was too hot to drink. He set his cup aside. "I know what you mean. It's been long enough that she should've reached out. She's gotta know that I'm worried sick. I just don't understand why she hasn't turned her phone back on. Would she have gotten a new one? But then changing your number is a hassle. I don't think she would've done that."

Sly poured himself a cup of coffee and sat in silence.

Edward hated the silence. "I hate to say it, but I think something bad has happened. I don't know what. But something in my gut is telling me it's bad."

Sly just sat and stared off into space. He knew the bad thing that happened to her. He also knew that he couldn't tell Edward about it.

All Sly knew to do was cry. He let the tears fall. Everything had finally caught up with him. Shame and guilt released in the form of liquid from his eyes.

The good sheriff placed an arm on Sly's shoulder. He had been his best friend for many years, but had never seen him cry before. Not only was he worried about his sister, his heart ached for his friend.

Sly was known for always looking good. He was always clean shaven and well rested. He barely even recognized Sly anymore with the scruff on his face and his head. It also looked like Sly had aged many years in the brief time period since Cindy disappeared.

A part of Edward wanted to lecture his friend. He knew that they shouldn't have gotten romantically involved. He knew that it would end badly. And now, he was right. He just wasn't sure how badly it would end.

It ended way worse than he could have ever suspected.

He knew that now wasn't the time to lecture his friend. Now was the time to console his friend. Sly might even be taking this situation worse than Edward did.

Edward felt awkward and didn't know what to do while Sly cried. He was a manly man and not very in touch with his emotions. He did the only reasonable thing he knew to do.

He changed the subject. "So, man. How's work going?"

Sly was relieved to think about anything other than Cindy. He told Edward about a huge commission he just got from the sale of a million dollar home.

Edward even offered up some stories about

the small town crime. There was never any bad crime in his jurisdiction. Most of the crimes were teens just looking to have fun. Theft, joyriding, and making out on the hill were the basics.

The friends actually sat and talked about anything other than Cindy. Even though she was in the back of both of their minds, they didn't speak her name.

CHAPTER 21

Sly was ashamed for crying in front of his friend. His whole life he had been great at controlling his emotions. He hated this mess of a man that he turned into.

After Edward left, Sly did exactly what he wanted to do. It was part of being a free man that didn't follow rules. He called into work, grabbed a vegetable peeler and made his way to his guesthouse basement.

Carl was still on his back, nailed to the wood that he laid on. Dried up blood seeped from his nail wounds. The one in the knee looked like it might be getting infected. Sly hadn't bothered with cleaning the nails before he inserted them into Carl's body.

Carl was groaning in pain. Sly just laughed at the man, and he reminded himself of dream Cindy. The way she laughed in a shrill tone at his pain.

Sly had one goal. To inflict the most pain humanly possible on Carl. He thought the vegetable peeler had been a genius idea. Plus, it wouldn't kill him. Also, he would have skin scraps to feed his pigs and Fluffy.

He thought about putting the gag in Carl's mouth, but decided against it. He wanted to hear the man scream. First, he offered him the hose. He knew that the man would need water to coat his throat before he screamed.

This time, Carl willingly took the water in his mouth. Sly was glad that he was hydrating. He was curious how long he could keep Carl around. How much pain could the human body possibly endure?

He remembered that Carl's sins were mostly sexual, based on his wife's musings on her laptop. Since the punishment must fit the crime, he started with Carl's dick.

With Carl's penis in one hand, and the vegetable peeler in the other hand, he laughed and couldn't believe what he was getting ready to do.

The realtor couldn't help but notice how little the man's sex organ was. That was enough to laugh about.

Carl felt the maniac wrap his hand around his cock. "Please. I can't take anymore. I'm begging you! Not my cock!"

Sly used his palm to create a hard surface to flatten the dick on. Then he ran the vegetable peeler down the shaft. Little pieces of skin curled up as it was being shaved away from his body.

The skin was so thick that the blade on the peeler was starting to clog up. Sly picked out the pieces of skin, and started a pile that he could feed to his pets.

Carl spent all night trying to raise himself from the nails. He knew that getting away would be his only chance of survival. When the realtor started peeling the skin from his private parts, he tried even harder.

No matter how much strength he exerted to raise his hand from the nail, the physical pain stopped him in his tracks. His dick being mutilated was the kind of motivation he needed to try harder.

Carl raised upward on both of his hands. His left arm didn't respond, due to the hammer shattering his elbow. But he tugged on his right hand, and he got it to slide just a tiny bit up the nail. The pain radiated down the whole right side of his body.

His hand felt like it was ruined, but he knew that he had to try again. Turning his head, Carl saw that the head of the nail was much larger than the opening in his hand.

He knew that it was pointless. Carl could do nothing but scream. He wailed in pain, but that didn't stop Sly from shaving the skin off his very delicate area.

"Why are you doing this? Please! I'll do anything."

Sly remembered his old rules. His old rules required him to tell the victim of their sins. Not today. Sly wasn't following any rules. He was doing whatever he pleased.

Sly got angry when the man asked why. He was partly angry with himself for casting away his own rules. He strapped the gag to the man's head to quiet him. At least he could still hear the man's screams, even though they were muffled.

Sly had collected a small pile of curled up skin. Knowing that it wouldn't be enough to feed his pigs and Fluffy, he realized that he had his work cut out for him.

He tried to think of what would be the most painful place to remove skin. He studied the unmoving man's body. His bare feet were out before him. He had never tortured someone on the bottom of their feet.

Placing the vegetable peeler to the curved part underneath Carl's foot, Sly applied some extra strength to really get down deep into the sensitive skin. The blades ate away the skin as he stroked it across Carl's foot. Still, there wasn't very much skin. He needed enough skin to feed his pets.

Sly grabbed his trusty hunting knife. He laid the blade flat against the sole of the other foot, with just a very slight angle to it. As he applied pressure, he felt the sharp blade glide into

Carl's foot. He pressed down on the knife, and it quickly peeled away the top layers of skin.

Now he was getting skin pieces large enough for his animals to snack on.

Even though Carl was screaming, Sly didn't feel like he was in enough pain yet. He wanted to really hurt this guy.

Then, a thought hit Sly, almost like he was being struck by lightning. Everything seemed so crystal clear in this moment. The worst kind of torture was mental torture. Dream Cindy had taught him that much.

Sly got down on the cold, concrete floor and laid next to his victim. He tried not to look at the drool that was pooling around the gag in Carl's mouth. Sly craned his neck so that he was close enough to whisper into Carl's ear.

Sly thought of the worst thing he could say. "I'm gonna go get your wife. I'm gonna make you watch as I have my way with her. You're gonna watch me kill her!"

Carl squirmed and made his usual muffled noises.

Sly had no intention of getting the man's wife. Afterall, the whole point of taking Carl was to protect her from her monster of a husband. He only needed his victim to think that he was going to hurt her. He wanted the man's mind to play tricks on him.

For the finishing touch, Sly grabbed the water hose. He sprayed the man to rinse him of the blood, drool, and urine. But it was also cold.

Sly had already noted how chilly it was in the basement. He couldn't imagine how cold it would be if you were wet. He hoped this was enough to hurt the man mentally.

He collected his skin shavings, and left the man to be alone with his mind.

Fluffy ran to Sly, happy to greet his master after his disappearance into the guest home. The dog sat on his hind legs, and kind of raised his front paws in the air. The dog sure knew how to beg for treats.

Sly threw a few of the skin peelings from Carl's dick on the ground. The dog smelled the small pile, then held them in his teeth. He ran away with the treats in his mouth, more than happy to go devour them in a secret hiding place.

The larger skin shavings from Carl's feet were reserved for his pigs. It wasn't enough to be classified as a meal, but he hoped that the pigs would be grateful for the snack. He mixed the skin with feed, and threw it into the pigsty.

The pigs ate around the feed, scooping up the skin first. He knew that human flesh was their preference, and wished he could feed it to them more.

Then Sly sat down and watched the pigs eat. He checked his watch. It was still early in the day. He didn't know what to do with his free time.

He just sat and watched. Mental torture sure was boring, but he figured the longer he left the man alone, the crazier Carl's mind would be.

CHAPTER 22

Sly sat still for so long that he eventually closed his eyes and drifted off into a dreamless sleep. He woke up after napping for a couple of hours.

Thankful that he didn't have any dreams of Cindy, he closed his eyes and tried to sleep some more. He was scared to go into the house. Since she wasn't outside, she had to be in the house waiting for him.

Then another thought hit him. Maybe he had transferred mental misery to Carl. Maybe since he was mentally torturing his victim, Cindy was content.

He knew her ghost's goal was to cause distress. Carl was in distress. He only hoped that her ghost was spending time with Carl. He needed for her to leave him alone. He needed his rest.

Just as he drifted off to sleep again, his cell phone rang, waking him with a startle. Sly jolted awake and quickly answered.

"Man, I have some bad news."

He quickly recognized Edward's voice. And

that was his luck. Just as he was getting some restful sleep, he would be disturbed with some bad news.

Sly wiped his own drool from his mouth and the mess on his hand disgusted him. He played coy. "Is it about Cindy?" He knew that it couldn't possibly be about Cindy. They would never find her body.

Edward shook his head no, as if his friend could see him through the phone. "That judge signed off on the search warrant. I'm sorry, but the state boys are gathering equipment to search your property. It looks like they're even gonna dredge your lake. I'm sorry, I have zero control over this. They're gonna tear your place up again."

Sly tried to calm himself. He needed to lower his blood pressure before he spoke again. He didn't want Edward to hear how anxious he was in his voice. He said nothing while he took deep relaxing breaths.

Then he came up with one word. "Okay."

"You seem pretty calm over this. It looks like they're supposed to be out there tomorrow with the equipment. I wish there was something I could do to help you."

Sly wiped the sweat from his brow. "Thanks for telling me. I'll make it a point to be home tomorrow. Are you gonna be here, too?"

"Yep. I told them since it's my jurisdiction I have a right to be there. Maybe I can stop them from totally trashing the place."

Sly tried to stop his tears. "Well, then I'll see you tomorrow." He told a bold face lie.

Sly had so much to do. He knew this time would come, he just didn't know that it would happen so soon. Even though he was tired, he knew that he only had one day to disappear. That was plenty of time to get south of the border before anyone would come looking for him.

Sly called his dog over to him, and patted him on his head. Saying goodbye to the pooch was one of the hardest things he ever had to do in his life. Then, he called for his pigs. He threw them extra feed, he didn't want them starving to death before the police got there.

A quick trip to the house, he grabbed his journal, a few personal items, and a large duffel bag. That's all he needed for now. There was plenty of time to stop by the bank and fill the bag with his cash.

American money went a long way in Mexico.

He walked through his house and even looked for dream Cindy. If her ghost were to appear, he would even tell her goodbye. He hoped that she wouldn't be able to find him in Mexico.

He had this time planned out in his head for some time now. He didn't know anything about Mexico, but he had heard one of his favorite television producers give an interview once, talking about their favorite part of Mexico.

Even though he didn't know anything about the place, it seemed as good a place as any to go. His plan was to hide and start a new life. Plenty of criminals hid in Mexico. And he felt like he was smarter than most of them

Afterall, it had taken many years before he was caught. It was a good run while it lasted, and surely there had to be sinners in Mexico.

With ghost/dream Cindy being in his house, he was almost excited about starting a new life. That's what he needed, a fresh slate.

The realtor laid out some extra kibble for Fluffy, and made his way out the door.

CHAPTER 23

He knew there would be cash on hand at the office, so he stopped there first. Cash was all that he needed for this trip. Anything else that he needed, he could buy. Sly acted as if nothing was wrong as he greeted Cindy.

He was cool as a cucumber as he walked past all his employees. They didn't see the fear and excitement in his eyes.

He went into his office and drained the petty cash box first. There was only a couple of hundred dollars in there, but at this point, every dollar counted. Then he opened the large safe. It had a few thousand dollars in it.

As he walked out of the office, he strolled casually. Stacy, his secretary was none the wiser that his life was on the brink of turmoil.

Next he had to go to the bank. When the realtor told them that he wished to close his bank account, they tried to talk him out of it. Naturally, it was good business to have an account as large as Sly's. They even offered him incentives to stay with the bank.

He eventually had to throw a small fit. Even though they agreed to close the account, the banker offered him payment in the form of a cashier's check. He couldn't cash a check. He was going to be a fugitive on the run.

Sly pounded his fist on the counter. The worker told him that they wouldn't be able to come up with enough cash until morning. He knew that banks were required to keep cash on hand to cover people's accounts.

After being rude and threatening enough workers, the manager agreed to get him his cash. Sly filled his bag with more green money than he had ever seen in real life. It felt like being a gangster in some Hollywood movie carrying around so much paper money.

Next, he had to rent a car. After tomorrow, he knew that cops would be looking for his car. Eventually they would figure out that he rented a vehicle, but that would take days. That would be more days for him to travel to his destination.

Sly rented the car, then he drove south.

As he neared the Mexico border, he thought about Carl. He had left in such a hurry that he forgot all about his victim. The last search, they hadn't found his hidden basement. Maybe they wouldn't find Carl this time.

Sly couldn't imagine how miserable it would be lying alone in the dank basement slowly starving to death. It would take days to die, and Sly was proud of himself. Maybe that was the worst form of torture imaginable.

Sly got close to the border and found a bus station. He wanted to leave the rental car at the border, and throw the police off by taking a bus. It would take them a long time to follow his trail.

As he got out of the car, he saw his own reflection in the window of his car. He didn't recognize himself. He knew that in a matter of time, the police would have a picture of him all over the news channels.

Luckily for him, he had lost weight and grown hair since the last picture of him was taken. A small beard had even started to form, hiding his face. Fearlessly, he bought his bus ticket, and was on his way to start his new life.

CHAPTER 24

Carl had been laying in the dark for so long, he had lost track of time. It felt like he had been alone for days. He spent his time praying that his realtor wasn't hurting his wife.

He couldn't stand the thought of someone hurting her. She was his whole world. He would rather die than for her to be hurt.

His mind still hadn't come up with a logical explanation as to why the realtor was doing this to him. It didn't make sense. In the first day or so, he kept hoping that he was dreaming.

The pain reminded him that he hurt too bad for it to be a dream.

He had tried to free himself. But the nails hurt so bad. Trying to raise his arms was an impossible task. Especially his left arm. He knew that the blow with the hammer had to break some bones.

His knees hurt worse than anything. He couldn't see them, and he didn't know what Sly had done to them, but it felt like they had nails through them, too. Plus he remembered the realtor beating his knee with a hammer. It had to be broken, too.

Carl had to pee, and let the urine out slowly. Where the crazy man had peeled the skin from his genitals hurt real bad. Then when he urinated and the warm fluid flowed over the raw skin, it hurt extra bad.

Not to mention how gross it was peeing on yourself. He didn't even know had he had any urine. How long had it been since he had water? It seemed like days.

His mind started playing tricks on him. Carl saw visions of the realtor raping his wife. Didn't he say he was going to make him watch? Was he raping her in private? Nothing was making sense.

He couldn't sleep due to the pain, but he was sure that he had lost consciousness a few times. Carl had no choice. All he could do was lay on his back, in pain, in the dark. He was miserable.

He had given up on life. He was trying to will himself to death. Then he heard something upstairs. He hoped that the realtor was making his way to the dungeon to kill him.

Death would be peaceful, death would ease his mind. Hopefully it wouldn't hurt any worse than he hurt right now.

If he was hearing correctly, he was hearing multiple footsteps. Then voices. Were there voices upstairs?

Carl tried to scream, and his tongue hit the gag in his mouth. He forgot all about the gag. He cleared his throat, and tried to make as much noise as possible.

His throat was dry and it hurt to make noise, but he knew it was his only hope. Even though the gag muffled his sounds, they were still sounds. His only hope was that someone upstairs would hear him.

Carl was persistent and he refused to give up. He could still hear the voices, but he couldn't make out what they were saying. If only he didn't have a gag in his mouth.

That just meant that he had to try harder. Just a minute ago, he had been praying for death.

Then God sent him hope. There were people just feet above him. Hopefully they were nice people.

CHAPTER 25

When Edward arrived with the search crew, he was surprised that Sly wasn't there. He hated it that the state boys came in to do the search. It meant that he had no control over whatever they did.

The sheriff hated the idea of the law men tearing up his friend's home. Not only would they leave a mess behind, they would also violate Sly's personal space. He cringed when he thought what it would feel like if complete strangers were at his home going through his things.

What made it worse was that he knew Sly was completely innocent. He'd been his best friend for many years now. He knew the man better than anyone else. Sly wasn't capable of hurting a fly. Nevertheless, he couldn't possibly be behind the disappearance of the police officer.

He did find it odd though that Sly's farm was the last place Cindy and the cop's phone registered. But he knew it would turn out to be some weird coincidence. There had to be a logical explanation.

The state sent in two dozen state troopers to complete their task. Everywhere Edward looked he saw a man wearing a brown uniform violating Sly's privacy.

Sly's farm was huge. It was well over 500 acres, and he guessed that they sent so many men to cover every inch of the farm. It would take days if they planned on dredging the lake and covering all the wooded area. He was glad that he was there to supervise. He had no intention of being involved in the search.

Mainly, he was there in support of his friend.

Even though Sly wasn't there, it didn't prevent the state troopers from their task. Edward was petting Fluffy as he watched a man kick in the front door of Sly's home. If Edward would have been thinking, he would have offered them his spare key. But it was too late now.

Edward walked inside while the men turned over drawers and threw Sly's items all over the house. By the time they were done, there was nothing but a pile of things in the middle of each floor.

Edward shook his head. He knew they wouldn't find anything. Fluffy walked with Edward while he took his time walking the mile back to the guest home. Edward acted as if he was out for a leisurely stroll.

As he approached the door of the guest

home, he saw that it had also been kicked in. He was glad that Sly had the money to fix the damage the state troopers were making. It was making Edward mad seeing the damage.

Edward peeked inside the guest home and was standing in the bedroom, watching a state trooper pull the bed sheets off the bed. As if there were going to find something between the sheets and the mattress.

The men were talking, even discussing some of the items they found. They looked through Sly's pictures and even conversed about how the place was decorated.

Edward thought he heard a whimper, and looked down expecting to see Fluffy. Fluffy must have still been outside. Then, once again, he heard something. A strange noise coming from beneath his feet. Maybe it was coming from the air vent.

Edward tried to listen but he couldn't hear anything over the voices of the other men. "Shush! Do you hear that?"

The men shut up and smirked at Edward. He had no authority here. They had only allowed him to be there out of courtesy.

One nameless officer perked his head sideways. "Shh! I hear something!"

Every man in the house listened, trying to identify where the noise was coming from. Edward thought maybe it was Fluffy or maybe a pig somehow burrowed under the home.

Edward took his foot and started tapping on the floor. He moved around the floor of the living room, just tapping his foot. Then, when he tapped his foot, it sounded hollow underneath.

He wanted to save Fluffy. He wondered how he got under the home. But instead of going outside and looking, curiosity got the best of him with that hollow noise.

There was a pile of stuff on the rug and Edward started moving the stuff around. He rolled up the rug, and saw some type of door. A type of hatch. He thought that was strange. He never knew that there was a basement in Sly's guest house.

Edward was determined to open the hatch. He had to get to Fluffy. He wanted to save the dog. As he lifted the hatch, and climbed down the ladder, he couldn't believe his eyes.

CHAPTER 26

Edward's jaw dropped. There was a naked man, somehow nailed to a wooden pallet. His first response was that it must be Sly. But it wasn't.

Nothing was making sense. A state trooper pushed Edward out of the way, wanting to see what was down there. He vomited when he saw the nails sticking out of the man's knees.

Edward was trying to make sense of everything. Why was there a bloody man in Sly's basement? The trooper got on his radio and called an ambulance while they discussed the best way to remove the man from the wood. They decided to wait until the paramedics got there.

As one man removed the gag from the man's mouth, he was asking him a ton of questions.

"Sir, are you okay? How did you get here? Who did this to you?"

The man had enough strength to say only one word. "Realtor."

Edward couldn't believe his ears or his eyes.

When the paramedics arrived, they kicked all the officers out of the basement. Edward was standing outside, trying to figure out what was going on.

He heard an officer's radio confirm that they found two vehicles in the pond. One of them fit the description of Cindy's car.

Edward had to sit down. His heart was racing. He was covered in sweat and he was having a hard time breathing.

How did this happen? Mostly he wanted to know where Sly was.

There had to be a logical explanation, but he couldn't think of one. Before he knew what was going on, there were news reporters on the scene reporting about a mutilated man being found in the high-profile realtor's basement.

Edward thought about Cindy. Was it possible that Sly had something to do with her disappearance? Could he have killed her? He already saw what Sly done to Carl Rait. Only a monster could mutilate another human being so badly.

When Edward overheard two officers talking about how Sly drained his bank account yesterday, he knew that he must be guilty.

Even though they searched, they didn't find any bodies. What did Sly do with Cindy's body?

Edward made it his life's goal to hunt down

Sly Verdict. He wouldn't rest until that man was either dead or behind bars.

CHAPTER 27

Sly rode on the bus for two days. He hoped that he was far enough away that the police couldn't find him. Surely, they had revealed his secrets by now.

He pulled his ball cap close to his face to try and hide his identity.

He didn't know anything about Mexico. He just remembered that when his favorite television producer had been suspended he did an interview saying that he had spent his 'vacation' in Mexico. Sly even remembered the name of the town.

The producer had explained it as being authentic Mexico, not being in a tourist area.

Sly figured if the place was good enough for that American, then it would be good enough for him.

Sly got off the bus and looked around. The streets were dirty, actually made out of dirt. The streets weren't even paved.

There were many undesirables hanging out in the street. Everyone looked too skinny. And it was so hot. The sun was beating down on him making him sweat.

The ex-realtor held the duffel bag extra close to him. It was full of a load of cash and he didn't want anyone to try and steal it from him.

Sly walked, hoping that he would eventually run into a hotel. He needed somewhere to lay his head. From the research he had done online, most of the places in Mexico weren't too strict about needing proper identification to rent a room.

Luckily, he came across a sign that said 'Hotel'. That was fortunate for him, because he didn't know any spanish. His hope was to find a local who knew english. Maybe he could pay them to show him the ropes of living in Mexico.

He rented a room and couldn't believe how cheap it was. His money would go far and last him a lifetime at this rate.

His room wasn't up to his typical living standards, but it was clean and had running water. He hid his bag under the bed and decided to go out exploring.

A small bar was just outside of the hotel, and Sly decided that he needed a drink. He ventured into the bar, and saw scantily clad women. That was another thing he read about online. Prostitution ran rapid in some parts of Mexico.

He noted all the sinners. In time, he could work out the mechanics and go back to following his rules. Mexico would be a perfect place for his hobby.

He pulled up a stool and ordered a 'cerveza'. That was beer in spanish. That was one of the very few spanish words that he knew. There was a television on, and it must have been on some channel with world news.

On the television screen was Sly's farm, a helicopter flying over the place. He quickly recognized his own farm, but couldn't understand a word that the spanish reporter was speaking.

Then a picture of him flashed on the screen. In the picture, he was still at his full weight and bald. He looked into the mirror behind the bar and was glad that he didn't even favor the man in the picture.

Then they flashed a picture of Carl Rait. Then, he knew that they even found his basement. He knew now that he was a fugitive and would have to spend the rest of his life on the run.

He wondered what Edward thought about the whole mess. They must have found Cindy's car by now.

Sly turned away from the television. There was no need to watch what he already knew. From behind, he heard a man order a beer. He recognized that the man had an English accent, and was speaking English.

He needed a man like this in his life. When he looked up, he couldn't believe his eyes! It was the producer!

The man had longer hair, and a beard, but there was no mistaking it. It was him.

The man had a tattoo on his arm. It looked like a red figure holding a pitchfork with a forked tongue. Maybe a devil.

Sly turned to face the man. "I'm such a huge fan! I'm here because you suggested it! I hated it that they canceled your show!"

The man with the devil tattoo turned his head and looked around. "No Ingles."

Sly laughed he knew he was also on the run. "It's okay. I'm here for the same reason you are."

The man turned his back on the stranger. He looked around for police but didn't see any. He didn't know if he should run or not.

Sly tugged on the man's shirt. He turned around and Sly pointed at the television screen.

"See, that's me, right there. That's my story."

The man with the tattoo smiled. "Hi. I'm Damon. It's a pleasure to meet you, Sly."

Okay, for those of you who have read the Deadly Reality Tv Series, you already know who Damon Dahmer is. For those of you who haven't read it, maybe now would be a good time to do so.

I'm starting a new series that will have both Damon Dahmer and Sly Verdict. Two deadly fugitives on the run in Mexico. I'm excited about the upcoming series.

Coming September 6, 2019 'Damon Dahmer and Sly Verdict 1. Extreme. Horror.' Now available. The second and last book of the Damon Dahmer series will be released September 20, 2019

Anyways, thanks so much for reading this book. Find me on Facebook (Sea Caummisar) or on Twitter (@SeaCaummisar).

I love hearing from my readers. Be sure to keep up with me for the release of the brand new Dahmer/Verdict Series. Coming soon.

I like reviews, too. No pressure, but they really help out authors and give them encouragement to write more.

Printed in Great Britain
by Amazon